BLOODY SEAS

Depth Force Thrillers
Book Three

Irving A Greenfield

SAPERE
BOOKS

BLOODY SEAS

Published by Sapere Books.

24 Trafalgar Road, Ilkley, LS29 8HH

saperebooks.com

ISBN: 978-1-80055-795-6

UNDERSEA ATTACK!

"Target bearing nine seven degrees," droned the radio operator. "Range nineteen thousand yards. Speed four zero knots and closing fast. ID one torpedo."

"Helmsman," Captain Boxer said, "come to course four three degrees."

"Coming to course four three degrees," the helmsman answered.

"Second target bearing nine seven degrees," the radio operator reported — this time with a little more agitation in his voice. "Range nineteen thousand yards. Speed four zero knots, closing fast. ID another torpedo, sir!"

Cowly looked at Boxer and exclaimed, "They're trying to bracket us!"

"And they're doing a damn fine job of it, too," Boxer said softly.

"What are you going to do?"

"Nothing."

"What?"

"Targets four five degrees. Range eight thousand yards. Speed four zero knots and closing fast..."

CHAPTER 1

Under a bright tropical sun, the American submarine *Shark* and the Russian submarine *Q-21* were still lashed together, dead in the water two hundred miles off the Skeleton Coast of west Africa.

With the bridge and deck details from both submarines watching, Captain Jack Boxer walked to the forward deck of the *Shark* and looked across the narrow ribbon of calm sea that separated him from his Russian counterpart, Captain 1st Rank Igor Borodine.

Each man was bearded. Boxer was slightly taller than Borodine, but the Russian was broader. Both men, though only in their thirties, were beginning to gray at the temples.

Boxer moved to the side. "Are you well, Captain?" he called across the open space between the two submarines.

"Yes. And you, Comrade Captain?" Borodine asked, speaking English with a Slavic accent.

"Well, Comrade Captain," Boxer answered, using the word comrade, knowing it would please Borodine.

Borodine tilted his head up and squinted at the blue sky. "I never thought I'd see it again," he said; then looking at Boxer he added, "I will put everything you have done in my report."

"And I will do the same," Boxer said.

Borodine moved toward the very edge of the *Q-21*. Without hesitation, he leaped on to the *Shark*'s deck and landed directly in front of Boxer.

The bridge and deck details on both boats cheered him.

"It would be a pity," Borodine said, offering his hand to Boxer, "if we did not take this opportunity to shake hands."

Boxer firmly grasped his adversary's hand. "Tell your men," he said, "I honor and respect them."

Borodine nodded. "And tell yours the same," he said.

"I am sorry about your casualties," Boxer said.

"How many did you lose, Comrade Captain?" Borodine asked.

"One third of my attacking force," Boxer replied.

Borodine nodded. "And all for gold," he said with obvious disgust. "But we do what we are ordered to do."

"Not always," Boxer answered with a smile. "At least I don't always do what I'm ordered to do."

Borodine raised his eyebrows.

"In a moment or two," Boxer said, "I'm going to do something that I wasn't ordered to do: I'm going to give you half the gold my men took from your undersea station."

"What?"

"Let's just say that I feel generous," Boxer said.

"But what about your command. Won't they object?"

"I'm sure they will. But it is a small payment for what you did to help save the *Shark*," Boxer said.

"But you and your men did no less to help save the *Sea Savage*," Borodine said.

"Ah, so that's what you call her, eh? I wondered about that. To me and my men your boat has always been the *Q-21*."

Borodine smiled. "She is the *Sea Savage*."

"Have your men stand by to take the gold aboard," Boxer said.

Borodine shook his head. "I don't understand you. We are enemies."

"We are enemies sometimes," Boxer said. "Do you know your Bible?"

Borodine shook his head. "We are not permitted to know it," he said.

"There is a line in the Book of Daniel in the Old Testament that goes like this: 'Thou art weighed in the balances and art found wanting.' After what your men and mine have experienced together, I would consider myself wanting if I did not share the gold with you."

"I think I understand, Comrade Captain."

"Good," Boxer said. "Then have your men stand by."

Borodine turned toward the *Sea Savage*'s bridge. In Russian, he said, "Send ten more men topside. Stand by to take on a gold shipment."

The officers on the *Q-21*'s bridge hesitated.

"Move," Borodine ordered. "I want those men on deck double quick."

"Aye, aye, Comrade Captain," the officer in charge answered.

Boxer keyed his executive officer, Cowly. "Start moving the gold topside," he said.

While the deck parties on each boat formed a human chain moving the gold bars from the *Shark* to the *Sea Savage*, Boxer and Borodine stood on the deck of the *Shark* and watched.

"I don't think anything like this has ever happened," Borodine said, offering Boxer a cigarette.

"No, but then I don't think any two captains ever fought the kind of undersea battle that we did."

Borodine nodded, then he said, "The future will see many battles like that and at greater depths than we fought."

"Three hundred feet was deep enough for me," Boxer commented. "We had trouble with sharks and killer whales. Your mine fields and oxygen-fired rifles took a heavy toll."

"Our forces were commanded by Comrade Major Alexander Petrovich from aboard the *Sea Savage*. He would have been at the sight of the conflict but we went off to answer a Mayday." He stopped. "That was part of the plan, wasn't it?"

Boxer nodded.

Borodine uttered a weary sigh. "The salvage operation was top secret," he said. "Comrade Colonel Petrovich's men did the actual salvage work. The *Sea Savage* was used to transport them to the salvage sight and then would have been used to return the men and the gold to Russia."

"Well, at least some of the gold will be going back with you," Boxer said.

"Yes, thanks to you," Borodine answered.

"Skipper," Cowly said, keying Boxer, "the last ten bars are moving topside now."

"Roger," Boxer answered. To Borodine he said, "That was my executive officer. He told me the transfer is almost complete."

"Time, then, to return to the *Sea Savage*," Borodine commented.

"Yes," Boxer answered. This time he was the one who offered his hand.

"I hope the next time we meet it will be in friendship," Borodine said.

"I hope so too," Boxer answered.

"Skipper," Cowly said, keying Boxer again, "the transfer has been completed."

"Roger that," Boxer answered. "Stand by to get underway."

"Aye, aye, Skipper," Cowly answered. "Standing by."

Borodine turned toward the *Sea Savage*'s bridge. "Stand by to get under way," he ordered.

"Standing by," Viktor Korzenko, his executive officer, answered.

Borodine faced Boxer and smiled, then turned around and leaped back on board the *Sea Savage*.

"Deck party," Boxer ordered, "stand by on the lines."

"Standing by on the lines," the chief in the charge of the deck party answered.

Borodine gave the same orders.

"Let go forward and aft lines," Boxer said.

"Aye, aye, Skipper," the chief answered. "Letting go forward and aft lines."

The deck party on the *Sea Savage* slipped the forward and aft lines free.

Boxer keyed the engineering officer. "Reverse four zero zero rpms," he said.

"Reversing four zero zero rpms," the EO answered. Slowly the *Shark* slid away from the *Sea Savage*.

"Mahony," Boxer said, keying the helmsman, "take her around one eight zero degrees once we're clear of the *Q-21*."

"Aye, aye, Skipper, around one eight zero degrees," Mahony answered.

Boxer watched the *Sea Savage* drop away from them.

Borodine was already on the bridge, waving to him.

Boxer waved back.

"Good luck, Comrade Captain Boxer," Borodine said over the MCA system.

Boxer keyed the *Shark*'s communications officer. "Patch me into the main MCA system," he said.

"You're patched in," the COMMO answered.

"Good luck, Comrade Captain Borodine," Boxer said.

Borodine waved again, then disappeared from the bridge. The *Sea Savage* was already beginning to dive.

Except for the *Shark*, the ocean was empty. In another few minutes the short twilight of the tropics would give way to night. Boxer had been on the outside bridge since the *Shark* and the *Q-21* separated, which was, according to the clock on the computer control panel, thirty-four minutes ago.

Other than to give a heading to the helmsman, Mahony, and telling the EO he wanted twenty knots, Boxer was silent. Meeting Borodine was a strange experience and giving him half the gold was an even stranger one. He was sure the Company chief, Kinkade, would really get his back up over it. But he wasn't so sure what Williams' or Admiral Stark's reaction would be. Well, he couldn't undo what was done. Besides, in his book, half the gold was a small payment for the *Shark*'s crew. Without the help of the *Q-21*, the *Shark* never would have survived that undersea storm. Never. Only by lashing the two boats together and using every bit of their combined power were they able to break free of the torrent of cold water that had pinned them to the bottom and would have kept them there until the weight of the water pouring over them had broken them apart. Sooner or later some structural part would have failed. No matter what the consequences might be, Boxer was certain he had done the right thing. He was also certain that if the situation had been reversed, Borodine would have done something similar, though his freedom to do anything on his own was certainly more restricted.

Darkness came and with it the Southern Cross appeared.

Boxer realized the red lights for night vision were on. He didn't remember giving the order and assumed that Cowly had. He nodded and was about to decide whether to dive or run on the surface awhile longer when Captain Steven Bush came alongside of him.

"You did excellent work," Boxer said, referring to Bush's action in the minisub against the trawlers that provided the surface protection for the Russian undersea station.

"Thank you," Bush responded. He was a handsome, narrow-shouldered man, with green eyes and a fair complexion. "Captain," Bush said, "I have something I want to discuss with you."

Boxer stopped himself from frowning. Bush was coming along but his use of captain instead of skipper put Boxer on his guard. This was Bush's second trip with the *Shark*. And both times he was on board to be Kinkade's watchdog.

"I'd prefer your quarters, if you don't mind," Bush said.

"Cowly," Boxer said. "You have the CONN. Keep her on the same heading. I'll be in my quarters."

"Aye, aye, Skipper," Cowly answered.

Boxer hurried down from the bridge and went straight to his quarters. Bush was directly behind him. Neither man spoke until the door was closed.

"Sit down," Boxer said, gesturing to a chair. He settled down on his bunk, chose a pipe from the rack on the shelf above it, filled the bowl with tobacco and lit up.

Bush remained standing. "I sent a message to Kinkade informing him of what was happening."

Boxer nodded. He had misjudged the man to think he was loosening up. "You had no authority to do that," Boxer said quietly. "I wanted to maintain radio silence —"

"Kinkade ordered me to do everything in my power to destroy the *Q-21*."

Boxer was on his feet. "He's a fucking idiot!"

"I obeyed his order," Bush said calmly.

"What?" Boxer asked, taking the pipe out of his mouth. "Just what the hell did you do?"

"I emplaced a time-delay bomb," Bush answered, looking straight at him.

Boxer restrained the desire to punch Bush in the face. "First thing first," he said. "Where was the bomb placed and what time was it set to detonate?"

"I'm sorry," Bush said. "I was ordered to tell you only as much as I have told you."

Boxer took a deep breath and slowly exhaled. If he ever hated a man, he hated Bush now.

"There's something else," Bush said.

Boxer nodded. "Go on, tell me."

"I'm relieving you of your command," Bush said. "Kinkade —"

Boxer reached over to the COMCOMP and pressed a button. In a matter of moments four men from Major Redfern's strike force were at the door. "Escort Captain Bush to his quarters," Boxer said. "Keep him there until I order his release."

"You can't —"

"Bush, I just did," Boxer said. "I'll radio Kinkade and tell him you'll take command of the *Shark* when I leave it. Now go to your quarters without a fuss, or you'll be taken forcibly."

Bush glared at him, turned and left the cabin.

Boxer keyed the COMMO. "Contact the *Q-21*. I want to speak to Captain Borodine."

"Aye, aye, Skipper," the COMMO answered. "But that might not be so easy."

"Try their known transmission frequencies," Boxer answered.

"Trying," the officer said.

Even though the interior of the *Shark* was air-conditioned, Boxer was sweating profusely.

"Nothing, Skipper," the COMMO said.

"Keep at it," Boxer answered.

"Aye, aye, Skipper," the officer said.

Boxer set his dead pipe down in an ashtray and went straight to the inside bridge.

Word about Bush being confined to quarters spread fast. The men cast furtive looks at Boxer as he started toward the COMCOMP; then changing his mind, he headed topside to the outside bridge. "I have the CONN," he said briskly to Cowly. Automatically he checked the course and heading. Both were correct. He looked back in the direction from which they had come. Somewhere out there was the *Q-21* with a bomb — or maybe the bomb had gone off and...

"Surface target, bearing two eight zero degrees," the radar office reported. "Range twenty thousand yards. Speed thirty knots."

"Course?" Boxer asked, instantly becoming alert.

"Eight zero degrees."

"ID?"

COMMO keyed Boxer. "Skipper, got through to the *Q-21*. Captain Borodine is standing by."

Boxer kept his eyes in the direction of the target. He flipped the radio communications switch. "Comrade Captain there is a time-delayed bomb emplaced somewhere on your hull."

"What are you talking —"

"Target ID: Sovremenny class guided missile destroyer," the RO said.

Boxer punched the klaxon twice. The bridge party hurried down into the sail. The last man in dogged the hatch shut.

Boxer ran to the bridge.

The diving officer flooded the bow tanks.

"Crash dive," Boxer said over the MC. "Crash dive. Flood main ballast. Diving planes one zero degrees. EO, flank speed."

"Main ballast flooded," the DO reported. "Diving planes at one zero degrees."

Boxer watched the needle on the manual depth gauge swing through fifty feet.

"Flank speed," the EO reported.

"Lower sail," Boxer said.

"Sail lowered," Cowly answered, pressing the control button.

"Contact with the *Q-21* broken," the COMMO said.

"Roger that," Boxer answered.

The *Shark* continued to slice through the water.

"Level her at one zero zero feet," Boxer said.

"Coming level at one zero zero feet," the DO said.

Boxer watched the depth gauge. The needle swung past one hundred feet then came back to it. He switched on the digital dep readout; in green numerics it registered one hundred feet.

"Steady at one hundred feet," Boxer said; then he punched the name of the Russian ship in the command computer and asked for details.

"Second surface target, bearing four zero degrees. Range eighteen thousand yards. Speed thirty knots. Closing on us. Target ID Sovremenny class guided missile destroyer."

Boxer had a mental image of the two ships converging on him. He looked down at the information on the screen:

SOVREMENNY CLASS (DDG)
displacement — 7,500 tons
length — 510 feet
propulsion — gas turbines
main armament — unknown SSM system

— unknown ASW system

— unknown gun system

— eight torpedo tubes

— twenty ASW rockets

— four single 30mm Gatling guns

aircraft — one HORMONE helicopter

Boxer ran his hand over his beard. Even without the unknowns, she was a formidable fighting machine, especially with the HORMONE ASW helicopter on board. He knew that whirlybird not only was armed with torpedoes, it also carried a variety of sensing devices.

"Surface target, bearing nine zero degrees," the SO reported. "Range twenty-two thousand yards. Speed three zero knots. Course three six zero degrees. Closing fast. ID Sovremenny class guided missile destroyer."

"Roger that," Boxer answered.

"Two more and we'd have all of them," Cowly said.

Boxer hadn't realized Cowly was standing directly behind him. "We'll have enough trouble with these," Boxer answered.

Suddenly the dreaded ping of the enemy sonar sounded through the *Shark.*

"They've got us," Cowly said in a low, dry voice.

"Helmsman, come to course five six degrees," Boxer ordered.

"Aye, aye, Skipper," Mahony answered, "coming to course five six degrees."

The pinging began to decrease, then stopped completely.

"Skipper," SO said, "three smaller targets between the three surface vessels."

"Sonar buoys," Boxer answered, switching the sonar display screen.

"Surface targets holding same courses. Closing fast," the SO said.

Boxer pursed his lips. The Russians had surrounded him — if the surface ships didn't get him, the helicopters would. "Activate ECM," he said, hoping the boat's electronic counter measure system would confuse their sonar operators for a few minutes.

"Surface target bearing one nine degrees. Range twenty thousand yards. Speed one five knots. ID trawler *Katya*."

Boxer glanced at the sonar display screen. Now he'd have to expect the trawlers that survived Bush's attack to join in the hunt for the *Shark*.

Suddenly the pinging started.

"Helmsman, come to course two five five degrees," Boxer said.

"Coming to course two five five degrees," Mahony answered.

Boxer switched on the grid display indicator and looked at a three-dimensional view of the ocean floor. There wasn't any place to hide. The bottom was still flat and featureless. They had outrun the subsurface storm but hadn't yet left the area where such storms occurred.

"Surface targets holding same course. Range fifteen thousand yards. Closing fast," the SO reported.

Boxer keyed CIC. "Give me some info on that storm we pulled out of. Given its speed of say three zero knots or better and ours — tell me where that storm is now?"

"Aye, aye, Skipper," the CICO answered. "I'll put on the COMCOMP."

"Roger that," Boxer answered. He glanced at the sonar display screen. The circle was getting smaller. "Cowly, have the minisub rigged for radio control. Load her with explosives. We'll give these bastards a run for their money!"

"Aye, aye, Skipper," Cowly answered.

"Helmsman, come to course four four degrees," Boxer said.

"Coming to course four four degrees," Mahony answered.

A buzzer sounded and the informational display unit signal light began to flash red. Boxer turned his attention to the screen:

Storm moving NNE at between three zero and four zero knots. Coming from south. Frontal edge should arrive one five to two zero min. END OF INFORMATION.

The screen went blank.

"Cowly, how long before the minisub can be launched?" Boxer asked.

"One zero minutes," Cowly answered.

Suddenly the deep boom of an explosion rolled over them. It was immediately followed by a second and a third.

The CICO keyed Boxer. "Pattern firing, Skipper. A salvo from each ship."

"Roger that," Boxer answered. Pattern firing meant that the Russians knew they were there but hadn't been able to lock on to them again. "Helmsman, come to course seven five degrees," Boxer said.

"Coming to course seven five degrees," Mahony answered.

"Minisub ready, Skipper," Cowly said.

Boxer nodded and keyed the EO. "Reduce speed to five knots. Stand by to launch minisub."

"Standing by," Cowly answered.

Boxer keyed Communications. "Switch minisub radio control system to COMCOMP control."

"Minisub radio control switched to COMCOMP control," the COMMO said.

Boxer brought up the image of the minisub in the launch bay on the fourth scan screen of the COMCOMP. He zoomed in on the diving planes and changed their pitch by manipulating controls on the COMCOMP; then he focused on the minisub's prop and rudder and activated each of them. Satisfied that the radio control system worked, he keyed the launching officer. "Flood bay and stand by to open bay doors."

"Aye, aye, Skipper," the LO responded.

"Targets maintaining bearing and speed. Range twelve thousand yards and closing fast," the SO reported.

Another series of explosions rolled over the *Shark*.

Boxer turned on the UWIS system. The bottom was flat and featureless. Several sharks swam into view.

"Launch bay flooded," the LO reported.

"Roger that," Boxer answered. He pressed a button that started the minisub's engines. "Stand by to open launch bay doors." He keyed the EO. "Zero zero rpms," he said.

"Zero zero rpms," the EO answered.

Another series of explosions rolled over the *Shark*. They were coming closer.

"LO," Boxer said, "open launch bay doors." On the scan screen he watched the doors open. Slowly he increased the number of revolutions per minute of the minisub's propeller. The boat began to sink down toward the opening doors. Within minutes it was out of the *Shark*. Boxer had it on the UWIS. "Close launch bay doors."

"Aye, aye, Skipper," the LO answered.

Suddenly the ping of the Russian sonar sounded throughout the *Shark*; another series of pings followed. Two of the Russian ships had found the *Shark*.

"Cowly," Boxer said, "get Bush up to the bridge."

"Captain Bush, report to the bridge," Cowly said over the MC. "Captain Bush, report to the bridge."

Boxer keyed the EO. "Flank speed," he said.

"Flank speed," the EO responded.

"Helmsman, come to course two zero zero degrees," Boxer said.

"Coming to course two zero zero degrees," Mahony answered.

Bush came up to the bridge under armed escort.

"Take over on the minisub," Boxer told him. "I want it used to destroy as many ships on the surface as possible."

Bush was about to say something.

"I don't want any discussion, Captain. I gave you an order. I want that ordered obeyed."

"Yes, sir," Bush answered.

"Blast a hole in their defenses so that we can go through. We're going back into that storm. But not to the bottom. We'll stay at the temperature boundary line. That should throw their sonar out."

Bush nodded. "That's if they don't sink us first," he said sarcastically.

Boxer flushed but didn't answer.

"Targets closing fast," the SO said. "Range now seven thousand yards. Bearing and course the same."

Suddenly an explosion shook the *Shark*. Boxer grabbed onto the COMCOMP. Bush was thrown against a bulkhead.

"That's from one of the helicopters," Boxer said. "Helmsman, come to course five three degrees."

"Coming to five three degrees," Mahony answered.

Another explosion smashed down on the *Shark*, forcing the bow down.

"Medic ... medic ... forward torpedo room," the torpedo officer shouted over the intercom.

"Get that minisub going!" Boxer told Bush.

"Skipper," the TO said, keying Boxer, "two men with cut scalps. One requires stitches."

"Roger that," Boxer said.

Another depth charge went off alongside the *Shark*, heaving it over to one side.

"Damage Control, any problems?" Boxer asked.

"Negative, Skipper," the DCO answered.

"Bush, have you gotten that minisub to where it will do some good?"

"Moving into position," Bush answered.

Boxer glanced at the control panel. The minisub was heading straight for the destroyer guarding the southern escape route. "Helmsman, come to course nine zero degrees."

The pinging of the Russian sonar had stopped.

Boxer watched the minisub on the UWIS. Suddenly a black object came hurtling down at her.

Bush skillfully swung her off to the right.

The explosion roiled the water. But the minisub was safe and back on course.

Boxer checked the water temperature. It was fifty-five degrees.

The pinging began again.

Boxer was sweating profusely. He had to stay on course if he was going to follow the minisub out of the ring of steel the Russians had thrown around him.

A sudden explosion dimmed the lights and caused the UWIS to momentarily go blank.

"Skipper," the damage control officer said, "we've got damage to the bow ballast tank on the port side."

Boxer switched on the DDC and put the information on one of the COMCOMP screens.

DDC READOUT — HULL DAMAGE
AREA — PORT SIDE
SYSTEM — BALLAST
EXTENT — UNKNOWN
REPAIR — NONE

"Captain," Bush said, "coming up on target."

Boxer looked at the UWIS. The minisub was in view; less distinct was the Russian destroyer.

Another explosion hammered down on the *Shark*.

"Launching torpedoes in salvo," Bush said. "Torpedoes launched."

The *Shark* jerked to the starboard. The lights went out. Boxer was thrown to the floor.

A moment later the lights came back on.

"Skipper," the DCO said, "pressure pump to reactor-cooling system leaking. Radiation level above max standard."

"Clear all personnel from pump area," Boxer ordered. "Activate decontamination system." He glanced at the UWIS screen.

Four almost simultaneous explosions rolled over the *Shark*.

Boxer watched the destroyer's hull disintegrate. "Good job!" he exclaimed. "We'll either go under her or very close."

"Secondary target coming up," Bush said.

"Ram it," Boxer ordered.

"Range four thousand yards and closing fast," Bush said.

Boxer keyed the SO. "Can you ID target approaching minisub?"

"Destroyer, moving in from the east at four five knots," the SO answered.

"Turning minisub toward new target," Bush announced.

A sudden explosion slammed against the hull of the *Shark*.

"DCO," Boxer said, keying the damage control officer, "anything from the last one?"

"Negative," the DCO answered.

Boxer checked the bank of instruments that check the ambient conditions of the water surrounding the *Shark*. The temperature was down to forty-five degrees. The storm was moving in.

"Captain," Bush said, "target two thousand yards and closing fast."

"Keep her steady," Boxer answered.

Another pattern of three explosions badly jolted the *Shark*.

"Medic! Medic! Medic!"

This time the call came from the communications center.

"Skipper," the COMMO said, "one man here with a broken arm."

"Roger that," Boxer answered. He looked at the temperature gauge again. The needle had moved down five degrees. "DO, stand by," Boxer said.

"Standing by," the DO answered.

"Captain," Bush said, "minisub five zero zero yards from target."

"DO," Boxer said, "come to five zero feet."

"Coming to five zero feet," the DO answered.

Boxer watched the temperature gauge.

"Skipper," the SO reported, "we've lost all target contact."

"Bush?"

"Target two five five yards —"

"Abandon attack," Boxer said, looking at the distorted image on the UWIS screen.

"But why?"

"Abandon attack!" Boxer roared.

"Attack abandoned," Bush answered.

"Bring the minisub back," Boxer said. "We're safe now. Cowly, have the men stand down from general quarters."

"Aye, aye, Skipper."

"Now hear this," Cowly said over the MC, "all hands stand down from the GQ. Stand down from GQ."

Boxer leaned forward and rested his elbows on the COMCOMP. The Russians had almost had him. Almost.

"I hope you don't think it was an accident or a coincidence that we ran into those destroyers," Bush said.

Boxer looked at him. "Meaning?"

"That they were alerted by your Comrade Captain Borodine."

Boxer shook his head. "He just doesn't think or operate that way" Boxer answered.

CHAPTER 2

Borodine had heard Boxer clearly: A bomb was emplaced somewhere on the hull of the *Sea Savage*. Then he heard the klaxon sound twice and knew the *Shark* was crash diving. All transmission was cut off.

Viktor was standing close by and heard the conversation too.

Borodine turned to him. He was very pale.

Communications signaled Borodine. "Comrade Captain, message coming in from Headquarters."

"Roger that," Borodine answered and put the message on one of the screens of the master control computer.

TO CAPT. 1ST CLASS IGOR BORODINE
JOIN ATTACK ON AMER. SUB SHARK IMMEDIATELY
CONTACT SQUAD 4 FOR EXACT POSITION ... USE CODE 11
ADMIRAL OF THE FLEET
GORSHKOV

"Now what the hell do we do?" Viktor asked.

Both men were silent.

Borodine knew the decision was his. "I have to believe Captain Boxer."

"Then what are we going to do?"

"Radio Headquarters we have a bomb aboard and as soon as we find and neutralize it we'll join in the attack on the *Shark*." He typed out a message. Keying Communications, he said, "Send this to Headquarters."

"Aye, aye, Comrade Captain," the COMMO answered.

Borodine switched on the MC system. "All hands," he said, "all hands this is the captain speaking. Listen closely —" he took a deep breath and slowly exhaled before he continued — "I was informed a few moments ago we have a bomb emplaced on the hull of the *Sea Savage.*" He paused and looked toward the CIC section. Every face was turned toward him. Every face was filled with fear. "Stand by for emergency surfacing. All systems will be on manual control." He glanced at the depth gauge. "We are one five five feet down. DO, diving planes one zero degrees up."

"Diving planes one zero degrees up," the DO responded.

"Prepare to blow all tanks," Borodine said.

"Standing by to blow all tanks," the DO answered tightly.

"Blow tanks," Borodine said.

The sound of rushing air filled the *Sea Savage.* She started to rise slowly at first, then with more speed.

"Engineering," Borodine said, "flank speed."

With her bow tilted up, the *Sea Savage* knifed through the water.

Borodine swallowed hard to equalize the pressure in his ears. The depth gauge needle was moving fast; it passed ninety feet.

"She'll break water with her bow coming out first," Borodine said to Viktor, "and fall back as the rest —"

The explosion shook the *Sea Savage.* She faltered in her race to the surface and began to settle down at the stern.

"Comrade Captain," the DCO reported, "the aft torpedo room has been blown out. All bulkhead doors automatically sealed."

Borodine looked at the depth gauge. The boat was holding at eighty feet. "Casualties?" he asked tightly.

"Everyone on duty," Viktor answered.

Borodine clenched his teeth: That meant ten men. He keyed the DCO. "Any other damage?"

"Starboard propeller shaft out of alignment," the DCO answered.

Borodine keyed the EO and ordered the speed reduced to five knots. Then he called the DCO to the bridge and said, "We must be able to make repairs and surface."

The DCO's face was set in tight lines. "We can send divers out to look at the damage but the hole is too large to repair under water. Too large." His voice was barely audible.

"We've got to get to the surface!" Borodine exclaimed.

"There's nothing left in the tanks to vent and —"

"Viktor," Borodine said. "Vent all our water supply."

Viktor hesitated.

"Vent it," Borodine said.

Viktor gave the order.

Borodine watched the depth gauge; the *Sea Savage* went to seventy feet.

"The waste system," the DCO said.

Borodine nodded. That system was blown clear every twenty-four hours. "Vent the waste system," Borodine said, "and keep it dry."

"Venting waste system," Viktor answered.

The *Sea Savage* moved to sixty-five feet.

"Anything else?" Borodine asked.

"We need the water in the reactor system," the DCO said.

Borodine put the schematic of the reactor cooling system on one of the screens. "How much does that hold?" he asked, pointing to a reserve tank.

"Three hundred gallons."

"Viktor, vent the reactor system reserve tank," Borodine said.

"Venting reserve tank," Viktor responded.

The *Sea Savage* went up another five feet.

Borodine began to smell something strange. He took several sniffs.

The fire warning light on the command console began to flash. The next moment the alarm sounded.

Borodine activated the damage-control system.

"Son of a bitch, it's in the air scrubber!" the DCO yelled.

Borodine switched on the MC. "All hands ... now hear this," he said. "Now here this: We have a condition red on board. All fire fighters report to the DCO for further instructions. All hands go to emergency air supply. The central ventilation system will be shut off in one zero seconds. Stand by... The central air system is shut down. All hands use your emergency air system." He turned to the DCO. "Get that fire out!"

"Aye, aye, Comrade Captain," the man answered, turned and hurried away to organize his fire fighters.

Borodine looked at the nearby air vents. Wisps of dark gray smoke were coming out of them.

Viktor approached him. He wasn't wearing his emergency air mask.

"Put it on!" Borodine ordered, pointing to the air mask. "Put it on and don't take it off until I give the order." Then he donned his own and raised his eyes to the depth gauge again. The *Sea Savage* was holding at fifty-five feet.

The DCO keyed him. "Comrade Captain, it's an oil fire. Oil is leaking into the scrubber system. We'll have to cut our way through a section of the duct work."

"Do it," Borodine said, sorry now that he had barked at Viktor.

"That means the scrubber system will be out for —"

"Do the fucking work!" Borodine snapped.

29

"Aye, aye, Comrade Captain," the DCO responded.

Borodine keyed the diving officer. "One five degrees on the diving planes," he said.

"One five degrees on the diving planes," the DO answered.

The *Sea Savage* gained another five feet. She was now at fifty feet and holding.

Borodine keyed the forward torpedo room. "Stand by to load and fire torpedoes."

"Standing by," the torpedo officer answered.

"Set all torpedoes for three-minute time delay. Fire all torpedoes at will."

"Torpedoes being loaded," the TO said.

Borodine waited, his eyes fixed on the depth gauge.

"Torpedoes fired," the TO reported.

The *Sea Savage* rose ten more feet.

"Fire all torpedoes aboard," Borodine ordered.

The smoke on the bridge was becoming perceptibly thicker.

"Torpedoes loaded," the TO said, as the boom of four simultaneous explosions rolled over the *Sea Savage*.

"Fire at will," Borodine responded.

"Torpedoes away!"

The *Sea Savage* gained another fifteen feet. Her sail was out of the water.

"Bridge detail, topside," Borodine ordered. "Viktor take the CONN."

Within moments the bridge hatch was thrown open and fresh air rushed into the *Sea Savage*'s smoky interior.

"All hands, stand by," Borodine said over the MC. "Pass everything forward that isn't part of the boat's operating equipment. All personal belongings, including clothing and shoes ... everything that you're not wearing. Colonel Alexander Petrovich, assemble your men into a chain. Have them pass everything to the bridge and over the side." Despite the flow of fresh air, the smoke was thickening.

Alex came to the bridge. He and Borodine were friends of long standing. They had served together at the embassy in Washington.

"We need another fifteen feet before I can open all the hatches," Borodine said.

Alex nodded. He was shorter than Borodine, solidly built. He had a fair complexion, blond hair and a bull's neck. He had come up through the ranks of the naval marines.

The men were already passing things to the bridge.

Borodine switched on the MC. "All bedding goes over the side."

He watched the gauge. The needle moved slowly. The *Sea Savage* was up another five feet.

"Alex," Borodine said, "send four of your men into the aft torpedo room. Have them jettison all the torpedoes."

"Anything else?"

"Any equipment that can be moved. But not the bodies of the men."

Within minutes a four-man scuba team was on its way to the bridge.

Borodine keyed the EO. "Stop all engines."

"All engines stopped," the EO answered.

Borodine waited and watched the depth gauge.

The leader of the team, Lieutenant Kasov, keyed Borodine. "Comrade Captain, we've reached the torpedo room. Ten-foot hole on the starboard side. Torpedoes being removed."

"Roger that," Borodine answered.

The needle on the depth gauge began to move again. It went through twenty feet ... eighteen feet ... fifteen feet. Then it stopped.

"All hands," Borodine said over the MC, "we need five more feet to surface. Rip out the chairs and tables from the mess area. I want everything not used to operate this boat to go over the side."

The tables and chairs were cut away from the deck and bulkheads and passed topside.

The depth gauge needle moved slowly through the remaining five feet. "Surface. Surface," Borodine shouted, sounding the klaxon three times. "Open all hatches. All hands stand by." Fresh air rushed through the *Sea Savage*, pushing the smoke out.

Borodine keyed the EO. "Start fans. I want the smoke cleared."

"Aye, aye, Comrade Captain."

"All hands," Borodine said over the MC, "all hands remove emergency air masks … remove emergency air masks." Then he keyed the COMMO. "Send a message to Headquarters informing them of our position and condition. Longer message will follow. Use the blue code system. Tell them we must have assistance. We cannot dive."

"Aye, aye, Comrade Captain," the communications officer answered.

Borodine removed his emergency air mask. Using a handkerchief, he wiped the sweat off his face and neck. Then he nodded to Alex and said, "Tell your men well done."

"They'd appreciate it more if it came from you," Alex responded.

"In a few minutes," Borodine said. "First I want to go to the bridge. I owe Viktor an apology."

CHAPTER 3

Boxer was topside, on the bridge, standing next to Cowly and looking at the spectacular night sky. He had come up a few minutes before, after having read a series of decoded transmissions that gave him the whole story of what had happened to the *Q-21*.

Boxer had more than a sneaking suspicion that Borodine purposely had sent those messages in a code that could be broken because he knew they would be picked up by the *Shark*, if she survived the attack.

"It was his way of telling us he had nothing to do with it and that his boat was okay," Boxer said.

"What?" Cowly asked, looking at him.

Boxer told him about the decoded messages and why he thought they had been sent in a code that every Russian captain had to know had been compromised.

"You could be right," Cowly answered. "A Russian might think that way. Especially a man of honor."

Boxer nodded. "Borodine is certainly that."

"Did you make any signal to let him know we're okay?" Cowly asked.

Boxer nodded. "But nothing so elaborate," Boxer said. "I had Communications play a tape for ten minutes, more than enough time for his people to get a fix on it."

"My God," Cowly exclaimed, "your thinking is becoming as Byzantine as theirs!"

"To know your adversary you must think like him," Boxer said, smiling. "Isn't that what we were taught at the Academy?"

"It's been too long for me to remember," Cowly answered.

Boxer didn't pursue the conversation. The battle for the gold, the subsequent lashing of the *Shark* to the *Q-21* in order to save both of them and then the battle with the Soviet destroyers afterward were only now having their full effect on him. He was physically and mentally exhausted.

Communications keyed Boxer. "Skipper, we have a six-code message from the *Mary-Ann.*"

"Read it," Boxer said. A six-code classification was the highest priority given to a civilian transmitting to the *Shark.*

"'To Captain Jack Boxer — slash — for your eyes only — slash — standing by for your transmission. Give ETA and coordinates. Congrats on a job well done. Immediate reply requested.' End of message. Standing by to copy your reply."

Boxer gave a snort. He wasn't about to give anyone the *Shark*'s position. "Ask the *Mary-Ann* for her position," he said. "Tell her we won't disclose our ETA. Tell her to hold her present position, or whatever her future one will be."

"That's it?" the COMMO asked.

"That's it," Boxer answered. "No, wait a minute." He smiled. He could at least be as courteous as Borodine. "Send the message in Code Yellow."

"Skipper, we know the Russians can monitor —"

"Code Yellow," Boxer said.

"Aye, aye, Skipper," the COMMO answered.

Boxer filled his pipe and lit it. The idea of spending more time aboard the *Mary-Ann* did not on first thought appeal to him. He would have preferred to return to the *Tecumseh*, or better still take the *Shark* all the way back to Norfolk, where she'd be put into dry dock for repairs. The depth charging had ruptured some piping and had knocked out a pump in the nuclear power plant cooling system. That portion of the boat was off limits to personnel, except those in the damage control section trained to deal with such failures. And even they had to wear special clothing. The five crew members who were exposed to massive doses of radiation immediately after the pump failed were already in the sick bay complaining of headaches and constant nausea. He hoped no one else on board would develop the symptoms of radiation sickness.

Communications keyed him again. "Skipper, the *Mary-Ann* will be at twenty-six degrees south latitude, one zero degrees east longitude in approximately one zero hours."

"Roger that," Boxer said. "Stand by." He checked the *Shark*'s position on the AUTONAVSYS, then set the coordinates just given to him into the COMCOMP, dialed a projected speed of twenty knots and asked for a projected course and an ETA readout.

Within seconds the COMCOMP responded with:

INDICATE SURFACE RUN Y/N

Boxer touched the N key.

INDICATE DEPTH.

Boxer typed in 150 feet.

COMCOMP answered:

COURSE — 14°

ETA — 7h 20 min

Boxer dialed in the course heading, then switched on the MC. "All hands, stand by. Prepare to dive." He struck the klaxon twice.

The bridge was cleared. The last man dogged closed the hatch.

Boxer checked the COMCOMP. The *Shark* was still on the surface. "All systems on automatic," Boxer said, changing several switches to place all of the ship's operating systems under the control of the COMCOMP. "Making one five zero feet," Boxer said, adjusting the electronic plane control for five degrees. The dive would be gradual. He watched the various instruments as they indicated which ballast tanks were being flooded. Boxer dialed in the speed of twenty knots; moments later, the twenty knots came up on the speed indicator.

Boxer moved his eyes to the DDROUT. The *Shark* was going through seventy-five feet. Everything was working smoothly. All systems showed green lights. Boxer sat back and said, "Lower sail."

"Lowering sail," Cowly answered.

Three minutes later, Boxer watched the bubble indicator come to a level position. He switched on the MC. "Dive completed. All systems being monitored by COMCOMP." He switched off the MC and turned to Cowly. "Take the CONN. I'm going to sleep. Wake me in an hour."

"Will do, Skipper," Cowly answered.

Boxer left the COMCOMP and went to his quarters. He was asleep almost as soon as he laid down.

Boxer was awake before the hour was up. But he remained in his bunk. He had a hearing to face when he returned, and some of what he had done during this mission was sure to bring him more difficulties ... perhaps even dismissal.

He sat up, swung his feet off the bunk and planted them on the deck. If he were dismissed, what the hell would he do? Who would have need for a submarine captain? Suddenly he found the idea of advertising his services funny and grinned. He'd bet the Russians would like to get hold of him. They wanted him so much they had already tried to kill him.

Boxer stood up and went to the washroom immediately across the passageway from his quarters. He washed his face and took a few moments to look at his face in the mirror. There were dark circles under his eyes but otherwise he looked as good as any other thirty-five-year-old man, except that his beard needed a trimming.

Suddenly he was keyed by the sonar officer. "Target bearing nine seven degrees. Depth one five zero feet. Range twenty thousand yards. Speed unknown. ID unknown."

"Roger that," Boxer said. "I'm coming up to the bridge now. Does Mister Cowly know about it?"

"Yes. He suggested I notify you."

"Roger that," Boxer answered. He went straight to the bridge.

Cowly stood up and pointed to the screen on the COMCOMP. "It just stays at twenty thousand yards ... where we can pick it up but not ID it."

Boxer studied the screen for a few moments. "We know it's not the _Q-21_."

"It could be another Russian sub," Cowly ventured.

Boxer shook his head. "Another sub, yes. But not a Russian one. Even they would know better than to send a conventional sub against the _Shark_." He keyed the EO. "Reduce speed to one zero knots for five minutes; then increase to twenty-five for one zero minutes; then return to two zero knots. Removing propulsions system from auto control."

"Aye, aye, Skipper. System off auto control. Going to one zero knots."

"Roger that," Boxer answered; then he keyed the SO. "Stand by to run ID on target."

"Standing by, Skipper," the SO answered.

Boxer watched the screen on the COMCOMP. Suddenly the target hung in the outer limits of the sonar's range. "Got him!" Boxer exclaimed.

"Running ID," the SO reported.

"He's stopped," Cowly said.

"He knows when he's been suckered in," Boxer said.

"ID complete," SO reported.

"Interface it with the COMCOMP," Boxer said. A moment later the information came up on the general data screen.

ATTACK SUBMARINE (SS): FOXTROT CLASS
Displacement — 2,000 tons surfaced
Length — 295 feet
Propulsion — Diesel-electric
Main Armament — Torpedo tubes
Supplementary Information: eight of these submarines have been provided to India, several to Libya and two to Cuba.

Boxer checked the *Shark*'s speed; it was still moving at ten knots. His eyes moved to the sonar display screen; the target was eighteen thousand yards away. "Libya or Cuba," Boxer said. "Take your pick. Either one is fair game." And he pressed the red general quarters alarm. A moment later he switched on the MC. "All systems going to manual. Section officers report."

One by one each of the *Shark*'s section officers responded conditions normal.

"Aft torpedo room ready torpedoes for tubes five and six. Range nineteen thousand yards. Set depth on one torpedo for one five zero feet, on the other one seven feet. Activate acoustical homing device. Arm detonator for proximity release."

"Time?" the TO asked.

Boxer had already run the torpedo's speed and the distance between it and the *Shark* through the COMCOMP. "Seven minutes," he answered.

"Torpedoes set," the TO responded.

"Load torpedoes," Boxer said.

"Torpedoes loaded," the TO reported.

A red light began to flash on the upper right side of COMCOMP.

"Stand by to fire," Boxer said.

"Standing by," the TO answered.

Boxer keyed the DO. "Stand by to shift ballast as soon as torpedoes are away."

"System equalizer on ready," the DO answered.

Suddenly the *Shark* was violently shaken.

"What the hell was that?" Boxer asked.

The damage control officer keyed Boxer. "Skipper, we've got a severe vibration pattern on number two driveshaft on the starboard side."

Again the *Shark* was violently shaken.

Boxer switched the COMCOMP to the damage control mode. A detailed plan of the *Shark*'s driveshaft system was displayed on the screen. The area of difficulty was highlighted by a red flashing circle.

Boxer typed: RECOMMEND REPAIR PROCEDURE?

COMCOMP: STRAIGHTEN SHAFT IMMEDIATELY. CHANGE SPEED IMMEDIATELY.

Boxer keyed the EO. "Go to one five knots," he ordered.

COMCOMP: 15 KNOTS SATISFIES PRESENT OPERATING CONDITIONS. SEVERE VIBRATION WILL OCCUR BETWEEN 6 AND 11 KNOTS.

Boxer checked the sonar display. The target was still within the system's range. He keyed the TO. "Stand by to fire torpedoes from tubes five and six."

"Standing by," the TO answered.

"Target bearing nine seven degrees. Range nineteen thousand yards. Speed forty knots and closing fast. ID one torpedo."

"Helmsman," Boxer said, "come to course four three degrees."

"Coming to course four three degrees," the helmsman answered.

"Second target bearing nine seven degrees. Range nineteen thousand yards. Speed four zero knots, closing fast. Depth one seven feet."

"Holy shit," Cowly exclaimed, "the son-of-a-bitch is trying to bracket us."

Boxer dialed the course change into the fire control system. "Fire torpedo five."

"Torpedo five fired," the TO answered.

"Fire torpedo six," Boxer said.

"Torpedo six fired," the TO reported seconds later.

"Target bearing nine seven degrees on new course of one zero zero degrees. Range twenty thousand yards. Speed twenty knots."

Boxer cranked the target's change of bearing and speed into the fire control system and into the COMCOMP for transmission to the two torpedoes.

"Two targets changing course to four five degrees. Range ten thousand yards and closing fast."

Boxer switched on the electronic counter measure system. "Now we'll see if we can play cat and mouse with those two fish."

"We could blow them out of the water," Cowly said.

Boxer shook his head. "We'll do it the hard way."

"Targets four five degrees. Range eight thousand yards. Speed four zero knots and closing fast."

"Captain, just what the hell are you doing?" Bush roared, coming up to the bridge. "Use two fish to get those torpedoes."

Boxer ignored him.

"You're crazy!" Bush shouted.

"Helmsman," Boxer said, "stand by to change course."

"Targets bearing four five degrees. Range seven thousand yards and closing fast."

"Come to course six five degrees," Boxer said.

"Coming to course six five degrees," the helmsman answered.

Bush switched on the MC. "Now hear this. All hands, this is Captain Bush. I'm taking command of the *Shark*."

Boxer keyed the EO. "Give me flank speed."

"Flank speed," the EO answered.

"You're officially relieved —"

"Bush, get the fuck away from me," Boxer said, "or I'll have you put in irons."

"Targets changing course. Bearing six five degrees. Range six thousand yards. Speed three five knots. Closing fast."

Boxer keyed the DO. "Make one zero zero feet."

"Making one zero zero feet," the DO answered. "Targets bearing six five degrees. Range five thousand five hundred yards. Speed thirty knots. Closing fast."

Boxer turned to Cowly. "In about two minutes those fish should drop to the bottom. Have them deactivated and brought aboard the *Shark*. Tell Tom to ready his bomb squad."

The boom of a distant explosion rolled over the *Shark*. Seconds later another followed.

"Then go get some sleep," Boxer said. "You look terrible." He turned to Bush. "You look terrible, too."

CHAPTER 4

Boxer boarded the *Mary-Ann* the same way he had left her four days before. It was 0300 and only a few trusted members of the *Mary-Ann*'s crew were on duty.

Sanchez was on deck to greet him with a hearty handshake and a slap on the back. "The Russians are going crazy," Sanchez said. "Absolutely crazy!"

Boxer nodded. "My men are standing by to offload the gold," Boxer said.

"Yes, yes," Sanchez answered. "My men are ready. How long do you think it will take?"

"An hour at the most," Boxer replied.

"Do your men want anything?" Sanchez asked.

"Nothing that you could give them."

Sanchez winked. "I've had some lovely women flown out —"

"Nothing!" Boxer said sharply.

Sanchez's hands flew up defensively.

Boxer keyed Bush, who was now in command of the *Shark*. "Captain, have the men offload the gold."

Sanchez summoned his men and the process of transferring the gold began. It took exactly fifty-five minutes. As soon as it was completed, the *Shark* eased away from the *Mary-Ann* and quickly slid beneath the water.

"I counted two hundred and fifty bars," Sanchez said. "I thought there would be more."

"There was," Boxer answered. "I gave half of it to the Russians."

"What? You did what?" Sanchez almost shouted.

"It's a long story," Boxer said. "I put it down in my report to Williams. Now, if you don't mind, I'd like to go to my cabin. Do I have the same one or —"

"No, no, of course you have the same one," Sanchez answered. He was visibly upset, but was trying very hard not to show it.

"See you in the morning — I mean, later today," Boxer said.

Sanchez followed him. "That was a fortune you gave away," he said in a pinched voice.

"Yes, I guess it was. But, you know, I never thought of it that way. I guess that's because I don't have a fortune to begin with and therefore didn't think about it when I did have it. Anyway, it wasn't my fortune."

They had reached the cabin door. "Looks like we'll have good weather today," Boxer said, looking up at the sky. "Well, goodnight." He shook Sanchez's hand, opened the door, entered the cabin and rushed into the bathroom, where he doubled up with laughter.

"What's so funny?" Tracy Kimble asked.

Boxer saw her reflection in the bathroom mirror. She was wearing a black diaphanous nightgown. The light streamed through it, giving the illusion that she was more naked than if she had been totally nude.

"Well, aren't you going to tell me?" she asked.

Boxer took a tissue out of the box and dried the tears from his eyes. Just five days before they had been less than friendly toward one another and not only wasn't he prepared to find her in his cabin, he wasn't even sure that he wanted her there. To have any sort of relationship with her meant he'd have to ride an emotional cyclone and he didn't want to do that.

"I was waiting for you," she said calmly.

"That was considerate of you," Boxer answered. "Before I left, I didn't think I was one of your favorite people."

"Ah, so you did notice that," she said with a slight laugh.

Boxer watched her breasts move. The left one had almost escaped out from under its covering.

"Frankly, I was annoyed with you," she said.

Boxer crumpled the tissue and dropped it in the waste basket. "I'm sorry about that," he said.

"You couldn't care less!" she exclaimed.

Boxer nodded. "You're right about that." And he started toward the door.

Tracy moved aside to let him pass; then she followed him into the bedroom. "That wasn't much of a greeting," she commented.

He shrugged and started to undress.

"Do you want me to stay?" she asked.

Boxer sat down on the edge of the bed. Looking up at her, he said, "I'm dog tired. I haven't had much sleep since I left here. I don't want to play games with you, Tracy. Stay if you want to stay; if you want to go, then go."

Boxer slipped off his shoes; then stood up and unzipped his pants. A few moments later he was completely naked. "I want to have a quick shower," he said.

She nodded.

Boxer didn't expect to find Tracy there when he returned. But she was already in bed, waiting for him. He stretched out alongside of her and, reaching over to the end table, switched off the lamp.

She put her arms around him.

Enjoying the soft warmth of her body and the scent of her perfume, Boxer closed his eyes. He felt himself sinking deeper and deeper into the dark depths of sleep…

He was on the bottom of the sea, where the gold was. Tom was close to him; they were watching the men advance toward the cylinder of gold. Then the mines started going off. Silently, tearing men to pieces. The fight brought the sharks — hundreds of them, swerving through the water. But the cylinders of gold gleamed brighter and brighter. The killer whales rushed in, devouring sharks and men alike and the water became colder and colder. Boxer saw the water moving toward them. It was pure white, so white that it looked more like snow than water. It was rushing at them from the south. He worked frantically to tie the two submarines together. Borodine reached through the hulls of the *Q-21* and the *Shark* to take hold of his hand. They made the surface together; then they separated and the depth charging began. Explosion after explosion came. The *Shark* was battered. Water began to pour in and then one of the sides gave way...

"No!" Boxer shouted. "Stand fast!" His body covered with sweat, he bolted up.

"Easy there," Tracy said. "Easy, Jack."

"I'm okay."

Boxer stood up, walked into the sitting room and went directly to the bar, where he poured himself a double Scotch. He drank it before he asked Tracy if she wanted a drink.

"No, thanks," she answered.

Boxer poured another. With the glass in hand, he walked back into the bedroom. He put the glass on the end table and sat down on the bed.

Tracy touched his cheek. "You're wet. I'll get a towel."

Before Boxer could say anything, she was gone. He picked up the glass and finished the Scotch.

Tracy returned and began toweling him.

"Thanks," he said, raising his arms to make it easy for her.

"That must have been some dream," she commented. "I brought some body powder, too." She began to sprinkle it on him and gently rub it over his back and sides. "Stretch out and I'll do your chest."

Boxer eased himself down. He was surprised how strong Tracy's hands were.

"How does that feel?" she asked.

"Good," he answered, closing his eyes.

"Do you often dream like that? I mean, as violently as that?"

"Violently?"

"You were thrashing around and making all sorts of weird sounds. Not words, just sounds."

Boxer didn't answer.

She stopped rubbing his body and said, "I'm a good listener, if you want to talk."

"You'll print every word of what I say and probably misquote at least half of it."

Tracy laughed. "I'm not even going to bother answering you."

"But anyway, thanks for your concern," Boxer said. "I'll try not to dream so violently again, at least not when you're in bed with me."

He was about to ask her if he should say more when the phone rang.

"Let it ring," Tracy said.

Boxer ignored her and lifted the phone. "Boxer, here," he answered.

"Captain, this is Julio. Please come to the bridge," Sanchez said.

"Now?"

"Now," Sanchez answered.

"I'll be there in ten minutes," Boxer said. "Have some black coffee ready."

"It will be ready," Sanchez replied.

Boxer put the phone down. "I have to see Sanchez," he said, switching on the light. He hadn't realized that Tracy had taken off her nightgown. He looked at her, nodded and said, "That body of yours will pass muster anytime, anywhere."

"Do you have to go?"

"It bothers me more than it bothers you," he said, putting on his skivvies. "But Sanchez wouldn't have called me unless it was important."

"I'll be here when you get back," Tracy said.

Boxer froze. Dee Long had used those exact words before he had left her and then she had been murdered.

"What's wrong?" Tracy asked, sitting up in bed with her leg folded under her. "You're absolutely white."

He couldn't tell her about Dee. "Lock the door when I'm gone. No, better still, take this." And he handed her his snub nose .38. "I'm taking the safety off. If anyone other than me comes through that door, point the gun at him and squeeze the trigger."

"You're joking!"

"I never joke, Tracy, when it comes to killing someone," Boxer said. "Just do what I ask." He put the revolver down on the end table.

"How will I know it's you?" she asked.

"I'll knock twice. Pause. Then knock three times. You'll ask who it is and I'll answer 'The *Shark*.'"

"This is crazy!"

"Do it," Boxer ordered.

"Alright, alright. You don't have to bite my head off."

"Just do it," Boxer said again, putting on a pair of pants and slipping his feet into a pair of sneakers. "I'll be back as soon as I can." He bent over and kissed her on the forehead.

"Is that all I get?" she chided.

"More later," he said as he hurried to the door.

"At the radar," Sanchez said as soon as Boxer entered the bridge.

Boxer looked at the scope. There were two targets at seventy-eight degrees.

"The captain says that they have been following us for the better part of two hours," Sanchez said. He was shorter than Boxer and was forced to tilt his head upward to look at him.

"That's just after I came aboard," Boxer commented.

"Who the hell are they?" Sanchez asked.

Boxer shrugged. "In this part of the world, there's no telling who they might be." He looked at the captain of the *Mary-Ann*. "They've kept the same distance?"

"*Si.* A range of seven thousand yards."

"I don't like it," Sanchez said. "I don't like it at all."

Boxer moved out onto the starboard bridge wing and looked at the two targets. They were just two dark masses spotted with some lights. "You wouldn't happen to have infrared glasses aboard?"

"We do," Sanchez answered and, in a quick burst of Spanish, told the captain what he wanted.

In a matter of moments, Boxer trained the night glasses on one of the ships, then moved them to the other. "They're bigger than we are. Fishing trawlers, from what I can see. How many hours to first light?"

Again Sanchez spoke to the captain in Spanish.

"I want the precise time," Boxer said.

Sanchez translated the request.

The captain looked at Boxer and said, "Zero five thirty will be first light."

Boxer trained the glasses on the two ships again. After several minutes of studying each of them, he said, "Their rigging and nets are too clean for them to really be fishing trawlers."

"What?"

"Everything is too orderly. Nets are fresh looking and the lines to the drag boom look as if they've never been used."

"If they're not fishing trawlers..."

"They're fishing trawlers all right," Boxer said.

"I don't understand you then. Just what the fuck are you talking about?"

"They're trawlers," Boxer said. "But they just don't do the kind of fishing most trawlers do."

"Then what do they do?" Sanchez asked, his voice going up in pitch.

"Well," Boxer said, "I think we will find out what they do some time between now and first light." He handed the night glasses back to the captain. "In the meantime, get every member of your crew on the fore deck. What kind of weapons do you have aboard?"

"You must be joking!" Sanchez exclaimed.

"Do I look or sound as if I'm joking?" Boxer asked.

Sanchez hesitated.

"I'll be in my cabin," Boxer said. "Let me know when you've made up your mind."

"Are you sure they're not just trawlers?"

"They are trawlers," Boxer repeated what he had said before. "Only they don't go fishing for fish."

"A dozen handguns, five M-22s, an equal number of Russian Zukoffs."

"Zukoffs?" Boxer questioned. They were the Russian's newest rifle, issued only to elite troops. They were capable of firing any size ammunition, but were best when used with belts of 30mm ammo especially made for it.

"I also have a thousand rounds of belted ammunition," Sanchez said, with a faint smile on his face.

"Nothing else?"

"Two dozen grenades; they come a dozen to a box."

"Not a bad little arsenal," Boxer said sarcastically, "for a yacht."

Sanchez shrugged.

Boxer looked at the radar screen again. The trawlers hadn't come any closer.

"Russian, you think?" Sanchez asked.

"Not likely," Boxer answered, "though this time I wish they were. They could be pirates. It really doesn't matter who they are; their intent is the same, or they wouldn't be following us. Okay, break out all your weapons. Arm your crew first — give them the Zukoffs; then arm all your male guests."

Boxer went over to the PA system, switched it on and said, "This is Captain Boxer. Everyone assemble in the saloon. There will be no exceptions. This is an emergency. I repeat, this is an emergency."

"We better get down to the saloon and explain what's going on," Sanchez said.

"You go down and explain; they're your guests. I'll be down in a few minutes. I want to send a few messages first. They couldn't be more than two or three hours from us. And there might be other ships nearby who could help. Before too long we're going to need all the help we can get."

"You think it's going to be that bad?" Sanchez asked.

Boxer nodded, then he asked, "Do you have scuba equipment on board?"

"Yes," Sanchez answered.

"Have it readied," Boxer said. "We're going to have to use it."

"Anything else?"

"I'll let you know if I need anything, of that you can be sure," Boxer said.

Sanchez walked to the door and said, "I just hope you're wrong about all of this."

"So do I," Boxer answered. "But I'm not."

Sanchez opened the door and left the bridge.

"Any change," Boxer said, pointing to the scope, "let me know immediately."

The captain nodded.

Boxer looked at the screen again: Nothing had changed. There had to be a reason why they hadn't made their move yet and he couldn't even begin to guess what it might be.

"Captain," COMMO said, keying Bush, "a code red is coming in."

Bush set several switches on the COMCOMP, then pressed the run-code button. The information came up on the screen to his left.

EMERGENCY ... BOXER TO BUSH ... MARY-ANN BEING TRACKED ... RETURN IMMED. TO FORMER POSITION ... MIGHT NEED ASSIST.

Bush keyed the COMMO. "Any other messages?"

"A general code red on the emergency frequency," the COMMO responded.

"Can we verify the first message?" Bush asked.

"No. The code is top security. Sending is its own verification."

"Roger that," Bush said and deleted the message from the screen.

"Are we going to respond?" Cowly asked. He was standing just to the right of Bush when the COMMO first keyed him.

"Negative on that," Bush answered. "Our orders are to rendezvous with the *Tecumseh* in approximately six hours and that's exactly what we are going to do."

Cowly said nothing. But he knew that Boxer wouldn't have sent that message if he didn't need help and need it fast. He waited a few minutes and then asked to be excused from the watch for a few minutes.

Bush scanned the COMCOMP. "Everything is working perfectly. I don't see why not. You're excused for ten minutes."

Cowly nodded, left the bridge and hurried to Redfern's quarters.

"Major, get up. It's Cowly," Cowly said, knocking on the door.

"What the hell time is it?"

"I've got to speak to you," Cowly said.

"Come."

Cowly entered Redfern's cabin.

Redfern was already sitting up in his bunk. He lit a cigarette and blew smoke out of his nose and mouth. "What the hell is going on?"

Cowly told him about Boxer's message.

"And you mean Bush isn't going to respond?"

Cowly shook his head. "He didn't say as much but I think he thinks the message is a Russian decoy of some sort."

"If he had half a brain, we might be better off," Redfern commented.

"It's not his brain that's at fault, it's his rigidity. The man won't bend from the rules. What the hell are we going to do?"

"Take him out," Redfern said calmly.

Cowly's eyes went wide.

"I don't mean kill him," Redfern said. "Just neutralize him so that you'll take command."

"Drug him?"

Redfern rubbed his hand over his chin. "No, that wouldn't look too good on a report. He has to have some sort of an accident."

"We don't have much time," Cowly said.

"Okay, you go back to the bridge. In five minutes I'll key him and ask him to join me to watch my men do some judo. He'll come. One of the men will accidentally flip over and fall on him. He'll be out for several hours."

"But how?"

Redfern put up his hands. "You do what you're supposed to do and I'll do what I'm supposed to do. A quick jab with a needle and Captain Bush will be in the land of sweet dreams."

"I thought you didn't want to use drugs."

"You said we don't have much time," Redfern answered. "Besides, what I'm going to use isn't easily detectable. I'll have his head bandaged so he'll think he had a bang on the head."

"With no concussion?"

"God protects us all," Redfern said, "even the rigid amongst us."

"Comrade Captain," the COMMO said, "there is a coded transmission from an unknown source."

"Can we decode it?" Borodine asked.

"No."

"Can you get a fix on it?"

"No, it was two transmissions sent only once."

"Roger that," Borodine answered and wondered whether the message could have come from the *Shark*. Even if it had, there was nothing he could do about it. The *Sea Savage* had been badly damaged and was in no condition to fight either on the surface or below it. She was lucky to still be afloat and moving under her own power.

Borodine went up to the outside bridge on the sail. The three escort destroyers formed a triangle around him. He uttered a weary sigh. There was something almost shameful about having to be protected by surface ships.

Boxer heard the noise coming from the saloon before he entered it. Everyone was talking at once. The crew in Spanish and Sanchez's guests in English.

The instant he stepped into the room, everyone turned toward him.

"I want to know what's going on?" one of the men called out.

"Julio says," another man said, "we're all to be armed."

Boxer walked to the side of the room. "Can everyone see and hear me?" he asked.

"Tell us what's happening," Byron Hayes said.

Boxer had almost forgotten about him. "First, as soon as you're dismissed from this room, go to your cabins and dress. The women in pants — no dresses."

"You still haven't told us anything," another male guest said.

"We are being followed by two ships," Boxer said.

Instantly a hubbub arose.

"Who are they?" one of the women called out.

"Where do they come from?" a man shouted.

Boxer held up his hands. It wasn't enough to quiet them. "Silence," he roared. "Silence. Next time you see my hands go up, I want silence."

"You have no jurisdiction over us," Hayes said.

Boxer went to Hayes, grabbed him by the front of his shirt collar and pushed him down into a chair. "One more sound from you," he said tightly, "and I'll beat the shit out of you. Do you understand?"

Hayes was red in the face.

"Do you understand? I want to hear it loud and clear."

"I understand," Hayes said.

Boxer walked back to where he had been standing. "Those ships are following us for a purpose. I don't know why they haven't attacked us."

"Attack us?" one of the women squealed.

"That's what I said. But if and when they do, I want to be ready for them." He looked toward Sanchez. "Translate what I just said to your men."

During the pause, Boxer took time to look at the guests. There were at least ten new women aboard and several new men. Then he spotted Tracy. She was standing off to one side, looking up at him. Her eyes were bright and her lips slightly parted. Suddenly he realized she was wearing a pair of his pants and one of his shirts.

"Go ahead, Captain," Sanchez said. "I told the crew what you want them to know."

"I don't know what they want," Boxer said. "But whatever it is, if we don't give it to them, they'll try to take it."

"You mean they're pirates?" one of the men asked.

"It doesn't matter what you call them," Boxer said.

"But some of us don't know how to use a rifle," another man protested.

"You don't have to aim it. Just put the ammo in it and point it in the general direction that you want to shoot and pull the trigger."

"Where will the women stay?" one of them asked.

"Here in the saloon," Boxer said. "Some of you will be given handguns. Use them to protect yourselves and each other. Are there any more questions?"

"Why can't we get help?" one of the women asked.

"Because," Boxer said, "we're too far away from anyone who'd be able to help us." He wasn't about to tell them about the radio message he had sent and give them any false hope. "Any other questions? None? Okay, go to your cabins and dress. Get back here in ten minutes, and I mean ten minutes — no more and no less. Sanchez, start passing out the Zukoffs to your men. Have all of the other arms brought up to the saloon."

Sanchez said something to his crew and they followed him out the door.

"Better go down and dress," Boxer said to Tracy, who hadn't moved from where she was standing.

"I am dressed," she said.

He went over to her. "This is no joke," he said. "We could be in real trouble."

"I thought Hayes would crap in his pants when you grabbed hold of him," she said.

"Tracy..."

She flung her arms around him and he could feel her braless breasts pressed hard against his chest.

He pulled her away and held her at arm's length. "Put some more clothes on," he ordered. "Do it now, or I'll have two of the crew help you do it."

She stuck out her tongue. "They might enjoy that a lot more than running around with guns."

The phone rang.

Boxer let go of her, crossed the room and picked up the phone. "Boxer here."

"Captain Boxer, there is another ship on the radar," the captain of the *Mary-Ann* said.

"Where?"

"One five degrees," the captain answered.

"What's her range?" Boxer asked.

"Twelve thousand yards."

"Speed?"

"One zero knots."

Boxer did some quick figuring. "That gives us a bit less than thirty minutes before we meet her. I'll be back on the bridge before that. Let me know if there are any other changes."

"*Sí, sí,* Captain."

Boxer put down the phone. "There are three of them," he said, going back to where Tracy was standing. "Hurry, go and put other clothes on. We don't have much time."

The phone rang again. Boxer answered it.

"Captain Boxer, the other two ships to the south of us have increased their speed. They are doing one five knots."

"Thanks," Boxer said.

Some of the guests began to drift back and Sanchez returned, carrying four rifles.

Boxer told him about the third ship to the north. "And the two south of us," he said, "have increased their speed."

"They were waiting for the third ship?" Sanchez asked in a high-pitched voice that betrayed his nervousness.

Boxer nodded. "So it would seem."

"This is for real, isn't it?" Tracy asked.

"For real," Boxer answered.

"I'll hurry back," she said and left the saloon.

The phone rang again.

"Answer it," Boxer told Sanchez.

After a moment's listening, Sanchez said, "We've been ordered to heave to and stand by to receive a boarding party."

Boxer rubbed his hand over his beard. "Tell your radio operator to buy us time. Tell him to pretend not to have heard the transmission."

Sanchez spoke in Spanish, then he put down the phone. "The *Mary-Ann* can make eighteen knots."

Boxer shook his head. "They probably could outrun us. Besides, they probably have a three-inch cannon aboard. No, we'll play a different kind of game."

The saloon was filled with guests and members of the crew.

"I need two good scuba divers," Boxer said.

"For what?" one of the men asked.

"To put explosives on the hulls of those trawlers," Boxer said.

"You're nuts!" the man exclaimed.

"Make no mistake about it," Boxer said, "those ships are coming for the kill."

"But why?" Tracy asked.

Boxer hadn't seen her come back into the saloon. Now she was dressed in her own slacks and blouse.

"To get whatever is of value aboard," Boxer answered.

"What do we have of value?" Tracy asked.

Boxer hesitated. But the people had a right to know. He guessed that the men aboard the trawlers knew what the *Mary-Ann* was carrying. "Gold," he said. "There is a fortune in gold aboard this vessel."

Everyone began to talk at once.

The phone rang again.

"Quiet down!" Boxer shouted. When they fell silent, he picked up the phone and said, "Boxer here."

"Captain Boxer," the captain of the *Mary-Ann* said. "All three ships have increased speed."

"Let them come within one thousand yards," Boxer said, "then head straight for one of them. Understand?"

"*Si, si.* I understand."

Boxer put the phone down. "Sanchez, have your men take up positions on the side closest to the ship we'll pass. I want them to fire at the bridge and at any man on the ship's deck who has a weapon. The other men get into position to fire their weapons at the ship itself. I need a few men with good throwing arms."

Two men volunteered.

"You guys take four grenades each. Go to the top deck. Each of you find separate cover. When we slide by the trawler, throw the grenades." Boxer went over to the box of grenades, picked one and said, "This is the pin. Once you pull the pin and release the plunger, you have ten seconds to let go. Make sure it lands on the other ship."

"What are we going to do about the other two ships?" Hayes asked.

"Sink them, if we can," Boxer said.

"They'll blow us out of the water," Hayes said.

"Maybe yes, maybe no," Boxer answered. "Okay, everyone to their positions."

The men filed out of the saloon.

"What are we going to do about the other two ships?" Sanchez asked.

"Fight them," Boxer answered. Then he said to the women, "The wounded and the dead will be brought here. Sanchez, have the cooks prepare coffee and have lots of hot water ready. I want all your medical supplies brought here to the saloon."

Sanchez went to the phone and relayed Boxer's instructions to the purser.

Two of the women began to weep.

"Crying won't help anything," Boxer said. "There will be wounded and there probably will be dead. We will be fighting for our lives." Then, looking at Sanchez, he said, "Grab a rifle and as much ammo as you can carry and come to the bridge with me." He took a rifle for himself, put four bandoliers of ammunition around his neck and fastened three grenades to his belt before he was ready to go.

"Jack?" Tracy called.

He stopped at the door and turned to her.

She came up to him. "*Vaya con Dios*," she said, kissing him lightly on the lips.

Boxer nodded. "See you," he said, closing the door. At that moment, he loved her. He knew in this kind of crisis he could absolutely depend on her.

Boxer checked the radar screen. The two ships to the south were three thousand yards away. The one to the north was less than eighteen hundred. "Tell your engine room to give me everything she has," Boxer said. "I'll take the helm."

The captain of the *Mary-Ann* rang up full speed.

Boxer motioned the helmsman aside and took the wheel. "Sanchez," he said, "send every man on the bridge down to the saloon to pick up the remaining rifles, ammo and grenades."

Sanchez barked out the order in Spanish.

"Captain," Boxer said, "kill all lights."

The *Mary-Ann* went completely dark.

Boxer swung the wheel hard over to starboard. The *Mary-Ann* seemed to shudder, but she began to respond. Within minutes they were rushing south.

"Give me the range on the two ships off our bow," Boxer said.

"Fifteen hundred yards," the captain said. "One is at seven nine degrees, the other at nine three degrees."

The men returned from the saloon.

"What the hell are you going to do?" Sanchez asked.

"Make them sweat," Boxer answered.

Suddenly the lights on the two ships in front of them went out.

Boxer swung the wheel hard over to port. The *Mary-Ann* trembled. But she turned.

"Tell the men on the starboard side to stand ready," Boxer said.

The captain relayed the order.

"What's the range of the ship off our starboard bow?" Boxer asked.

"Five hundred yards," the captain answered.

"Helmsman," Boxer said, "bring the *Mary-Ann* alongside. Get us as close as you can without hitting her."

The captain translated.

"*Sí, sí,*" the man answered, taking the helm.

Boxer picked up a rifle and loaded it.

Suddenly a beam of light reached out from the approaching ship and illuminated the bridge.

Boxer threw the rifle up to his shoulder and squeezed the trigger. The glass window shattered and the light went out. "Stand by," he shouted. "Pass the word: Everyone stand by!"

Sanchez relayed the order in Spanish.

Suddenly their bows were passing.

"Fire," Boxer yelled. "Fire!"

The guns on the *Mary-Ann* opened up.

"Get those grenades off!" Boxer shouted, pulling the pin of one and hurling it onto the deck of the passing ship.

One explosion took place forward, another against the side cabin. Boxer's grenade exploded just aft of the wheelhouse.

Return automatic fire was coming in; then 20mm rounds began chewing on the *Mary-Ann*.

"Get that gun," Boxer shouted.

Two crew men rushed along the deck and were cut down. Boxer threw another grenade. It landed amidships and caused a fire.

The 20mm was still firing.

One of the guests threw a grenade at it. The explosion hurled the gunners into the sea and threw the gun on its side.

The *Mary-Ann* slid past the trawler.

"Casualties?" Boxer shouted. "How many casualties?"

"Four wounded. One bad," one of the men answered.

"Get them into the saloon," Boxer said.

Suddenly an explosion ripped the middle of the trawler and a huge orange flame shot up. She broke in half.

"Take her to course nine zero degrees," Boxer said.

The captain translated and the helmsman put the *Mary-Ann* hard over and brought her to her new course.

The other two ships were firing their 20mm. Slugs were tearing into the *Mary-Anne*'s cabin.

Boxer didn't need a radar reading to tell him the ships were only several hundred yards away. "Put us between them," Boxer said.

Sanchez translated.

The helmsman hesitated.

Boxer pushed the man away from the wheel and gave a few spokes to starboard.

The trawlers put their searchlights on.

A burst of rifle fire from the *Mary-Ann* killed the lights.

"Sanchez," Boxer said. "Take the wheel and hold it steady."

"I'll take it," the helmsman said.

Boxer gave him the wheel and shouted to the men on deck. "Stand by to repel boarders. Stand by. I want grenades thrown."

The firing began.

The *Mary-Ann* was sliding between the two trawlers. Men from both trawlers leaped onto her deck. Boxer, Sanchez and the captain fired down at them.

The 20mm were slamming into the *Mary-Ann*. A fire had started forward.

Several grenades were thrown. The wheelhouse of one of the trawlers blew out.

A second fire started on the *Mary-Ann*.

The phone on the bridge began to ring. The captain answered it. "We got fire in the engine room," he said.

"Can it be controlled?" Boxer asked.

An explosion blew off part of the aft deck.

The face of the *Mary-Anne*'s captain went white. He dropped the phone and crossed himself.

The trawlers were turning away. One of them was burning but still able to fight.

"Where's the PA switch?" Boxer asked.

"Over on the wall," Sanchez said.

Boxer flicked the switch into its On position. "Stand by to abandon ship," he said calmly. "Stand by to abandon ship. Lifeboat stations. Lifeboat stations. Launch life rafts. Launch life rafts."

The *Mary-Ann* was beginning to settle at the bow.

One of the crew reported that two of the four lifeboats aboard were shot up.

"Get the women in the other two," Boxer said. "The men will use the rafts. Abandon ship. Abandon ship."

"What about the gold?" Sanchez asked.

"Nothing about the gold," Boxer said, thinking for a moment about all of the men who had died for it. "Abandon ship. Everyone abandon ship."

"You go," said the captain of the *Mary-Ann*. "I will follow."

"Now, Captain," Boxer said, pointing a rifle at him. "Now."

"Come," Sanchez said. "It is no use to argue with him."

Boxer was out on the flying bridge. The first trawler was listing badly to the starboard side. She would probably sink. A second ship was afloat, but black smoke was still billowing out of her hull. Only the third ship was unscathed, though Boxer was sure she had several dead and wounded aboard. He looked down at the two lifeboats and the rafts. All of the guests and the wounded were aboard. He took a moment to search for Tracy, found her and then hurried off the bridge, grabbing four grenades from the box and attaching them to his belt. He wasn't at all sure what the attackers would do, but he wanted to have a surprise for them if they came close enough to the lifeboats or the rafts. He left the bridge, ran toward the bow and was actually able to walk into the sea. Then with powerful strokes, he swam toward one of the rafts and was quickly hauled aboard by several crew members of the *Mary-Ann*.

Boxer looked toward the east. It would be dawn; then the full blaze of the tropical sun would beat down on them. "How much water do we have?' he called.

"Two ten-gallon cans," one of the women called from a lifeboat.

"Two more on this boat," Tracy shouted.

"How many wounded?' Boxer asked.

"Eight," a woman called out. "One dying."

"Four dead," Tracy said. "All crew members. We didn't take their bodies with us."

Suddenly another explosion rocked the *Mary-Ann*. She was standing on her bow. In a few minutes, she would go straight down.

"Get those lifeboats close to the rafts," Boxer said. "That's right; put out the oars and pull on them."

"Captain," Sanchez said, tapping Boxer on the shoulder. "She's coming for us."

Boxer looked up. The undamaged trawler had come about and was now bearing down on them. He guessed it was less than a thousand yards away. "We'll stay aboard as long as we can," he said. "Then everyone in the water. I have four grenades. I want to get that bastard."

"I'll take one," one of the male guests said.

"Gi'me one," the helmsman said, putting out his hand.

"Me, too," the captain of the *Mary-Ann* said.

Boxer handed each of them a grenade and kept one for himself. "Move those lifeboats off," he called out, motioning them away from the rafts. "Move them away."

"Holy Christ," Sanchez exclaimed, "look at the flag!"

"Libyan!" Boxer answered.

Suddenly the bow of the trawler exploded. The rest of her rose out of the water; then she came down on her side.

"Jesus!" one of the men exclaimed.

"There," Boxer shouted, pointing to the northwest. "The *Shark*!"

She broke surface between the rafts and the other two trawlers. Thirty seconds after the hatches were opened the gun crews were firing at the two trawlers.

The survivors of the *Mary-Ann* cheered.

Within a minute both vessels were sinking.

The *Shark* came close to the rafts. Boxer looked up at Cowly, who was on the bridge. "Get the women and wounded aboard first," he shouted. Cowly waved to him.

Redfern and several of his men came out on deck.

"The lifeboats first," Boxer yelled.

Four men went over the side and swam out to the lifeboats; four others came toward the rafts.

Within minutes, Boxer stepped aboard the *Shark*. He grabbed hold of Redfern's hand. "Not much time to spare," he said.

"Next time we'll come a bit sooner," Redfern answered with a smile.

"Let me have your radio," Boxer requested.

"Cowly is in command," Redfern said.

Boxer arched his eyebrows but didn't ask any questions. He keyed Cowly. "We have wounded. One critically. Alert the *Tecumseh* to change course and come toward us."

"Aye, aye, Skipper," Cowly answered.

Boxer waited until everyone was below before he left the deck and went into the sail. A few moments later he was on the bridge. He looked out at the debris and the oil slicks. There were no survivors. "A damn close call," he said to Cowly.

"The close ones don't matter," Cowly answered.

Boxer nodded, then he said, "We'll go down to the bottom and send a team of scubas out to recover the gold from the *Mary-Ann.*"

He checked the fathometer: The bottom was 250 feet down. "Take care of the details," Boxer said. "I'll see to the survivors."

"Sure, Skipper," Cowly answered. Then, putting out his hand, he said. "Glad to have you back on board."

"Glad to be on board," Boxer answered, shaking Cowly's hand.

Cowly hit the klaxon twice. "Diving," he said over the MC. "Diving. Clear the decks. DO make two five zero feet."

Boxer went through the hatchway into the depths of the *Shark.* Even as he was going down the steps, he felt her tilt at the bow. It was a good feeling ... a safe feeling.

All of the survivors from the *Mary-Ann* were in the mess area. When Boxer joined them, he was greeted with cheers and back slaps. With Redfern at his side, he moved to the far side of the room.

He held up his hands for silence and immediately got it. "Has everyone been given food and something hot to drink?" he asked.

Satisfied that they had been taken care of, Boxer said, "In a few hours we will rendezvous with our mother ship, all of you will be more comfortable. In the meantime you cannot leave this area. Should you, Major Redfern's men will stop you. As you probably guess by now, the *Shark* is a very special submarine and all of its operating equipment is highly classified. In addition, we have a problem in one of our aft compartments involving a high concentration of radioactivity; therefore, for your own safety, I urge you to remain here in the mess area. Major Redfern's men will be here to help you, should you need help."

"Skipper," Cowly said, keying him, "we're going down to the bottom."

"Roger that," Boxer answered. Then, to the people, he said, "In a few minutes we will come to rest on the seabed at two hundred and ninety feet. A team of my men will go out and board the *Mary-Ann* to recover the gold. When they return, we will get underway again and rendezvous with our mother ship. Are there any questions?"

"Hundreds," Tracy said.

"They'll have to wait," Boxer answered.

Tracy ignored him. "What the hell are you doing here, Tom?" she asked.

Redfern flushed.

"Any questions about the next few hours?" Boxer asked again. He waited a few moments. "None? Good. All of you have been great. See you soon." And with Redfern at his side, Boxer left the mess area.

"Do you think Tracy will let go of it?" Redfern asked.

Boxer shrugged. "You never know what she'll do."

CHAPTER 5

It took three days after the *Shark* was safely stowed inside the *Tecumseh* for Boxer to have any leisure to spend on deck, or even dine with the survivors of the *Mary-Ann*. He spent eighteen hours a day assessing the damage done to the *Shark*, writing special evaluation reports and supervising the decontamination of the radioactive area.

When he finally did come on deck, it was late in the afternoon of the fourth day. The *Tecumseh* was off the eastern edge of Brazil, just over the horizon, where there were giant cumulonimbus clouds that moved slowly across the sky as if they were part of a procession of prehistoric animals.

Boxer took several deep breaths, then rested both hands on the railing. It felt good to be out in the sunshine. Only when he stopped working did he realize how tired he was and how much the mission took out of him.

"A penny for your thoughts," Tracy said, coming up behind him.

"Not worth even that much," he said, facing her. She was wearing the same clothes she had worn when the *Mary-Ann* was sunk. But her face was deeply tanned and without makeup, she was startlingly attractive.

"You're staring at me," she said.

"I'm sorry," Boxer said with a smile, "but you look better than I have ever seen you."

"I'm not sure that's a compliment," Tracy responded.

"It was meant to be."

"Accepted as such, Skipper," she said with a nod.

Boxer gestured toward the horizon. "Over there is Brazil," he said.

"Not terribly important," Tracy said, "if you're not going there."

Boxer fished out his pipe, which he filled and lit before asking, "How are the other people getting along?"

"Fine. Julio says his insurance will cover all our losses and then some. He and his purser are busy compiling lists for the insurance claims. Didn't you lose some personal items?"

"I'll mention it to Sanchez another time," Boxer said.

"You know," she said, "you were absolutely magnificent."

Boxer felt the color rise in his cheeks.

Tracy stepped closer to him. "Everyone says so," she said.

"It was one of the times," he said, trying to play down his role, "I earned my pay. It doesn't happen that often."

"That's not what Byron Hayes says," she answered.

Boxer stiffened.

"Just what do you do? I know you command the *Shark* and this ship, too, when you're aboard. But who runs the *Shark*? The Navy?"

"Let it alone, Tracy," Boxer said, gently taking hold of her arms. "Please, let it alone. You really don't want to know too much about what I do, or who runs the *Shark*."

She looked up at him; then with a slow nod, she said, "All right, Jack, I'll let it alone."

"Thanks," he said and he let go of her.

The *Tecumseh* entered the Chesapeake Bay a week after she and the *Shark* had rendezvoused off the northwest coast of Africa. The ship's anchors were let go at 2200. Boxer was on the bridge with Rugger, the *Tecumseh's* skipper when Boxer wasn't aboard.

"Everyone from the *Mary-Ann* asked to be put ashore tonight," Rugger said.

"I'm leaving a skeleton crew aboard the *Shark*," Boxer said. "Just enough to get her into dry dock. Then a special company detail will take over."

"You look tired," Rugger said.

"I am," Boxer answered.

Neither man spoke.

"Skipper," the *Tecumseh*'s radar man said, "I've got contact with the birds coming in. Bearing two nine five degrees. Range two five miles. Altitude three thousand feet. Speed seven zero knots."

Rugger switched on the landing lights. "I had the people wait in the mess area," he said. "It's cold out there and feels colder with the wind blowing the way it is."

"I'm sorry we didn't spend much time together," Boxer said.

Rugger nodded. "There'll be other times. Besides, Sanchez proved to be a damn good chess player and a better art connoisseur."

"Meaning he bought one of your paintings," Boxer said with a smile.

"Three of them," Rugger said proudly.

The sound of the choppers filled the bridge. "Time to get going," Boxer said, extending his hand.

"Good luck," Rugger responded.

Boxer left the bridge and hurried down the steps onto the deck.

The *Mary-Ann*'s survivors were already boarding the first bird. The other two remained aloft over the port side of the ship.

Tracy came up to Boxer. "You taking this one out, too?" she asked.

"So it seems," Boxer answered.

The roar of the helicopter's engines made it impossible for them to speak until they were airborne.

Tracy leaned close to him. "Are you going anywhere in particular?" she asked.

"To a hotel for tonight," he answered.

"Stay with me," she said.

Boxer nodded. "Thanks. I'd like that."

"I don't like to leave things unfinished," Tracy said, linking her arm with his.

"I never realized you had a fetish about tidiness," Boxer answered.

She nodded. "That proves how very little you know about me," she said, pressing his arm against her right breast.

"But what I do know, I know pretty damn well." He grinned.

"If you didn't have that shit-eating grin on your face," she said, "I'd be inclined to agree with you."

Tracy's apartment was a three-room affair on the twenty-sixth floor of a brand-new building a few minutes' walk from the Mall.

"You want to shower first, or —"

"You first," Boxer said. "I'll pour myself a drink and make a few phone calls."

"Make me a very dry martini," Tracy said, "and we'll shower together."

"Not a bad exchange," Boxer said, putting his valise down on the floor and dropping his trench coat over the back of a chair.

"The bar cart is in the living room and the ice is in the freezer," Tracy said, disappearing into the bedroom.

Boxer switched on the light and walked over to the bar cart. Directly behind it was a glass sliding door that opened to a corner terrace with a spectacular view of the Mall. He was half tempted to open the door and step out on the terrace. Instead he poured himself a straight Scotch, drank it quickly, poured another and drank that one too before he went into the kitchen for the ice.

Boxer mixed a martini, misting it with vermouth. "Drink's ready," he called out.

"Be there in a jiffy," Tracy answered.

Boxer dropped three cubes of ice into a glass and poured two fingers of Scotch over them; then he went to the phone and dialed his former wife's number.

Her new husband answered.

"This is Jack Boxer. May I speak to Gwen?"

There was silence on the other end. Boxer figured the man must have put his hand over the mouthpiece while he spoke to Gwen.

Suddenly Gwen was on the line. He heard her breathing before she asked, "What is it?"

Her tone instantly bothered him. "Sorry if I disturbed what you were doing," he said, hoping the innuendo wouldn't be lost on her.

It wasn't. "We weren't — I mean, I wasn't doing anything."

Boxer smiled. "I called to find out how my son is," he said.

"At one o'clock in the morning?" she asked.

Boxer glanced at his watch. He hadn't realized what time it was. "I just came ashore," he said.

Gwen didn't answer.

"Tell John I'll be up to see him in a few days," he said.

"I'll tell him."

"Have you spoken to Mom or Dad?" Boxer asked.

"Mom is okay," Gwen said. "And Dad is holding his own."

Boxer nodded.

"Anything else?" Gwen asked impatiently.

"No. Go back to whatever you weren't doing," Boxer said and he hung up. He went back to the bar cart, picked up his glass and drank.

"Now I'll have the martini," Tracy said.

Boxer turned around. She was nude. He handed her the drink.

"I walk around here this way all the time," she said. "Only the birds can see my charms and they're not interested in them."

"That doesn't say much for their taste, at least when it applies to women."

Tracy laughed. "That's where they win wings down; they don't have to apply it to women, only to other lady birds. I'm told by my paper's nature editor, they have their own standards."

"You are a…"

"Piece of ass?"

"I wasn't going to say that."

"It wouldn't bother me, if you were," Tracy said, raising her glass to him. "Now what should we drink to?"

"You tell me," Boxer said.

"To a night of good sex," she said.

He touched her glass with his. "I'll drink to a night of good sex with you any time."

Tracy nodded and drank, keeping her green eyes on Boxer.

Boxer's hearing was set for three days after he returned, at ten a.m. in Kinkade's office at Langly. Williams was there, sitting to Kinkade's right; Admiral Stark was on his left. Bush sat next to Williams; Cowly was next to Bush and he sat next to Stark.

There was pad and ballpoint pen in front of every man. Equidistant between them on the table was a tray with a pitcher of ice water and six glasses around it.

Kinkade began by giving the date and time of the meeting, then he said, "Everything said during the course of this hearing will be taped."

"I wouldn't have it any other way," Boxer said.

Kinkade glared at him.

"Before this meeting begins and everyone's time is wasted," Boxer said, "I resign."

Kinkade started to cough.

Williams shifted uneasily in his chair and Stark looked questioningly at Boxer.

"I resign," Boxer said, "because Kinkade is a horse's ass and I for one will not risk my life, or the lives of the men aboard the *Shark*, to follow the dumb directions of Mister Kinkade. I hope the tape recorder is on."

"You can't resign," Williams said quietly.

"You wouldn't want to go down to the wire with me on that one, would you, Mister Williams?" Boxer asked. "I'm ready to take this entire matter to the President, if that's the way you want it, or to the people of the United States."

Williams flushed.

Boxer pointed his finger at Kinkade. "You sent Bush to look over my shoulder. Well, you're lucky I didn't kill him. Yes, he's an excellent officer and a very brave man, as my reports both written and taped have shown. But like yourself, he's a rigid horse's ass."

Bush was out of his chair. "I don't have to take that —"

Boxer jumped to his feet. "You planted a fucking bomb on the *Q-21*, when she was under my protection."

"On my orders," Kinkade said.

"Listen," Boxer told him, "without the *Q-21* everyone on the *Shark* would be dead. Your boys didn't count on us being caught in a cold-water storm three hundred feet down. It's in the report. We survived because we were lashed to the *Q-21*."

"Let me remind you they survived because they were lashed to the *Shark*," Kinkade said.

Boxer looked down at Stark. "For God's sake, will you tell him which end is up?"

"Captain Boxer means," Stark said, "that the two submarines were operating under a flag of truce. Planting the bomb was a violation of that truce."

"More than that," Boxer said, "it was a violation of my word to Captain Borodine."

"Your word to a Russian —"

Boxer's face was very red. Again he pointed his finger at Bush. "Listen, I'm going to tell you this once and only once and when you find yourself a new captain, tell him what I'm going to tell you. Captain Igor Borodine is probably the finest submarine captain in this fucking world. But more important than that, he is one of the finest men in this fucking world. I would have gladly chosen him to be my brother if the fates had given me that choice. He honored his word to me. But on your orders, Bush broke my word to him."

"We are not getting anywhere with the matters before this hearing," Kinkade said in a low voice.

"Sir," Cowly said, "I have something to say."

"Let him speak," Stark said.

"The skipper — I mean, Captain Boxer — is the best we have. I've served under very good captains, but Captain Boxer — well, sir, every man on the *Shark* knows he can trust him in a tight situation. They know because they've been in tight situations with him and he has always gotten them out."

"Just what are you trying to tell me, Commander?" Kinkade asked.

"If the skipper goes, the whole crew will go. They won't sail under another captain."

"That's nothing short of mutiny," Kinkade shouted, striking the table with the palm of his right hand. "I won't have it."

"Sorry, sir," Cowly said, "but you already have it. The men knew about this hearing and before they went ashore they took a vote on it. The vote was unanimous. Captain Boxer remains our skipper, or we don't sail. By the way, Major Redfern and his men voted the same way."

Boxer was too surprised to show any reaction.

Stark cleared his throat several times before he was able to speak. "This is very irregular and not within the experience of the Navy. Since the men serving on the *Shark* are not completely under the control of the Navy, the application of the courts-martial manual would not be advisable."

"Are you telling me," Kinkade asked, "that you're not going to do anything about this?"

"No," Stark answered, "I'm telling you that you must decide whether or not you want the *Shark* operational."

"That is not the question here," Kinkade roared.

Williams held up his hands. "There's no need to shout," he said. "We all know that the *Shark* must remain operational. Even now it is in dry dock being repaired and refitted and several new pieces of gear are being added to her, based on Captain Boxer's excellent technical reports. Captain, would you mind if I asked you a few questions?"

"Go ahead," Boxer said, finally sitting down.

"Why did you answer the Mayday when you knew it —"

"If you heard the sound of a plane going down near your home," Boxer said, "would you go and try to rescue the people in that plane?"

"I would," Williams answered. "But I wouldn't be in any danger of being shot at by a Russian."

"I did not think Borodine would answer the distress signal," Boxer answered.

"What was the young woman Dee Long doing in your bed?" Williams asked.

Boxer looked at Stark.

"Give it to them straight," Stark said.

"Dee — Miss Long — was on her way back to go to prison. She came to my quarters and was waiting for me."

"Having a woman in —" Kinkade started to say.

"You make it sound like an act of mercy," Williams said.

"It would have been an act of great pleasure."

"And you have no regrets?" Williams asked.

"Only that she was murdered," Boxer said.

"My final question, Captain. Would you tell me why you gave the Russians half of the gold you took from them?"

Boxer smiled.

"I fail to see anything humorous in your actions," Williams said.

"It was my gift to Borodine," Boxer said.

"Your gift," Kinkade said, jumping to his feet. "The gold wasn't yours. How would you consider it your gift?"

"The gold wasn't yours either," Boxer answered. "The gold belonged to me and the members of my crew. We fought and died for it."

"That was your mission," Kinkade stormed.

Boxer nodded. "My mission was completed; then came the undersea storm. That storm changed matters. I figured

Borodine deserved something for having helped save the *Shark*."

"You still fail to realize that you helped save his boat, too," Kinkade said.

"But I had the gold. He had taken heavy losses to protect it and had failed. I gave him half of what we had taken from him as a goodwill gesture."

"We are not in that business," Kinkade said.

Boxer shrugged. "Borodine and his men earned it. I can't and won't say more than that."

"I don't think there's any need to continue this hearing," Williams said.

"That's my feeling, too," Boxer said wearily. "I'll have my resignation on your desk tomorrow morning, Admiral."

"We'll let you know what our decision is," Williams said.

"You don't seem to understand," Boxer said. "Your fucking decision doesn't count. Unless I'm given a free hand to run all future operations the way I see fit and unless you take Bush, or anyone else like him off my back, you can find yourself another captain and, according to Mister Cowly, another crew."

"Be that as it may," Williams said, unruffled by Boxer, "you will be notified of our decision later this afternoon. Please be in your hotel at sixteen hundred hours."

"I'll be there," Boxer answered, catching Stark's almost imperceptible nod.

Boxer left the table and went to the door. Cowly followed him. Bush hesitated.

"C'mon, Bush," Boxer said. "They don't want you around either. Besides, I owe you a drink for sinking a couple of Russian trawlers. Don't look so surprised. When I owe a man a drink, I always pay."

Boxer, Cowly and Bush cabbed it back to Washington and wound up in bar on East Capital Avenue.

Boxer was drinking vodka, Cowly was a bourbon man and Bush was sipping at a very dry martini.

"What you don't understand," Boxer said to Bush, "is that the rules are there for guidelines; they can't be the last word."

"Kinkade gave me a direct order," Bush answered. "A direct order."

"But he wouldn't have given you that order if you hadn't contacted him."

Bush put down his glass. "You want it straight?" he asked.

"Straight," Boxer said.

"I didn't want to waste the opportunity."

"Waste what opportunity?"

"The chance to sink the *Q-21*," Bush said. "Now she'll have to be killed the hard way."

Boxer drained the last bit of vodka from his glass, pushed it toward the back of the bar and, gesturing to the barkeep, he said, "Do it again. You guys ready for another round?"

Both men pushed their glasses toward the barkeep.

"Yeah," Boxer said, "she'll have to be killed the hard way and that's the way it should be. Not the way you wanted to do it. Not by blowing her hull out when Borodine doesn't expect it. That's too fucking easy."

"You see," Cowly said, "we make the rules to this game."

"Game? Game?" Bush said, his voice becoming so screechy that Boxer motioned him to speak lower. "This isn't a game. You're trying to blow one another out of the water."

"The stakes are higher," Boxer said. "But it's a game. Deadly, yes. But still a game."

The barkeep returned with their refills.

Boxer looked around for a phone, spotted one near the rest rooms and told the other two that he had promised to phone someone.

A couple of minutes later, he was speaking to Tracy. He had spent two nights with her and earlier that morning he had moved to the hotel he usually stayed at.

"I figured," he said, "I'd better tell you I moved to my hotel."

After a momentary pause, Tracy asked, "Anything wrong with the service you were getting at my place?"

"Too much of a good thing can spoil a man," he answered.

"When will I see you again?"

"I'll be around," Boxer answered.

"Call me when you want some good fucking," she said and hung up.

Boxer returned the phone to its cradle. Tracy was upset. He thought about calling her again, but dismissed the idea. They had had similar partings before. Some more abrupt and with a great deal more anger. He shrugged and went back to the bar.

"I bet Cowly, here, you were bluffing Kinkade," Bush said.

"How much did you bet?" Boxer asked.

"Fifty."

"Give Cowly fifty bucks," Boxer said. "I meant every word I said, including what I said about having you aboard the *Shark*. I'll drink with you, Bush, but I won't ever again sail with you."

Bush flushed.

"I'd only wind up killing you," Boxer said, looking straight at Bush. After a few moments passed, he said, "That doesn't mean I don't respect your courage or your seamanship. I just don't happen to play the game the way you think it should be played."

"For all you talk about being loose, about bending rules, you don't bend much, if at all."

Boxer nodded. Bush started to hand Cowly a fifty-dollar bill.

"Keep it," Cowly said. "No, better still, you buy the drinks."

"Done," Bush exclaimed. "Done."

His hands locked behind his back, Kinkade was pacing up and back.

Kinkade was smoking a cigar and Williams was doodling on the yellow pad in front of him.

Kinkade suddenly stopped pacing. Standing directly behind his chair, he said, "Boxer is just not the man for the job. That's the long and the short of it. He's not the man for the job."

"Has he failed to carry out any of the missions?" Stark asked, blowing smoke toward the empty end of the table.

"It's the way he has carried them out," Kinkade said, "that worries me."

"Does it worry you, Thomas?" Stark asked, looking across the table at Williams.

"Not really," Williams answered. "But I know what Kinkade means. Boxer is unpredictable. Not totally, mind you. But enough to worry Kinkade."

"Are you saying it doesn't worry you?" Kinkade asked, looking toward Williams.

"I'm not quite as bothered by it as you seem to be."

"What about you, Stark?"

"I admit that I wouldn't do some of the things he has done. But then again I have never been in the circumstances that he has been in."

"Giving that Russian captain half the gold was not exactly an act of a normal man," Kinkade said.

"If Boxer were normal," Stark answered, "he would not be in command of the *Shark*. He is not normal, at least not in terms that most men are. To do the things he has done, he has to be different."

"Then you're willing to give in to his demands?" Kinkade asked.

"It's not so much a case of giving in to his demands," Williams said, "but rather the fact that he is the best man we have for the job."

"There's Bush," Kinkade countered.

"An excellent officer," Stark said. "He's yours to use."

"I don't like to be told what I can or cannot do," Kinkade said.

"Use Bush," Stark said. "The matter is closed and I can go back to my office and get some work done."

"I'm not going to make up my mind now," Kinkade said. "I'll let Boxer stew for a while. I'll tell him that his resignation is being considered."

"He won't go for it," Stark said.

"Tell him," Williams said, "that his resignation has been accepted. You can always change your mind."

"You agree with that?" Kinkade asked, turning his eyes to Stark.

"I agree," Stark said.

"Everything will remain the same," Kinkade said.

"Yes," Williams answered.

"Yes," Stark said.

"He's back in his hotel," Kinkade said, "and our lady will make contact with him sometime within the next few hours. She'll be able to give us a very precise reading of how he reacts to the news that his resignation has been accepted."

"Too bad you don't like him," Stark said. "He's really quite a nice person."

"Boxer doesn't play the game by the Company rules," Kinkade answered.

CHAPTER 6

Two hundred kilometers southeast of Moscow, Paul Hardy stood on a small hill waiting for the Pick-Up One satellite to pass overhead; then for approximately ninety-five seconds he could communicate directly with CIA headquarters in Langly.

Hardy had chosen this particular spot because from it he and the two other agents with him — Dean Foster and Roy Ellis — were able to overlook the smoking ruins of the Kzagka Chemical Installation, where forty-four percent of the solid fuel for the Russian space program was produced.

Hardy, a broad-chested man of middling height with black hair and black eyes, looked nervously at his watch. "This is one contact I don't want to miss," he commented. "I want to get out of this fucking country before it's too late."

Neither of the other men commented.

"Still burning," Hardy said.

"Should for at least a week," Ellis commented. A tall, sharp-featured man, he was the group's demolition expert. For the last ten years, he had worked for the Company. Before that he taught chemistry at Erasmus Hall High School in Brooklyn, New York.

"We're thirty kilometers away from it and I still can see it. I wonder what it looks like from close up."

"Like hell itself and twice as hot," Ellis said.

"Stand by," Foster said, adjusting the range and azimuth controls on the SATDIRFND. "Target ... two five nine. Range twenty-five thousand miles. Ten seconds to go ... eight ... six ... five..."

Hardy picked up the mike and pressed the scrambler button.

"You're on," Foster told him.

"Mission completed," Hardy said.

"Roger that. Have it on the seismograph."

"Coming out as planned."

"Negative. Go to Moscow. Follow plan L. Follow plan L."

"Roger that," Hardy said and lowered the mike.

"What was that all about?" Foster asked.

"We've been ordered to Moscow," Hardy answered.

"Kinkade must be nuts!" Ellis exclaimed.

"I wouldn't doubt it," Hardy said. "I wouldn't doubt it at all."

Boris Donskoi, the civlian photogrammetrist in the naval ministry, who first identified the *Shark* for the Russian naval authorities, left his office promptly at five. As he stepped out of doors, he sniffed at the air. Though it was only the eighteenth of October, it smelled of snow.

Boris pulled up his collar and walked toward the metro station. The house he lived in was one station away from the end of the line. Because of his connections to people in high places, he was able to rent a four-room apartment in one of Moscow's loveliest residential areas.

Boris was a short, plump man with a cherubic face, pale blue eyes and thinning light brown hair. He sauntered along. It was not his way to hurry anywhere for anything and since he was a bachelor, he did not have to be home for dinner at a particular time.

Suddenly Boris was aware that a man was walking alongside of him. He didn't like having someone walk so close to him and was about to slow his pace even more to let the man pass.

"Do not change your pace," the man said. "And do not look at me. The most you have is forty-eight hours. You will be taken out by our people."

The man quickened his pace and disappeared into the maw of the metro station.

Boris was sweating profusely. None of the nightmares he ever had about how it would happen came anywhere near the reality. He always awoke from the dreams trembling and terrified. Now he was so frightened, his bowels churned. Afraid he'd shit in his pants, Boris actually ran to the toilet in the metro station.

Trying to calm himself, Boris sat in the stall for the better part of a half hour. That the man told him he still had forty-eight hours meant that another double agent, probably someone in the KGB itself, was protecting him. And sometime between now and the end of the allotted time, he was going to be taken out, or at least an attempt was going to be made to take him out. If it failed ... the thought of what could happen to him made his bowels contract and his sphincter muscle opened again.

Dr. Natalia Jannovich sat at a table in a small cafe. She sipped at her coffee and barely ate the cheese sandwich in front of her.

"You must be ready to leave at a moment's notice within the next forty-eight hours," the woman seated across from her said.

Natalia nodded. "Tomorrow I start a week's holiday," she answered.

The other woman nodded. "Then at least you won't be missed from the laboratories. Is there a man or men —"

Even before the question was finished, Natalia dismissed it with a wave of her hand. "Six months ago there was a man who would have been concerned about me, but now there isn't anyone in particular."

"Family?"

"In Odessa. A sister and a brother. I see them every couple of years. My parents are dead."

"You will be going out with other people," the woman said.

"I don't care who I go out with," Natalia answered, "as long as I get out."

"The risk is very great."

"I am suffocating here," she answered in a whisper.

The woman gave no indication that she had even heard her.

"Any special information I should know?" Natalia asked.

"The less you know," the woman answered, "the safer you will be."

It was Natalia's turn to remain silent. She reached for part of the sandwich she had already bitten into and took another bite.

The waiter came to the table and asked if either of them wanted anything else.

Since the woman hadn't ordered anything, she said, "Coffee and a piece of honey cake."

The waiter smiled and went toward the kitchen. Natalia watched the woman follow him with her eyes.

"You never know," she said when the man disappeared behind the kitchen door, "whether they're KGB or not. Someday we won't have to worry about it."

Nicole Pushkin, great-granddaughter of the famous poet, was on her way to the agricultural ministry. She walked at a brisk pace. Her cheeks were red from the cold and she was concerned about the ten-thirty meeting she was scheduled to have with the deputy minister.

Suddenly she found herself on a collision course with a man wearing a shabby brown coat and an equally shabby brown fur hat. "You have forty-eight hours," he said, suddenly stepping out of her way.

Nicole stopped. She glanced over her shoulder.

The man continued.

Suddenly she realized one of her colleagues, Comrade Leo Kronovich was coming toward her. She was suddenly afraid.

"Is anything wrong?" Kronovich asked, coming up to her.

She shook her head.

"You're absolutely pale," he said.

"Did you see the man who passed me?"

He nodded.

Saying the first thing that came to her mind, she said, "He said he wanted to fuck me."

Kronovich looked at her, moved his head a bit to the right and said, "So do I. So do several other men in the ministry." Nicole felt the heat rise in her cheeks. She was twenty-eight years old. Red-haired with green eyes, a narrow waist and good legs. She had one love affair when she was at the university. She had given herself to a middle-aged mathematics professor who claimed his wife did not understand him. By the end of the semester she found out he had taken the virginity of several other young women by telling them exactly what he had told her. The experience robbed her of any desire to know another man intimately. "I'm not telling you something you don't already know," Kronovich said.

She managed a smile, put out her hand and lightly touched his arm. "Thank you for the compliment."

He nodded. "It was my pleasure and would be more my pleasure to do it."

"It's my pleasure to be your friend," Nicole said.

He took hold of her gloved hand and brought it to his lips. "If you would let me," he said in almost a whisper, "I could love you."

"Take me to dinner Saturday night instead," she responded.

"Not much of an exchange," he said. "But I'll take it."

"Good," Nicole answered, knowing that by then she'd be on her way to freedom.

Kinkade sat at the head of the conference table. He helped himself to the pitcher, poured a glass of water, and drank a little before he said, "Hardy is coming out with three big prizes. One of them has been one of our men for several years. We're going to move them slowly. From Moscow to Odessa; then to Cracow and finally across the East German border. The movement is to throw the KGB off. It should take about six to eight weeks to get them out. It's October eighteenth now. They should be out by the first week in January, at the very latest."

"Chief, do we know how much the KGB knows?" a man with a crew cut and square jaw asked.

"All three have been reported missing," Kinkade said. "All three have been worked on by makeup artists. I doubt if their own mothers would recognize them. They have completely new identities and the necessary papers to prove who they are. The entire operation should be a piece of cake, as the expression goes. But to make sure of it, I want each of you to alert your group leaders that we have people in transit and to be on the alert for any indications that the KGB is becoming more active in one area than another. We'd want to know that immediately."

The half dozen men around the table nodded.

"James," Kinkade said, directing his attention to a tall, owlish-looking man who sat on his right two chairs down from where he was, "I want to fly out to Moscow in the next day or so and monitor the exit operation."

"Traveling with them or parallel to them?" James Conners asked.

"Use your judgment," Kinkade answered. "You will probably have to vary your routine to fit the circumstances."

"Probably," Conners answered. Then he leaned forward, put his elbows on the table and, clasping his hands in front of him, asked, "Once I make contact with Hardy, which one of us runs the operation?"

Kinkade raised his eyebrows.

"It's just that I know Hardy and Hardy knows me," Conners said. "He'll have his way of doing things and I'll have mine."

Kinkade took another drink of water.

"Hardy was never my favorite person," Conners said.

"He's one of our best," Kinkade answered, putting the glass down.

"I wouldn't argue that," Conners responded. "I just want to know which of us gives the orders?"

"Hardy does," Kinkade answered. "After all, it's his mission."

"That's okay with me. Then any mistakes are his and not mine."

"That's the way it will be," Kinkade answered.

Conners unclasped his hands, lifted his elbows off the table and, a satisfied expression on his face, moved back into the chair. "I'll leave the day after tomorrow."

Kinkade nodded.

CHAPTER 7

Borodine was on the bridge, waiting for the sight of the low hills that rise above Vladivostok's harbor. Lieutenant Popov was standing next to him.

"It's been a long, slow voyage," Borodine said, watching the wavy shafts of sunlight suddenly appear and disappear.

"I'll be glad to be home," Popov said. "Glad to see my girl again."

Borodine smiled and nodded. "That's always good," he answered, remembering how eager he used to be to see Galena. But now he wasn't sure what his feelings for her were. Their last parting had been anything but tender. And, since then, he had spent a night with one woman and could easily fall in love with another. Still, Galena was his wife and —

"Land, Comrade Captain!" Popov exclaimed. "Land, zero five points off the port bow."

Borodine saw the low-lying smudge on the horizon.

"Comrade Captain," the radar officer said, "we have land at two seven six degrees. Configuration shows harbor and surrounding hills."

"Roger that," Borodine answered.

Suddenly the COMMO keyed Borodine. "Signal from base Commander, Comrade Captain."

"Read it," Borodine said. "Go straight to the message."

"The *Sea Savage* proceed to dry dock four. Entire crew to have ten days shore leave. Captain Borodine report to base CO office as soon as possible."

"Thanks," Borodine answered, then to Popov he said, "We're going into dry dock immediately."

"I'll have the EO and the DCO have their reports ready for the base CO," Popov said.

Borodine nodded.

"Comrade Captain," one of the other members of the watch said, "Comrade Colonel Petrovich asks permission to come to the bridge."

"Permission granted," Borodine responded.

Petrovich came up through the open hatch and settled next to Borodine. "It's always a good sight to see land," he said, "even if it is as desolate as the land in front of us." Then he smiled. "But home is where the heart is, isn't that so, Igor?"

"Yes, where the heart is," Borodine answered. Then he said, "Everyone on board has ten days shore leave."

"Then I shall go home and see my wife and family. It's a long way between here and Kiev. I imagine I could get a flight that goes there."

"With some luck, yes," Borodine said. "But even if you don't get a direct flight —"

COMMO keyed Borodine again. "Comrade Captain, your orders have been changed. You are to report immediately to the base KGB officer."

"No explanation?" Borodine asked.

"No," the COMMO answered.

"Answer that I will be there as soon as the *Sea Savage* is safely in dry dock."

"Aye, aye, Comrade Captain," the COMMO answered.

"I'm ordered to the base KGB commander," Borodine said to Petrovich.

"It could just be routine," Petrovich said with a frown.

"Nothing they do is ever just routine," Borodine answered.

There was a car waiting for Borodine to take him to the base KGB office, which was a large stone structure at the far end of the base, several kilometers away from any other facility.

It not only housed the offices of the KGB, it also served as a military prison for those members of the armed forces in the Vladivostok military district who were either convicted of, awaiting trial for, or being suspected of having committed a crime against the state.

Borodine settled back in the car. He was disappointed that Luba wasn't his driver. Like every officer in the armed services Borodine had to deal with the reality of the KGB. Markov, the political officer and KGB agent assigned to the *Sea Savage*, had been killed when the trawler he had been aboard had been sunk by the *Shark*.

Borodine suspected he would be questioned at length as to why he had put Markov aboard a trawler instead of keeping him aboard the *Sea Savage*. Markov and those like him were members of the GRU, the department of the KGB that watchdogged the military.

Borodine entered the building and reported to the duty officer, who immediately picked up the phone and, after pressing three buttons, announced him to Colonel Andra Stepanovich, the military district KGB commander.

"Comrade Captain," the duty officer said, "please sit down there." He pointed to a group of three straight-backed chairs across from his desk. "Comrade Colonel Stepanovich will see you in a few minutes."

Borodine nodded.

"Please feel free to smoke," the duty officer said.

Before Borodine could thank him, the man began to shuffle the papers on the top of his desk. Borodine did light a cigarette and let the smoke linger inside his throat and nose before blowing it out toward the floor. He had met Stepanovich at several of the base social functions. A thin man with a pockmarked face, who seldom laughed and whose dark blue eyes roamed nervously over the guests, there were many rumors about his personal habits. He had heard, he forgot from whom, that Stepanovich seldom showered, but masked his body odor by using a great deal of American deodorants and cologne.

The phone on the duty officer's desk rang. The man answered it, looked at Borodine and began to talk in a barely audible voice.

Borodine knew the conversation was about him and he also knew that having him wait was part of Stepanovich's "treatment." Suddenly he decided not to take part in a game where one player always has the advantage. He stood up, went to the desk, ground his cigarette into the duty officer's ashtray and said, "Tell Colonel Stepanovich that I have more important things to do than wait on his whim. I am returning to my boat."

The duty officer flushed, said something hurriedly over the phone and then told Borodine, "The colonel will see you now, Captain. Just go through that door on the right."

Borodine nodded, crossed the room and, without knocking, opened the door and walked into Stepanovich's office.

"Terribly sorry, Captain, about keeping you waiting," Stepanovich said in a surprisingly sincere voice.

Borodine decided to become a player in the charade on his own terms. "You're not and I don't expect you to be. But I just arrived with a damaged boat from a mission that —"

"Was not very successful," Stepanovich said, dropping down in a luxurious black leather chair. He had been standing when Borodine had entered.

"The *Sea Savage* had most of her complement returned," Borodine said.

"That's hardly a measure of success," Stepanovich answered. "Why don't you sit down? You'll be more comfortable."

Borodine sat down in a chair with red velvet armrests. He was directly in front of Stepanovich.

"Vodka?" Stepanovich offered.

Borodine was about to refuse; then he changed his mind and said, "Yes, vodka."

Stepanovich left his chair, went to a side bar that was against the right wall and poured two drinks. "Ice?" he asked.

"Yes," Borodine answered, really looking at the contents of the room for the first time. Besides the desk and the chairs, there was a couch, which looked as if it could be converted into a bed, and several shelves of books, the titles of which Borodine couldn't see. On three of the walls there were landscape paintings of considerable beauty. Then he realized there weren't any windows in the room.

Stepanovich returned with the two vodkas and handed Borodine his. "A toast," he said, returning to his chair.

Borodine nodded.

"To your lovely wife, Galena, may her absence be easily explainable," Stepanovich said, raising his glass.

Borodine's heart jumped, then raced.

"Aren't you going to drink, Captain?" Stepanovich asked.

Borodine forced his hand to be steady and his voice to be calm. "You're a bastard, Colonel." And he threw the vodka in Stepanovich's face.

Stepanovich's hand went to his revolver. "I could kill you for that," he rasped.

"You won't," Borodine said.

"I could arrest you."

"On what charge? Throwing vodka in your face? Come now, Colonel, you wouldn't want to be made the laughing stock of your department. And I don't want to have anyone, even you, try to play games with me. What about my wife?"

"Two days after you sailed," Stepanovich said, "she was reported missing by the neighborhood political officer."

"And?"

"She has apparently gone underground and is trying to defect to the West," Stepanovich said.

Borodine looked at the KGB officer and said, "How do you know she hasn't been killed?"

"We checked every morgue in the country. None of them had a body resembling your wife," Stepanovich answered.

Without asking permission, Borodine stood up, went to the bar and poured himself another vodka. He drank it and, before he returned to his chair, he poured another and drank that one, too.

"We know that you and she argued before you left," Stepanovich said.

"That proves nothing," Borodine answered.

"We also know that you had sexual contact with a military driver."

"Luba?"

"She is one of ours," Stepanovich said.

"She's very good," Borodine said.

"Your wife has put you in a very serious situation," Stepanovich said.

"I was at sea when she disappeared," Borodine said. "I knew she was unhappy living here. But I never thought —"

"It doesn't matter what you thought, Captain. The fact remains that she has vanished. When a person does that, we can only draw one of two conclusions: either she's dead, which, in this case, doesn't seem to be so, or she has gone underground, which does seem to be the case. And when a person does go underground, we have found that it is either to carry out sabotage against the government or to defect. Your wife's past history eliminates the first reason, but, certainly, you must admit, points to the second."

"I was at sea," Borodine said.

Stepanovich nodded. "You are not being accused of a crime, Captain, unless it is the unwritten one that makes a husband responsible for everything his wife does. You should have reported her anti-government attitudes before they got out of hand. She could have been placed in one of our very effective thought-modification programs. People can be made to change their minds about anything and everything."

Borodine knew about the thought-modification programs. Most of the people who were sent to them wound up spending the rest of their lives in a mental institution, or were returned to the normal world more zombie than human. As far as he was concerned, Galena would be better off dead than in any thought-modification program.

"From the expression on your face," Stepanovich said, "I see that you don't approve of —"

"Colonel," Borodine said, cutting him short, "you brought me here to tell me that my wife is missing, that she has gone underground, presumably to defect."

"That is correct."

"I was at sea at the time she was reported missing," Borodine said.

"Captain, can you honestly say that you knew nothing of her intentions?"

"Absolutely nothing," Borodine answered.

"You realize that your wife's actions have certainly put your career in danger."

Borodine said nothing.

"How much does your wife know about your work?" Stepanovich asked.

"Very little. She knows I command a large boat. I never told her anything more."

"Well, that remains to be seen," Stepanovich said. "That really remains to be seen."

"I don't understand," Borodine said.

"As of this moment you are relieved of your command of the *Sea Savage*. You will fly to Moscow and present yourself to Admiral Gorshkov, who will determine what you will do while we wait."

"Wait for what?" Borodine asked.

"Until your wife surfaces in the West and is debriefed by American agents," Stepanovich said. "Then and only then will we know how much you actually told her about your boat and what it does."

"But that could take weeks, or months," Borodine said, forcing himself to speak in a moderate tone.

"In certain cases," Stepanovich said, "it has been known to take as long as three years."

Borodine clenched his jaws.

"If of course she is found by us," Stepanovich said, "she will be debriefed by our people and your life will resume a more normal course."

"And if she is found dead?" Borodine asked.

"That would present problems. We could never be sure who she met and what she told them."

Borodine stopped himself from shaking his head. He did not want to give Stepanovich the pleasure of seeing how very upset he really was. "Then let's hope," he said, "that she is alive. Either here or in the West."

"The plane for Moscow leaves at twenty-three hundred hours," Stepanovich said. "In the meantime you are free to go anywhere except back to your house. And since your boat is in dry dock no one has to be in command. Oh, yes, I thought you would like to have Luba for your driver again. She is waiting outside for you."

"You are very considerate," Borodine said.

Stepanovich sighed. "In my profession, it is a luxury that cannot often be afforded."

Borodine wasn't interested in Stepanovich's problems. He had more than enough of his own.

CHAPTER 8

Wrapped in a blue terry cloth bathrobe, Boxer stood at the hotel window and looked out. A wind-driven November rain hurled itself against the pane, distorting everything in the late afternoon light that lay beyond it. Earlier in the day, Boxer had heard a TV weather forecaster predict that the rain would change to snow because a huge storm was working its way up the Atlantic coast and was supposed to bring the first snow of the season to the Washington area.

"Jack, I came all the way over here just to be with you," Kathy Tyson complained, "and now that I'm here in your bed waiting for you, you're gazing out the window."

Boxer turned. She was completely naked.

Kathy was a natural redhead. Her features were classic and, gifted by nature with a svelte body, she was indeed as sexy as she looked.

"We should take a trip somewhere," Kathy said, drawing her naked body up so that she was able to lean back against the two pillows behind her. "Washington is the pits now. We could go south to Mexico, or Antigua. My father has a membership in one of the best clubs on the island. We could stay there."

"Can't go," Boxer said. "My dad is too sick for me to go anywhere now. I was actually thinking of going to New York to spend some time with my folks. You could come along, too. There's plenty to do in the city."

"When would we be going?" she asked.

"As soon as the storm that's supposed to hit us passes," Boxer said. "If it's as big and powerful as the Met guys think, then it will probably take the better part of a couple of days to clear the snow. We'll take the train up and spend a few days with my folks."

"Then can we go away?" she asked.

"Maybe between Christmas and New Year's," he said. "I have an invitation to a New Year's Eve party at the Redferns and I want to go. I want to see Tom and Cowly and some of the other people from the *Shark*."

Kathy made a face. "Sue-Ann doesn't like me," she said.

"That's because she doesn't know you the way I do," Boxer answered.

Boxer slipped the robe off and let it fall to the floor. He bent over Kathy and kissed her navel. He loved her more than he thought he could love a woman. He had loved Gwen, his former wife, but that love was very different from the way he felt about Kathy. He couldn't explain the difference, but he knew it existed. Kathy was not only the woman he had in bed, she was also the woman who had buoyed him up during these past months … months of waiting to hear what Kinkade had finally decided, months of frustration, months of waiting for his father to die.

Kathy eased over, making room for him on the bed, when the phone rang.

"Let it ring," Kathy said.

"I thought I had unplugged it," Boxer said.

"Don't answer it," Kathy responded.

"Could be about Dad," he said, reaching over to the phone and picking it up.

"It's Tracy," the voice on the other end said. "I have to see you."

"Now?" Boxer asked.

"Now. It's very important."

"Where are you?"

"Downstairs in the lobby," she said. "I thought I'd better call you before I came up."

"Don't come up. I'll come down," Boxer said. "I'll be down in five minutes," he said and put the phone back in its cradle.

"What's this all about?" Kathy asked.

"Tracy wants to see me now," he said. "I told you about her."

"She came here now, in this weather?" Kathy asked.

Boxer got out of bed and began putting on his skivvies.

"She said it was important," he explained.

"I shouldn't have come here today," Kathy said. "I knew it wouldn't be a good day the moment I got up. I just knew everything would go wrong."

Boxer bent over her and put his hands on her shoulders. "I'll be back and we'll make it a wonderful day; then later we'll go down to the cocktail lounge and have a few drinks and dinner. I promise you it will be a wonderful day."

Kathy reached up, entwined her arms around his neck, and easing his face down to hers, kissed him passionately on the lips. "I want you so much, it hurts," she whispered.

"I'll be back soon," he said, gently extricating himself from her embrace. He went to the door, turned, blew her a kiss, then left the room and locked the door behind him.

Boxer stepped out of the elevator and into the lobby.

Tracy was seated in a high winged-back chair facing the elevator banks. She was wearing a simple dark blue pants suit and her hair was held in place by a blue rope headband. A raincoat was draped over her lap.

She stood up, embraced and kissed Boxer on the cheek. "Long time, no see," she said, shifting her raincoat to her left arm.

"There was never anything serious between us," Boxer said. "You know that and so do I."

She nodded, and as they walked toward the cocktail lounge, she leaned close to him. "Nothing but good sex and that, whether you believe it or not, mister, is no small thing for a woman."

The cocktail lounge was almost empty. There were two men and women at the bar watching a football game that was being held in Los Angeles.

They sat down at a booth. Boxer ordered a vodka on the rocks and Tracy asked for Scotch on the rocks.

"Now tell me what's so important," Boxer said. "You made it sound as if it were a matter of life or death."

"It's important to you, Jack," Tracy said, taking a cigarette out of a gold case.

"I'm listening," Boxer said.

"Let's wait until we have a drink," Tracy suggested.

"If it's that important…"

"I guess there just isn't an easy way of telling you this," Tracy said, leaning slightly forward to allow Boxer to light her cigarette.

The waiter returned and set their drinks down on the table.

"Well," Boxer said, "the drinks are here. Now let's have it!" He half suspected that Tracy was playing some sort of game.

Tracy picked up her drink and sipped it. Still holding the glass, she asked, "How much do you know about the woman you've been sleeping with?"

Boxer flushed. He was almost angry. "That's what I would call putting a question squarely on the table," he said.

"Can you give me an answer?" Tracy asked.

"She comes from money," he said. "She's a Bryn Mawr graduate."

"The last part is right," Tracy commented.

Boxer raised his eyebrows.

"Have your drink," Tracy said. "You're going to need it and more."

Boxer drank.

"I've been doing some digging," Tracy said. "It started when Hayes told me about how you fished him and some thirty other people out of the Pacific, then of course my own experience aboard the *Mary-Ann* and then the *Shark*. I wanted to do a full-length story on you and the *Shark*."

"The Company would never allow it," Boxer said.

"That's my paper's worry. Not yours or mine. Anyway, I started to do some digging on all the people involved. I came up with Kinkade, head of the CIA; you and every member of your crew; Admiral Stark, CNO; and James Hicks, a friend of mine, who thinks you're the bravest man he has ever known; and another Navy captain named Bush."

"You've got the whole team," Boxer said. "But I'll bet you a thousand dollars your paper won't print a word about it."

"The *Shark*'s cover has been blown. The Russians know about it."

Boxer nodded. "But not all the names of the men who sail on her, or some other pieces of information the Russians might be able to use to figure out the kind of equipment she has on board."

"That's not my concern, or your concern. The Company has a copy of my article. Their people will decide what they want to cut out; then my people at the paper will argue with them. In the end some sort of a compromise will be worked out."

"Is that what you wanted to tell me?" Boxer asked, finishing his drink.

"No. I told it to you in order that you would understand how I came to find out who and what Kathy is," Tracy said.

"Kathy is the woman I intend to —"

"She's a member of the Company; she was assigned to you and only to you while you're here. When you go to sea, she has a different assignment."

Boxer could feel the heat come to his cheeks. He took a cigarette from her cigarette case and, though his hand trembled, managed to light it.

Tracy signaled the waiter. "Two more of the same and make that a double vodka," she said.

"Kathy Tyson was born in Brooklyn, New York, on September tenth in nineteen sixty. The Tysons now live in Palm Beach. Mister Tyson worked for the Post Office and Mrs. Tyson worked in the main branch of the Dime Savings Bank. Kathy has been with the Company since she graduated from Bryn Mawr."

The waiter brought the second round of drinks.

"You couldn't be wrong?" he asked, not looking at her.

"For your sake, I wish I was," Tracy said, reaching across the table and taking hold of his left hand.

"Did you write about any of this?" he asked, still not looking at her.

"No. Nothing," Tracy answered.

He nodded. "Thanks," he said, finally raising his eyes to look at her. "Thanks." Then he picked up his glass and quickly drank the vodka. "I started to say, before you told me about her, that I intended to marry Kathy." He pursed his lips and rubbed his beard. "It was another one of my dumb ideas."

"There was no way you could have known," Tracy said gently.

Boxer shrugged and stubbed out the cigarette.

"Do you love her?" Tracy asked.

He nodded.

"Maybe I did the wrong thing by telling you," Tracy said.

"No," Boxer sighed, "you did the right thing."

"What are you going to do now?"

Boxer signaled the waiter and asked for another round.

"I've had enough," Tracy said, covering the top of the glass with her hand. "Jack, are you sure you can handle it?"

"I'm sure," he answered. "Bring me another double vodka on the rocks," he told the waiter.

"She might really love you," Tracy said.

"She might," Boxer answered. "But it wouldn't matter. It wouldn't make any difference now."

"I'm sorry," Tracy said. "I'm really sorry."

Boxer took hold of her hand and brought it to his lips. "You did the right thing," he said.

The waiter returned with the double vodka on the rocks and set it on the table.

"Here's to love, honesty and fidelity between men and women," Boxer said, raising his glass.

Tracy bowed her head.

Boxer finished the drink quickly, then he said, "If you'll excuse me, Tracy, I have to take care of something that's very important."

"Are you sure you want to do it now?" Tracy asked.

Boxer nodded. He fished out a ten-dollar bill and dropped it on the table. "That should cover it. See you around, Tracy," he said, getting to his feet. "See you around." And he walked straight toward the door.

Boxer left the elevator and walked slowly toward his room. Suddenly, he realized how tired he was of living in a hotel. How really tired he was of everything.

He unlocked the door, opened it and walked in. Kathy was still naked in bed.

"How did your meeting go?" she asked.

Boxer went to the window. Huge flakes of snow were whirling around. Those that touched the pane melted instantly.

"It wasn't what I expected," he said.

"Oh!" she exclaimed and pushed herself up, leaning back against the pillows again.

Boxer looked at her reflection in the window. All he could see was the upper part of her body.

"You don't look right," Kathy said. "Is something wrong?"

He turned to her. "I know," he said.

She looked at him quizzically.

"About your work," he answered.

He watched the color come into her cheeks.

"That's what Tracy told you?"

"That's what she told me," he answered.

She pulled herself higher up on the bed.

"I don't want a scene. I don't want any explanations. I want you to go," Boxer said quietly.

"Would it make any difference," Kathy asked, "if I told you I loved you?"

Boxer shook his head.

"I do, you know."

"Now," he said, "I don't want to talk about it."

Kathy left the bed and began to dress.

Boxer faced the window again. "Don't report this conversation to the Company," he said. "I want to see Kinkade myself."

She didn't answer.

Boxer felt his anger mounting. "I said something to you a moment ago and I didn't hear an answer. I want to hear an answer."

"Today is Sunday. I file my report on Wednesday. The Company will want to know —"

He went straight to her and grabbed her arms, saying, "I don't give a fuck what the Company wants or does not want. You report nothing about this. Understand?"

"Is that a threat, Jack?"

"It's a threat," he said, staring down at her. "Believe me, it's a threat." Then he let go of her and went back to the window.

"No goodbyes?" she asked, going to the door.

Boxer stood motionless and silent. Even when he heard the door close, he did not turn around.

CHAPTER 9

Boxer waited until Monday to call Stark. "I want a meeting arranged with Kinkade and Williams," he said. "I want that meeting today."

"Listen, mister, you're still under my command," Stark answered. "I don't give a fuck what you want."

"Admiral," Boxer said, "I respect you. But this is very important. It can't wait, or stand on the usual protocol between us."

Stark was silent for a few moments, then he said, "I'll call you back in fifteen minutes."

"I'll be here," Boxer said.

The line went dead.

Boxer pressed the disconnect button, then he dialed his parents' number in Brooklyn.

"How's Dad?" he asked as soon as his mother answered.

"He had a restful night," she said.

"Good. Listen, Mom, I'll be home sometime this evening or tonight."

"Travel is very bad. The airports have been closed for hours."

"I'll take a late-afternoon or early-evening train. With any luck, I should be home for dinner."

"I'll make meatloaf for you," she said.

"There's no need to fuss," Boxer told her.

"Don't worry about it," she said.

"Ma, don't tell Dad I'm coming. I want to surprise him."

"He'll be glad to see you," she said.

"I'll be there soon. See you, Mom," he said and put the phone down. For several moments he didn't move, then he went to the window. It was still snowing but not nearly as bad as it had been earlier. Now the wind was moving huge curtains of snow in front of his line of sight.

The phone rang.

Boxer crossed the room, picked up the phone and said, "Boxer here."

"Be at the Watergate hotel by eleven-thirty," Stark said. "Room ten fourteen. Williams was caught in the city by the storm. The room is in his name."

"I'll be there," Boxer said.

"Kinkade is very angry and so is Williams," Stark told him.

"Admiral, I couldn't care less," Boxer answered.

"Be there on time," Stark said and hung up.

Boxer replaced the phone and looked at his watch. It was ten o'clock. With the weather the way it was, he knew he wouldn't have much chance of finding a cab, and public transportation would be almost non-existent. He decided to walk the two miles between his hotel and the Watergate. He put on thick-soled, waterproof boots, a heavy woolen sweater, his pea coat and the woolen watch hat.

Outside, he was surprised to discover that it had really stopped snowing. But the wind was piling the snow, in various places, into large drifts. There were abandoned cars on all of the streets and those buses that were moving were going at a snail's pace.

Boxer walked with his head bent into the wind and his stride sure. He arrived at the Watergate a half hour before the meeting and went directly into the coffee shop.

He sat down at the counter, summoned the waitress and ordered a black coffee and a Danish.

"I thought it was you," a man said from behind Boxer. Boxer made a half turn and found himself looking at Stark.

"The pea coat and watch hat threw me."

"I walked here and was chilled," Boxer explained. "I need the coffee and the Danish is a substitute for breakfast. Why don't you sit down and join me?"

Stark settled on to the stool to Boxer's right. "If you needed transportation —"

"The walk was good for me," Boxer said. "I haven't been doing much lately."

The waitress came with Boxer's order and put it down in front of him.

"I'll have the same," Stark said. "Only I want very light coffee."

"Thanks for setting up the meeting," Boxer said.

"Can you give me some idea what it's all about?" Stark asked.

"I'm sorry, Admiral, I can't," Boxer answered. "But, believe me, it is important."

"If I didn't think it was," Stark answered, "I wouldn't have bothered."

The waitress returned with another cup of coffee and a Danish.

"After the meeting," Boxer said, "I'm going to see my father."

"Oh?"

"He's dying," Boxer said. "And I want to spend as much time with him as possible."

"I'm sorry to hear that," Stark said.

"I'll be sorry to lose him. We're very good friends."

"How are you traveling?"

"Probably by train," Boxer answered.

"No, you're not. You can use one of our helicopters. You have the fucking thing land in Fort Hamilton. There'll be a car waiting there for you. For Christ's sake, Jack, you're still being paid by us."

"Thanks," Boxer said.

"Before I left the office, I got a Met report. By fourteen hundred everything will be out to sea."

Boxer nodded. "After the meeting, I hope you're not sorry you made this offer."

"Jack, I respect you as a man and I respect the fact that you want to be with your father. What takes place upstairs has no bearing on that respect."

Boxer looked at his watch. "It's time that we went up," he said.

"I'll pick up the tab," Stark said, motioning to the waitress that he wanted the check.

Williams actually occupied a four-room suite, the windows of which overlooked the Potomac River.

Kinkade and Williams were having a late breakfast when Boxer and Stark entered the foyer.

"You look very much the sailor," Kinkade commented.

"That's exactly what I am," Boxer snapped back.

"There's enough breakfast for the two of you," Williams said, "if you care to join us."

Stark declined and Boxer said, "I didn't come here to breakfast with you, Kinkade."

"Then tell me why you came," Kinkade answered.

Boxer moved closer to the table. His eyes narrowed. "It's bad enough that you can be blind when you want to be," Boxer said, "but to be arrogant as well goes beyond the special rights your position gives you."

"Oh!" Kinkade responded and wiped his lips with a napkin.

"I don't care whether I command the *Shark* again but I want you to know this — you too, Williams — I want the both of you to know that if you ever mix in my life again, I'll kill the two of you."

"Captain —" Stark started to say.

"These two gentlemen set me up, Admiral. They set me up with a woman named Kathy Tyson."

"You couldn't be trusted with too many women," Kinkade said.

"Who determined that?" Boxer suddenly roared. "You, Kinkade? Or you, Williams?"

"It was a matter of security," Kinkade answered. "It was done to protect —"

"You're not listening to me," Boxer said. "I don't care why you thought it had to be done. If it's ever done again, you're dead. Do you understand that?"

"Admiral," Williams said, "there's some Scotch on the bar. Would you please pour Captain Boxer a drink."

"We were just discussing the situation," Kinkade said. "Miss Tyson informed me last night that her assignment had come to an abrupt end."

"She said she'd wait to tell —"

With a wave of his hand, Kinkade dismissed what Boxer had started to say. He said, "She is a very good agent. She did what she knew she had to do."

Boxer didn't answer.

"So you came here to threaten —"

"Kinkade, you didn't listen to what I said," Boxer told him. "I don't want anyone assigned to my bed. I'm more than capable of getting my own women."

"There's absolutely no doubt about that," Kinkade said.

Boxer turned to Stark. "Admiral, I don't want —"

Kinkade got to his feet. "It's what I think is necessary," he said. "Not what you want."

"Kinkade," Boxer said, in a low, flat voice, "you're not dealing with one of your agents. I'm not at all like them. They have to kiss your ass. I don't. I'm not in the least bit afraid of you."

"Nor I of you," Kinkade answered.

"I don't expect you to be afraid. I do expect you to believe me. Should you ever assign a woman to me again, I'll kill you. It's that simple."

"The reason why you're so upset," Kinkade said, "is that you fell in love with her. This time it was you who —"

Boxer went straight to Kinkade and slapped him across the face. "That's just for openers," he growled.

Kinkade turned very red.

"Captain," Stark said, "why don't you pour yourself a drink."

Boxer nodded, walked to the bar, poured more than a double Scotch and drank it. Then he came back to the table.

"Why don't you sit down," Williams suggested, looking up at Boxer.

Kinkade had gone back to his chair and Stark had also sat down.

"I am sorry," Williams said, "that you developed a deep emotional interest in Miss Tyson. I understand she has the same interest in you."

Boxer sat down. "It's over," he said in a tight voice. "It's over."

"Gentlemen," Stark said, "I think all of us here owe Captain Boxer our profound apologies — myself included, for not stepping in and stopping it, when the idea of assigning a female agent to him was first suggested."

"You knew about it?" Boxer asked, looking at Stark.

"Just that it was being taken care of," Stark answered.

"What was being taken care of?"

"Your sexual activities," Williams said. "In any case, I agree. We owe you an apology."

"Not good enough! I want a guarantee that it will never happen again."

"We can't give you that," Kinkade said.

"I think we can and must," Stark said.

"I do, too," Williams added.

After a few moments, Kinkade nodded.

"There's one other item to clear up," Boxer said, "before I leave. I want to know where I stand with the *Shark*."

"We absolutely cannot give you an answer on that," Kinkade said.

"I'll take that as a negative response," Boxer said. "That leaves me free to do whatever I want to."

"And just what do you want to do?" Stark asked.

"Resign. And I will. I will not let you keep me dangling. If I have to, I'll go straight to the President."

Williams looked at Kinkade, then he said, "It was never our intention to keep you from commanding the *Shark*."

"Then why all the games?" Boxer asked. "I've been sitting in a damn hotel room for the last few months when I should have been working —"

"There'll be plenty of time for that," Stark said. "You're scheduled to take her out to sea trials immediately after the New Year."

"What about Bush?" Boxer asked.

"He won't go, if you don't want him," Stark said. "But before you give me your answer, I'd like you to think it over for a few days."

"I owe you one, Admiral," Boxer said. "I'll think about it."

"Well," Williams said, "this has been a most productive meeting. Now, Captain, will you at least take coffee with us?"

Boxer nodded.

"And you, Admiral," Williams asked, "do you have time to have coffee with us?"

"Yes," Stark said, "I certainly do."

"My God," Kinkade exclaimed after Boxer and Stark left, "he walked out of here with everything he wanted. We don't have anything to hold him on."

"He's not the kind of man you play games with," Williams said. "He was hurt and he reacted."

"I don't give a shit about him being hurt," Kinkade shouted. "He runs things his way. I want them run my way."

"Until you get someone as good as him," Williams said, "you better learn to live with him."

Kinkade paced back and forth, then suddenly he stopped. "I want that Tracy woman taken out."

"What?"

"She's the damn source of all our trouble. That damn article she wrote will cause feathers to fly over half the fuckin' world. I want her taken out."

"If Boxer suspects —"

"Have it done by someone who knows his business. I don't want Boxer or anyone else to suspect. Have it done when he's at sea."

"Are you sure that's what you want done?"

"I'm absolutely certain," Kinkade said.

CHAPTER 10

"I've read your report with great interest," Admiral Gorshkov said, leaning back into his high back leather chair. "This Captain Boxer is an extraordinary man. Too bad he is not on our side."

"I have thought the same thing myself," Borodine said.

Gorshkov nodded. "Amazing that he should have warned you about the bomb. Absolutely amazing."

Borodine leaned forward. "I have a request, Comrade Admiral. It is not for me, but for Comrade Captain Boxer. I have heard it rumored there was an attempt to kill him outside of his home by several of our KGB agents, who in turn were killed."

"That's true," Gorshkov answered. "Did you also hear that he subdued two skyjackers aboard the plane while he was en route to Cannes?"

"No, I didn't hear that," Borodine answered. "But I'm not surprised."

"Get on with your request," Gorshkov said.

"I ask that no more attempts be made on his life by the KGB," Borodine said. "I make this request because without his help the *Sea Savage* and her entire crew would have been lost."

Gorshkov was a man of middling height, but he had a way of puffing himself up when he wanted to appear to be larger and he did just that. "You're asking me to interfere in the operations of another —"

"Admiral, you were at sea in the boats during World War Two. You know how dangerous it was then. Well, what the *Sea*

Savage and the *Shark* do is a thousand times more dangerous. We confront one another at depths and with weapons the submarine commanders during that great war couldn't even imagine. Leave Comrade Captain Boxer to me and to the men of the *Sea Savage*."

Gorshkov left his chair and began to pace back and forth behind it; then suddenly, as he passed the desk, he stopped and helped himself to a cigar, which he lit and began to smoke before he resumed pacing.

Borodine watched him.

"You have problems of your own with the KGB," Gorshkov said, continuing to walk as he spoke. "Your wife has put you in a very difficult position. Colonel Stepanovich seems to have taken your wife's disappearance as a personal matter. Apparently he thinks it reflects badly on his ability to know and control the people in his command area."

"I cannot undo what she has done," Borodine answered. "My service record is the only thing I have to show my loyalty to the country."

Gorshkov stopped, took the cigar out of his mouth and pointed it at Borodine. "Nothing good will come out of this for her. If she gets out, the West will use her. If she is caught — well, she'll get what she deserves."

Borodine moved his eyes down. He didn't want to think about what would happen to Galena if she were caught.

"Do you love her?" Gorshkov asked, putting the cigar back in his mouth.

Borodine uttered a deep sigh before he said, "No, not anymore." He raised his eyes to look at his commanding officer. "She did what she did knowing what the consequences would be for me. I do not believe she loves me anymore."

"Will you arrange for a divorce?"

Borodine shrugged. "I don't have any other choice," he said. "And I really don't want any other."

Gorshkov nodded and sat down. "I'll keep you here in Moscow until I need you for the *Sea Savage*. She's being refitted. And as for your request, I will speak to the premier about it."

"Thank you, Comrade Admiral," Borodine said.

"We never did have those drinks together, did we?" Gorshkov asked.

Borodine shook his head.

"The time will come," Gorshkov said. "Believe me, the time will come."

Two days after Boxer returned home, his father was taken to the hospital and put on life-support equipment. Boxer seldom left his father's room.

Several times his father opened his eyes, looked at Boxer and smiled.

Just before his father lapsed into a coma, he motioned to Boxer to bend close to him and said, "Have them pull the plug, son. It will be easier for me if that's done."

Boxer took hold of his father's hand and gently squeezed it.

"Never had a brother," his father said. "You became my brother and were my son."

With his free hand, Boxer moved his father's gray hair away from his forehead.

"Take care of Mom," he said. "She'll be lost for a while."

"You know I'll take care of her," Boxer said.

"I want my ashes scattered at sea."

"They will be," Boxer answered.

"Sorry about you and Gwen. I loved her, too."

"Once," Boxer sighed, "so did I."

"Try to be happy," his father whispered. "Try to be happy, son." Then he closed his eyes and slept.

Boxer held on to his father's hand for a long time; then he slowly let go of it and stood erect. He moved to the chair in the corner of the room, sat down and looked at his watch. It was two o'clock in the morning. He had been in the hospital for more than thirty hours.

He looked at the equipment around his father's bed. There were a dozen tubes going into the man's body; the EKG machine to the right of the bed beeped with every beat of his heart.

Boxer stood up and went to the door of the room. The hospital corridor was eerily quiet. He walked to the elevator and went down to the cafeteria, which remained open all night. He picked up a tray, put a wedge of apple pie and a cup of black coffee on it, then he walked to a table and sat down.

Boxer mechanically sipped the coffee and ate the pie. That his father was dying was almost beyond his ability to understand. His brain and his body were numb. He wasn't one of those people who pretended to themselves that their parents would live forever. But watching the man waste away was something for which he had not been prepared. He had seen many men die violently and quickly. But to die slowly was the worst kind of death. He looked down at the empty cup. The coffee hadn't done anything for him. He needed a drink. Something that would give him a jolt.

Boxer suddenly felt that someone was looking at him. He turned to the right: no one was there. Then he turned to the left. There was a doctor and three nurses at a table halfway across the room.

He took his pipe out, filled it with tobacco and lit up.

"That smells good," a woman said.

Boxer turned around. He recognized her. She was one of the night duty nurses who took care of his father. She was black and, from her high cheekbones, he guessed she had some Native American blood. Her name tag said she was Louise Ennis.

"The food isn't much to rave about this time of night," she said. "But then again it never is."

"I just need something to pick me up," Boxer said.

She nodded sympathetically. "How's your ma doing?" she asked.

"Holding up," Boxer answered.

"What about you? The nurses say you've been here a long time."

"Seems like a lifetime," Boxer said.

"It's never easy waiting," she commented.

"Never," he agreed. "And I spend a good deal of my time waiting."

"No way would I want that kind of job," she said. "I have to be doing things."

"Would you mind if I asked you something?" Boxer said.

"I can't tell you that before you ask," she said.

Boxer picked up his tray, stood up and took a seat opposite Ennis. "I want the doctor to shut off the life-support equipment," Boxer said in a low voice. "My dad asked me to have it done. Do you think the doctor will do it?"

"They'll do it, if you have a court order," she said, "and then reluctantly."

"Thanks," Boxer said. "I'd offer to buy you a cup of coffee—"

"I've already had one," she said. "I go off duty at six. If you're still here, I can offer you breakfast. I live two blocks from here, off York Avenue."

"I'll take you up on that," Boxer said.

They left the table together and rode the elevator up to the eighteenth floor.

Louise went into the office behind the desk at the nurse's station and Boxer asked to see the duty resident.

"I'm not sure he's available," the nurse told him.

"Make him available," Boxer said sharply.

The nurse picked up the phone, dialed a number and said, "There's a Mister Boxer who wants to see you... Yes, now."

"Give me the phone," Boxer said. Taking it from her before she could object, he said, "This is Captain Jack Boxer. Get your ass up here on the double, doctor. And I mean on the double." Then, handing the phone back to the astonished nurse, he said, "I'll be in my father's room."

"Yes, sir," she managed to stammer.

Boxer went back into the room and closed the door behind him. One by one he removed the IVs from his father's arms and legs. He disconnected the EKG and finally the respirator. Then he bent down and kissed his father on the forehead. "Go swiftly," he whispered.

Boxer sat down and waited for the doctor to arrive. He sat with eyes closed and remembered things about his father that he hadn't thought about for years. The walks in Prospect Park, the visits to the ships he commanded, the vacations...

Boxer heard the footsteps outside the room. He opened his eyes. The door opened and the doctor entered.

Boxer stood up. "About ten minutes ago I stopped all the life-support equipment," he said. "You can do one of two things: make a fuss, or nothing. Make a fuss and I'll make sure you have very bad press."

The doctor's jaw went slack.

"I'd appreciate it if you examined him," Boxer said.

The doctor went over to the bed and felt for Mr. Boxer's pulse; then he put on his stethoscope and listened to his heart. "Your father is dead," he said, dropping the stethoscope around his neck.

Boxer nodded.

The doctor started for the door.

"Which way will it be, doctor?" Boxer asked.

"No hospital can afford bad press," he answered.

"You make out the death certificate and sign it and I'll take care of everything else," Boxer said.

"It's hospital policy to have the attending physician call the deceased's wife or —"

"Doctor, I don't give a damn about hospital policy. I said I'd take care of everything else and I meant it."

The doctor nodded and left the room.

Boxer went to the side of the bed and, looking down at his father, he said, "Well, Skipper, you're in safe harbor now. I'll never meet anyone like you again, Dad." And, reaching down, he took hold of his father's cold hand and brought it to his lips.

When Boxer turned to leave, he came face to face with Louise.

"I'm sorry," she said. "I didn't mean to interrupt … but what you did was beautiful."

Boxer swallowed hard and said, "I loved him very much."

"I'm sure he knew it," she said.

Boxer glanced over his shoulder at his father's body. "Yes, I think he did."

"Listen, if breakfast would be too much for you to handle…"

"No, it would be just fine," Boxer answered, looking at her again. "I need some time before I face my mother. I'd only wind up walking the streets until I could get a drink. I'll go down to the lobby and call her. I'll wait for you down there."

"See you at six," she said.

"At six," Boxer answered and left the room.

Boxer and Louise left the hospital at six. The streets were still wrapped in darkness. But even as they walked, the sky to the east was beginning to lighten, and here and there in the windows of the various buildings they passed, a slab of bright yellow filled the windows. Mounds of dirty snow littered the sidewalks and it was cold enough to have put down in spots a thin sheet of ice from the previous day's melt.

Louise linked her arm with his. "To keep from slipping," she said. "I don't want to wind up a patient where I work."

Boxer accepted what she said without comment. He was grateful for the silence between them and the silence in the streets.

They stopped briefly at an all-night food store where Louise bought a quart of orange juice, a container of heavy cream, cream cheese and lox and bagels. The last two items Boxer had often heard Jewish officers refer to as Jewish soul food.

Louise's apartment was around the corner from the store and they were there in a matter of minutes. She had the front flat of a two-story old brownstone. The hallway smelled of polish and the wooden staircase and balustrade gleamed brightly.

"I have four rooms," she said, unlocking the door. "I use one as a studio. The place is a mess." She stepped aside to let Boxer in first. "The light switch is on the wall to the left."

Boxer reached over and turned on the foyer light. Louise followed him in, locked the door and then said, "Let me take your coat and hat."

He gave her his pea coat and woolen watch cap.

Louise put them and her own coat and hat in the foyer closet and said, "Well, I'm going into the kitchen to make some coffee. Why don't you go into the living room and relax, or come into the kitchen and watch me work."

"The kitchen will be fine," Boxer said.

"Okay with me," Louise replied. "But I warn you, I'm a tyrant there."

Boxer smiled and followed her into the kitchen. It was a bright room, with wallpaper showing sheaves of wheat stacked in a field. The table and chairs were finished with a birch stain and there were things on the wall that gave the room an altogether homey touch.

"I know your last name," Louise said as she worked, "but not your first."

"Jack," he answered.

She laughed. "I thought it might be something like that. But not Claude or Ian or Seth. It had to be a simple, straightforward name."

"Jack is that," Boxer answered.

For a moment, she stopped laying out the table. "The name may be simple and straightforward; the man isn't."

"You're not seeing me at a particularly good time," he said.

Louise continued to work, putting the bagels, cream cheese and lox on separate plates. "Would you mind if I used coffee mugs instead of cups and saucers?" she asked.

"As long as they won't change the taste of the coffee," he answered. "It smells great. Aboard ship the coffee is good, but never as good as the home-made variety."

"So the pea coat and the watch cap are for real, not just something you wear?"

"They're for real," Boxer said with a smile.

"And that captain bit you used on the phone —"

"You heard that?"

She nodded. "Everyone on the floor probably heard it."

"That's for real, too," he said.

Her face suddenly creased into a smile. "I think the doctor knew it, too, or he wouldn't have come flying up to see you. He'd have remained in bed with his girlfriend. Well, Captain Jack Boxer, you did it!"

"Jack, please," Boxer said.

"Okay, Jack, how do you like your coffee?"

"Black and strong," he answered, picking up a bagel and watching what Louise did with hers.

"Are you from the city?" she asked.

"Brooklyn," he answered. "But the neighborhood didn't have any Jews in it when I was growing up, and the only Jewish boys I knew went to the same high school as I did. But except for gym, I never really had much to do with them."

Louise put bits of lox over the cream cheese, which she had liberally spread over half the bagel. She bit into her bagel and began to chew it.

Boxer did the same. "Hey, this is really good!" he exclaimed.

She laughed and said, "I've made a convert."

"To Jewish soul food," Boxer answered.

"This goes great with champagne, or vodka and orange juice," Louise said.

"I'll remember that," Boxer said.

For several minutes, neither of them spoke. Boxer was content with the silence. He had a need for it. But at the same time he also had a need for human contact.

"More coffee?" Louise asked.

"Yes, please," Boxer answered.

"Have you any more phone calls that you want to make?" she asked as she poured coffee into his cup.

"Only my ex-wife," Boxer answered. "My father was very fond of her."

"There's a phone in the living room and on extension in the bedroom. You might want to use that one if you want more privacy. It'll take me a few minutes to clean up. I hate to leave dirty dishes around."

"The one in the living room will do fine," he said. He took out his pipe and started to fill it, then he remembered that not everyone liked the smell of tobacco. "Mind if I smoke?" he asked.

"No, go ahead."

Boxer lit up and eased back into the chair.

"You look very tired," she said.

"I need a shower, a shave and a few hours' sleep and I'll be okay. I'm used to going long hours without sleep. I guess you'd say it comes with the job."

"I have some coffee cake in the fridge, if you want it," she said.

"I've had more than enough," Boxer said. "It was very good. I'll remember bagels, cream cheese and lox."

"You should also try a lox, onions and eggs combination," she said. "That's really very good."

"How and where did you learn all about this stuff?"

"From Jewish friends. I sometimes go out with a Jewish man."

Boxer wondered if she also slept with him.

"Besides," she said, "I like trying different kinds of food. New York is probably the best city in the world to do that." She stood up and began putting the dishes in the sink.

"Let me help," Boxer said, standing.

"No, you make your call."

"You sure you don't mind? I wouldn't mind helping."

She shook her head. "The phone is on the end table alongside the big easy chair. It lights up as soon as you pick it up."

Boxer walked into the living room. There was sufficient light coming from the kitchen to enable him to find the phone without having to switch on another light. He sat down in the easy chair and punched out Gwen's number. The last time he had phoned, her husband answered. He hoped this time she would. He put his pipe down in a ceramic dish, which was the nearest thing around resembling an ashtray. The phone was ringing. Suddenly, he remembered what Gwen was like in the morning: her hair tousled from sleep, her body warm and smelling from sleep and —

"Hello?" Gwen answered.

"It's Jack," he said.

"Christ, Jack —"

"My father died this morning," he said, cutting her short. "The funeral is set for Thursday at noon. It will be out of the Moran Funeral Home on Fourth Avenue and Eighty-first Street."

"I'm sorry, Jack," she said in a softer tone. "I was very fond of him."

"He was fond of you," Boxer responded.

"Hold on a minute," she said, "I have to change my position."

Boxer didn't answer. He knew what she really meant was that she was telling her husband what the call was about.

She came back on the line and said, "I'm leaving on Wednesday. I'm really sorry."

Boxer was about to answer with, "I bet." But he fought the impulse down and instead said, "I want John there."

"That would be impossible."

"Gwen, I'm not asking you," Boxer said. "I'm telling you to have John there."

"But how?"

"Getting him there is your problem; getting him home is mine."

"Why must you be so damn difficult?"

"Thanks for your sympathy," Boxer said and hung up. He was much too angry to immediately go back into the kitchen. He sat hunched forward, his elbows on his knees, his hands clasped. He looked down at the floor.

Gwen's indifference to his anguish was in itself another kind of anguish. He couldn't understand why he had allowed himself to love her for so long. Why hadn't he been able to accept the reality that it had been over between them? Whatever they had once had was over. The only thing left of the rubble of their marriage was John.

Suddenly he caught the faint scent of perfume. He looked up and saw Louise standing in front of him.

"Why don't you shower," she said, "and go to sleep for a couple of hours. There's an extra bed in the studio."

"Thanks. But sooner or later I have to go home and I know my mother will be needing me."

"Are you sure you want to leave now?"

Boxer stood up. "I don't want to leave, but I must." He picked up his pipe and emptied the bowl into the ceramic dish.

Together they walked into the foyer.

Louise opened the closet, took out Boxer's coat and watch cap and handed them to him.

"After the funeral is over," he said, "I'd like to see you again."

"I'm in the phone book," she answered.

"Thanks," he said. "Thanks for introducing me to Jewish soul food and thanks for caring about me." He put his arms around her, drew her to him and gently kissed her on the lips.

The day of the funeral was very cold, and the sky was filled with high scudding clouds.

Boxer and his mother sat in front of the chapel. John wasn't there. The casket was draped with the flag. Off to one side there was a detail of blue-jackets standing at ease while the minister delivered the eulogy about a man he really didn't know.

Though his mother attended church every Sunday, his father seldom went. It was the one real bone of contention between them. His mother, raised as a Lutheran, eventually found herself drawn to Episcopalianism; his father became more and more atheistic.

The eulogy was brief and, since his father was going to be cremated, there would be no cortege to the cemetery.

"And now," the minister said, "will the mourners please rise and join me in reciting the twenty-third psalm."

"Before you do that, minister," a man said, "I'd like to say a few words about my friend and long-time shipmate Captain George Boxer."

Boxer recognized Admiral Stark's voice even before he turned around and looked at him.

"Please," the minister said, moving away from the lectern.

Stark was in uniform. He walked up to the lectern and stood in front of it. "Jack," he said, "you didn't know that I knew your father and mother. I know them well enough to know that they never would have told you. Their relationship with me goes back many, many years. Once I asked your mother to marry me. She turned me down and married your father instead. Now you know one of the family secrets. I also want to tell you that your father and I served in World War Two together. We were shipmates aboard the *Yorktown*. It was your father who pulled me out of a flaming plane when I crash-landed on the carrier's back. He was our landing officer and, though he never flew a mission, the guys who did knew he flew every one of them with them. He was loved and respected by everyone aboard that ship from its skipper to the cooks. That's about as good as can be said about any man when his time comes." Then he turned to the minister, nodded and took a place alongside Mrs. Boxer to join in reciting the twenty-third psalm.

When they finished, two men came through a side door, removed the flag from the coffin, and carefully folded it; then one of them handed it to Mrs. Boxer.

The blue-jackets were called to attention by the officer in charge and saluted the casket.

Stark came to attention and saluted, then he said to Mrs. Boxer, "Come, it's time to go."

She nodded and let herself be led out the aisle.

"I'll join you in a couple of minutes," Boxer said.

Stark looked at him.

"I need a couple of minutes," Boxer said. "I'd appreciate it if you'd escort my mother to my car."

"I'll do better than that," Stark said. "I'll drive her home in mine."

"Thanks," Boxer said. "I'll be there shortly."

Boxer turned and said to the men who were about to wheel the coffin out, "Let it be. I'll call you when I want you. Now I'd like to be alone with my father."

The men looked at the minister.

"It's alright," he said.

Boxer thanked him, walked up to the closed casket and put his right hand on the highly polished surface. There wasn't anything he could tell himself to ease his grief. This would be the last time he'd be able to be as close to him as he was.

Boxer pursed his lips. Like his father, he didn't believe in God or in the hereafter. It would be much easier if he did believe; then he could take comfort from the thought that, sometime in the future, he would again meet his father.

He swallowed hard and whispered, "Well, Skipper, this is really where we part ways. What can I say that we don't already know?" Suddenly he began to weep. He didn't even realize he was crying until he felt the tears on the sides of his face.

Boxer stepped back, removed a handkerchief from his back pocket and wiped the tears away. "Goodbye, Dad," he said. Then he turned and walked slowly out of the empty chapel.

CHAPTER 11

Chief of the KGB, Valentin Yedotev, gave a cheerful good morning to his beautiful blond secretary and entered his office with the feeling that the day would be a good one. Even before he removed his coat, he picked up the phone and, with the ringed forefinger of his right hand, punched out six numbers.

The phone on the other end rang twice before a man answered. "Comrade Major Labonov here."

"Major, how's our new guest?"

Labonov instantly recognized Yedotev's voice and said, "He is very quiet."

"I will be there later to talk to him," Yedotev said. "Arrange for the usual conveniences."

"Certainly, Comrade General."

Yedotev put the phone down and crossed the carpeted room to the closet, where he took a few moments to place his coat and fur hat and to appraise his reflection in the full-length mirror in back of the door.

Yedotev would be fifty years old on Saturday. But he looked ten years younger. He was a tall, muscular man, with good features, hair that was still jet black, and a naturally dark complexion. His eyes were dark gray, bright and unbelievably penetrating, so he was told by the variety of women he had bedded and the variety of individuals he had interrogated. Satisfied with the way he looked, he stepped back, closed the closet door and went to his desk, ready to begin the day's work.

There were two folders on his desk. One was the dossier of an American agent named Roy Ellis. The other was the dossier of a Russian woman named Galena Borodine, the wife of a submarine captain.

The phone rang.

"Comrade Yedotev," his secretary said, "your coffee and bun are here."

He smiled. "Bring them in," he said and put the phone down. He liked to have his coffee and bun first thing in the morning. It gave him a few minutes to relax and think.

The door opened and the secretary entered. She carried a tray with a thermal pitcher, a saucer, a plate with a sugared bun, a creamer, two packets of artificial sweetener, and a spoon, knife and fork wrapped in a white linen napkin.

"You're looking very well, Tanya," Yedotev said, spreading the napkin out on his lap.

She smiled at him. "It's a good day, Comrade General. The sun is shining and Moscow looks beautiful covered with snow."

Yedotev nodded. Tanya was a recent addition to his staff. He had seen her in the office of the second directorate and decided he wanted her to be his secretary. He also wanted her to be his mistress. But that would come later; he was sure of it.

The red phone on his desk rang. He motioned to Tanya to leave. As soon as the door closed, he picked the phone up. "General Yedotev here."

"Chernenkov," the voice on the other end said.

"Good morning, Comrade Premier," Yedotev said. He had expected the premier to call some time during the morning. But not the first thing. Obviously his sources of information were getting much better than they had been in the past.

"I was informed early this morning that you have picked up an American agent named Roy Ellis."

"He is resting comfortably in Lubyanka," Yedotev said.

"And I was also informed that several other agents managed to get away," the premier said.

That was something Yedotev did not know. He was not told anything about other agents by the duty officer who had called him at home at two o'clock in the morning.

"You did know about the other agents?" the premier asked.

"Yes," Yedotev answered casually. "We've known about the group for some time," he lied.

"Can you tell me when you will have the other agents resting comfortably in Lubyanka?"

The cat and mouse game had started. Yedotev neither respected nor liked Chernenkov. In Yedotev's eyes, he was a weak man who understood very little about the realities of world politics. Had he been in Chernenkov's place when the Americans destroyed the missile base on Torpay Island, he would have launched a missile attack against one of their remote bases to teach them a lesson.

"It would be a wonderful propaganda ploy if we could put all of them on trial at one time," Chernenkov said.

"I cannot give you an exact day," Yedotev answered. "But you have my word that it will be soon. I have yet to interrogate my guest."

"I don't want your guest dead," the premier said. "Dead men can't be convicted."

Yedotev felt the heat rise in his cheeks. "I assure you, he will be alive."

"Does the American embassy know you have him?" Chernenkov asked.

Unwilling to commit himself, Yedotev said, "I'll be better able to answer that later this morning."

"In other words, you don't know?" Chernenkov pressed.

"Not at this time," Yedotev was forced to admit.

"Call me as soon as you find out," Chernenkov said. "We will not release any information about his capture until it suits our purpose."

"If it were up to me, I'd never release any information about the people we take."

Chernenkov answered with, "Call me when you know something more."

"Yes, Comrade Chernenkov," Yedotev said.

The line went dead.

"Bastard," Yedotev growled. "The fucking bastard!" He slammed the phone down, picked up the other one and stabbed out a series of numbers. As soon as it was answered, he shouted, "Why wasn't I told about the other agents?"

"The information about them is included in Mister Ellis's dossier which was delivered to your secretary first thing this morning and should have been on your desk by now," the voice on the other end said calmly.

Yedotev dropped the phone back into its cradle and opened Ellis's folder. The information about the other agents was on the first information sheet. He scanned it quickly. Apparently Ellis was traveling with two other men. The other two escaped because the three of them went off in three different directions. It was the quick thinking of one of the KGB agents that made possible the capture of Ellis. They might have lost him, too, if the agent in charge hadn't decided to concentrate on one. The capture took place at a metro station. Ellis tried to leap in front of a train to prevent his capture. He was stopped by the second agent.

"At least two other agents," Yedotev said aloud. He picked up the thermal pitcher, removed the stopper and poured coffee into the cup, put cream into it and stirred the mixture until it was a light brown. Then he emptied one of the packets of sweetener into it and stirred it again. He cut the bun into three equal parts, picked one up and began to eat.

It occurred to him that the presence of three agents in one place was most unusual and could have ramifications far beyond anything he might be able to think of at the moment.

Yedotev glanced at the report again. The arresting officer said that the three had been under surveillance for several weeks. Two of them had done a great deal of traveling in the company of a woman companion. The description of the woman matched the description of two women who had been reported missing. One of them was Dr. Natalia Jannovich, a geneticist involved in important government operations; the other, Nicole Pushkin, was a computer programmer, responsible for developing mathematical models for the agricultural industry. Their extensive traveling had alerted the authorities. Then when the three men were spotted together, the agents assigned to follow them decided it was time to bring them in for extensive questioning.

Yedotev sipped his coffee and found himself wondering if there was any connection between the two missing women and the fact that Boris Donskoi vanished twenty-four hours before he would have been arrested by the KGB and charged with committing espionage for the Americans. That there might be a connection was an interesting possibility. Even an exciting one.

He finished his first cup of coffee and poured a second. From the traveling they did, it was clear that the group was trying to throw the KGB off their track and then find a way to get to the West. Possibly through Poland. Yedotev ate the second piece of the bun. Whatever he had to know about the group would have to come from Ellis. That much was very clear to him. There would be no other way for him to get the kind of information he needed to capture the other members of the group.

He drank his second cup of coffee slowly and before he finished it he ate the remaining piece of the bun. Then he opened the middle drawer of his desk, removed an American pack of cigarettes and helped himself to one.

Yedotev riffled through the other papers in Ellis's dossier until he came to a piece of information that made him stop. Ellis was a demolition expert. He gave a long, low whistle. It was time to interrogate Mister Ellis.

As soon as Yedotev entered the cell, he said in English, "Come, Mister Ellis, it is time for us to get to know one another."

Ellis stood up. His belt had been taken from him and he hitched his pants up.

"We would talk here," Yedotev said. "But a six-by-six cell has very little to recommend it."

They left the cell and walked down a long corridor that was harshly lit with naked electric bulbs and completely monitored by TV cameras.

"Have you had anything to eat?" Yedotev asked.

"No," Ellis replied.

"An oversight, I assure you," Yedotev commented. "I will take care of that as soon as we reach our destination."

They went down several flights of steps, through two more corridors, made several turns and then up several flights. "I am sorry we have to do so much walking," Yedotev said. "But it will help you work up your appetite."

"It will also serve to disorient me a little," Ellis commented matter-of-factly.

Yedotev smiled. "That too. I'm sure you use similar techniques in the United States. Perhaps you will tell me about them when we finish with the main business at hand."

Finally they stopped in front of a door, exactly like the doors in all of the other corridors. Yedotev opened it, stepped back and, gesturing to Ellis, said, "Please enter. Sit in the chair at the table." He followed him into the room. Two men were already there. Both were standing off to one side. He said nothing to them. He sat down opposite Ellis and offered him a cigarette.

"I don't smoke," he said.

"Ah, excuse me. I forgot. Your dossier says that you are very keen on physical fitness. That's good, very good," he said, lighting the cigarette with an American-made lighter. "Now, tell me what you'd like to eat and I'll order it."

"Hot cereal and milk would be fine," Ellis answered.

"If I were you," Yedotev said, "I would, until this matter between us is settled to my satisfaction, eat very lightly."

"The matter is already settled," Ellis answered.

Yedotev raised his eyebrows.

"You want certain information from me, which I will give you."

Yedotev was taken aback. He had expected a victory, but not so easily won.

Switching to Russian, Ellis said, "I am in Russia because I fell in love with a Russian woman the last time I was here. Her name was Maria Kosytin. But she is dead. She was killed in an automobile crash nine months ago."

"Mister Ellis, it's a sad story but not a true one," Yedotev said.

"Maria worked in the typing pool in your section," Ellis said.

"I'm sure she did, if you say she did. But that is not the reason why you are here, now is it?"

"I am here because two of your agents arrested me."

"You have false identification papers. You were doing a great deal of suspicious traveling in the company of a woman named Nicole Pushkin, who has been missing from her job for several weeks."

"Is she troubling you?"

"The two of you are troubling me," Yedotev answered.

"We became lovers," Ellis said. "Well, not really lovers. She felt sorry for me when I told her about Maria and suggested that making love to another woman for a while might help me get over my grief and look at it in the right perspective."

"You do admit that you were carrying false identification papers?" Yedotev said, dropping the cigarette on the floor and grinding it out with his heel.

"Yes, but only because I was so in love with Maria and you would not let me in this country of yours if I used my real name."

"Mister Ellis, you are a demolitions expert."

"That's right. I am also a construction engineer."

"You are a CIA agent, Mister Ellis," Yedotev said.

"I work for them, but I'm hardly an agent."

Yedotev lit another cigarette. "Who were the other men you were with immediately before you were captured?"

"I was alone," Ellis said.

"What type of explosive did you use to blow up the chemical plant?" Yedotev asked.

Ellis hesitated a moment too long.

"So that was why you came to this great and glorious country," Yedotev said.

"I told you why I'm in Russia," Ellis responded.

Yedotev nodded. "Sooner or later, I will have the whole story. Now tell me why you're in Moscow? And please don't tell me about Maria."

"If you don't want to hear about Maria, then I have nothing to tell you."

"It's my guess that after you and your friends blew up the chemical works, you were ordered here to take out several people, isn't that right?"

"You should write suspense novels," Ellis said.

"If I am wrong, tell me where?"

"I already told you," Ellis answered.

Yedotev shifted his eyes to the men standing at the other side of the room.

Suddenly, Ellis was thrown out of the chair and hurled to the floor.

"Stand up, Mister Ellis," Yedotev said.

As soon as he regained his feet, he was knocked down again.

"Stand up, Mister Ellis," Yedotev said.

Ellis pulled himself up and was knocked down again.

Yedotev repeated the procedure a dozen times before he said, "I do not like doing what I am doing, but experience has proven that pain is sometimes the only way to make a foolish man clever."

Ellis looked up at him and said in Russian, "You won't get anything more out of me."

"Beat him," Yedotev said, lighting another cigarette.

The two men attacked Ellis with short rubber clubs. They beat him until he vomited; then he passed out.

"Take him back to his cell," Yedotev said. "As soon as he regains consciousness, continue to beat him. Stop only if he says he wants to talk to me."

"Yes, Comrade General," one of the men answered.

Yedotev dropped the cigarette on the floor and squashed it with his heel, then he opened the door and left the room. A few minutes later he was back in his office. He flung himself into the chair behind the desk and closed his eyes. The Ellises of the world disturbed him. He did not understand their reasons for defending a social system that was doomed. He did not —

The phone rang. He picked it up.

"Comrade General," Tanya said, "you have a call from the interrogation section."

"Put it through," Yedotev said.

"Comrade General, this is Major Labonov. I am sorry to report that Mister Ellis is dead."

"What?" Yedotev shouted, leaping to his feet. "Ellis dead?"

"The result of a massive heart attack," Labonov explained. "He was dead when he was brought back to his cell. The body will be disposed of in the usual manner."

"No. Hold it until I tell you to dispose of it. Put it in the morgue."

"Yes, Comrade General," Labonov said.

Yedotev put the phone down. There was no way to hide the fact that the man had been beaten to death.

He opened the middle drawer and took out a cigarette, lit it and began to pace. He hadn't the slightest doubt that Chernenkov would demand a full-scale investigation. And there were many members of the Politburo who would like nothing better than to see him stumble and fall from power. A man in his position had more enemies than friends. Chernenkov would be among the first to pull him down. He did not expect the man to die of a heart attack. The bottom line was, of course, that he could have used other methods to obtain the information he wanted. But he wanted to prove he could break Ellis, make him plead to be allowed to give the information.

Yedotev stopped pacing and sat down. With the cigarette dangling from his lips, he looked at the red phone and waited with mounting fear for Chernenkov to call him.

Borodine and Comrade Lt. Irena Glazunov went to see the ballet *Swan Lake*; before they had gone to the theater they had had dinner out and now they were walking hand in hand along the snow-covered street where Irena lived.

"Thank you, Igor, for a wonderful evening!" Irena exclaimed. She was a blond woman, with pale blue eyes and a youthful body.

"And thank you," he answered.

She gripped his hand a bit tighter.

"My divorce came through two days ago," he said matter of factly.

For several moments, Irena said nothing, then she asked, "Does it make you sad or happy?"

Borodine uttered a deep sigh and the air in front of his face turned to steam. "Neither sad nor happy," he answered. "It was a formality which I had to go through."

"Do you think she's still in Russia?"

"No," he said quietly. "I think if she were, I would have heard."

They continued to walk without speaking until they reached the building where Irena lived. Then she said, "Come upstairs and I'll make coffee. I bought cake for us this afternoon."

"If I go upstairs," Borodine answered, "I'm not going to want to leave."

She suddenly stopped walking. "We'll talk about it upstairs," she said. "I don't like having private discussions in the middle of the street." She bolted away and hurried up the steps.

A few minutes later they were in her apartment. The aroma of brewing coffee filled the small apartment. Borodine stood in the kitchen doorway watching Irena set the table. She had tied a white apron over the black cocktail dress she wore. The way she set the table made him smile.

"What do you find so funny?" she asked, looking at him.

"Funny is the wrong word," he said.

"Oh! Then perhaps you could tell me the right one?"

"Pleased would be more accurate," Borodine answered. "Pleased by what I see."

Color came into her cheeks.

He went directly to her and swept her up in his arms. "You know I've wanted you from the first time I saw you."

"Make love to me, Igor," she whispered.

He kissed her passionately on the lips. She opened her mouth and gave him her tongue.

Breathless, they separated.

"I was never going to let you leave tonight," she said. "Never."

He scooped her up in his arms and carried her into the bedroom. The herbal-scented perfume she wore filled his nostrils and quickened his heart.

The bed was already turned down.

"I told you," she said, "that I wasn't going to let you leave."

He kissed her again, then he put her down.

They undressed quickly and for the first time he saw her naked. Her body was lovely. "Don't move," he said. "Just let me look at you."

"You're embarrassing me," she chided.

"No, I'm complimenting you," he said, bringing her against him and moving his hands over her bare back. Her skin was soft and warm. Her breasts rapidly rose and fell. "You're lovely to look at."

"And so are you," she responded.

Borodine picked her up again and moments later, he gently lowered her onto the bed.

She raised her arms and, embracing him, drew him down to her. "I've wanted this for almost as long as you have," she told him.

"Then why did you wait so long?" he asked, pausing to kiss her nose and forehead as he spoke.

She shrugged. "I wanted to be sure that you loved me, at least for a while."

"I want you," Igor answered. "I can't tell you anything more."

Borodine pressed his face into the valley between her breasts.

"You don't know how many times I imagined this," she said.

Borodine gently entered her.

"Yes, oh, yes," she whispered, placing her arms around his neck and drawing his face down to hers.

He kissed her passionately on the lips; their tongues met. He moved slowly.

She met each of his thrusts with her own gyrations. "Like that?"

"It's marvelous. Absolutely marvelous!"

Borodine quickened his pace.

"I'm almost there," she gasped, grabbing hold of his bare shoulders.

Borodine's passion mounted quickly. The heat in his groin became a fire.

"Oh, Igor, Igor, I love you!" she exclaimed.

Borodine felt the tension in her body suddenly implode.

She bit him on the shoulder.

His own passion burst out of him and hurled him into a world of vividly flowing reds, brilliant shades of orange and trembling yellows. Slowly the colors dimmed and dissolved into an ever-deepening blue. The orgasm was intense and it was taking him a delightful length of time to return to reality. When he did, when he opened his eyes, he was still on top of Irena. He looked down at her and smiled.

"Was it good for you?" she asked.

"Very good," he answered.

"For me, too," she said, embracing him. "It was very good for me, too."

"I love you, Irena," he said.

"Now … this moment."

"Now … this moment," he said "is all I can give you."

She nodded. "Then it will have to be enough," she answered softly.

He kissed the tip of her nose, then her lips.

Chernenkov summoned Yedotev to his office. He waited a full three days to do it: a full three days after his source of information not only had told him about Mr. Ellis's death but also exactly how it happened. And now Yedotev was seated before him trying very hard to look as if he didn't have a care in the world.

Chernenkov smiled. He was a roly-poly man with a pleasant smile. "It's good of you to have taken time to come see me today," he said.

"My schedule isn't very heavy today," Yedotev answered. "Besides it's good to get away from one's desk now and then."

"That's true," Chernenkov answered. "I was saying the same thing to one of my associates just the other day. We stay too long behind our desk and we lose perspective. It's a fact." He paused a moment before adding, "Don't you think?"

"Oh, absolutely," Yedotev answered.

"A drink?" Chernenkov offered.

"Scotch, please, on the rocks."

Chernenkov went to the bar and fixed the drinks himself. "I could never get used to the taste of Scotch," he said, handing Yedotev his drink. "To me it tastes like iodine, whereas vodka is smooth, as lovely as Mother Russia herself," he commented, raising his own glass.

"To Mother Russia," Yedotev toasted.

"Certainly, to Mother Russia," Chernenkov answered. He drank a bit, then sat down behind his desk. "Cigar, Comrade?" he asked.

"No, if you don't mind, I'll smoke a cigarette."

"Please do," Chernenkov answered, taking a cigar out of the humidor. "There's something very pleasant about the smell and feel of a good Cuban cigar." He smelled the cigar and twirled it between his fingers before he cut one end and lit up. "So," he said, settling back in his chair, "we have lost Mister Ellis, I understand."

"Heart attack," Yedotev answered. "I have a complete medical report."

Chernenkov nodded. "Good. Always good to have the necessary paperwork to cover one's mistakes."

"Mistake?" Yedotev exclaimed. "What mistake?"

"Come, come, Comrade General, we all make them. But now and then we make one which could have serious consequences."

"The Americans will not —"

Chernenkov waved him silent. "Certainly they won't protest. But I do. I protest that you had a man beaten to death who would have been of enormous value to the state."

Yedotev stubbed out the cigarette and immediately lit another one.

"I told you to keep that man alive," Chernenkov said. "Do you think I told you that because I really wanted him dead? No, no, Comrade General, that is not my way. I am a very direct man, a very simple man. I have often been accused of being too simple," he added with a chuckle. "But I never thought that you above everyone else would make the mistake of thinking that I was too simple."

Yedotev shook his head.

"You don't know how glad I am to hear that," Chernenkov said. "It will facilitate an understanding between us that will go a long way toward saving your career."

Yedotev blanched.

"I was thinking of calling for a full-scale investigation into the nature of Mister Ellis's death," Chernenkov said, "though of course I know exactly what caused his heart attack. But, I said to myself, is there any real reason that I want to destroy Comrade General Yedotev? The answer of course was no. Rather than destroy him, I'd like him to be more cooperative. Now certainly that is the more civilized way of working things out, don't you think?"

Yedotev nodded.

"Would you like me to tell you how you could be more cooperative even today? You see, Comrade General, you don't have to wait for a special occasion to exercise your new-found attitude."

"Tell me," Yedotev answered, stubbing out his cigarette.

"Comrade Admiral Gorshkov is a very good friend of mine. He tells me that you have a Comrade Captain Igor Borodine under surveillance because his wife has gone underground, presumably because she is trying to defect."

"That is so."

"I see no real reason to have Comrade Captain Borodine followed," Chernenkov said, purposely blowing a cloud of smoke across the desk.

"She might try to make contact —"

"No reason at all," Chernenkov said. "In fact, I think it is a waste of the state's money."

Several moments passed before Yedotev answered, "I see your point. Yes, I most certainly see your point."

"Then I can tell my old friend that that will be taken care of to his satisfaction?"

"Yes," Yedotev answered.

Chernenkov smiled. "I don't know why you have the reputation for being an unreasonable man," he said. "I certainly don't find you in the least bit unreasonable."

"Is there anything else?" Yedotev asked.

"Not that I can think of for the moment. Ah, yes, there is. I want the other American agents captured so that we might be able to hold a public trial. I want the Russians who are with them captured so that they might be tried for treason. I want them captured before they manage to get out of Russia. Do I make myself clear, Comrade General?" The tone of his voice suddenly took on an edge. "And when they're captured, I want them kept alive. Is all that very clear?"

"Very," Yedotev said. "Is there anything else?"

"Only that from now on, Comrade General, you belong to me," Chernenkov said. "The KGB will be run from this office. Should you suddenly have any ideas of becoming its head again, I'll have you removed. Killed if necessary."

"That won't be necessary."

Chernenkov smiled. "You don't know how much that pleases me."

CHAPTER 12

The sky above Langly was gray with the promise of snow or rain. Which one would come would depend on whether or not a storm off the coast of North Carolina would stay over water or more inland. Conners hoped it would snow. He wanted to get some skiing in over the weekend. He sat in a chair next to Kinkade's desk and looked out the window.

"Christ," Kinkade complained, "can't anything go right?"

James Conners shrugged. "You told me Hardy was in charge. I'm lucky I got away. I was sure I was recognized."

"What the hell were all of you doing in one place?" Kinkade asked.

"Ask Hardy when he comes in," Conners said.

"That's not funny," Kinkade said. "I lost one man already. I don't want to lose another. And I want to bring those other people out."

Conners shifted his weight toward the side of Kinkade's desk. "I'll tell you this: They're not coming out through the West. It's sealed tight. The KGB is looking for someone. I think we just happened to be trying to get people out at the wrong time."

"The longer they stay inside the more likely they'll be caught," Kinkade said.

"That's for sure!"

"I can't let that happen," Kinkade said, slamming his right hand down on the desk. "Whether or not you think so, Hardy and Foster are good men and the people with them are important to us."

"I don't see how you could stop it," Conners responded.

Kinkade touched a button on the side of his desk. A huge map of the Soviet Union filled a screen that came down from an opening in the ceiling. "We're going to find a place where we can take the five of them out."

"The West is closed," Conners said.

"You already told me that," Kinkade snapped.

"The Turkish border?" Conners suggested.

"They'd be competing with too many smugglers and several of our own people who have to cross back and forth."

"Take them out through Siberia," Conners said offhandedly. He wasn't in the least bit interested in how Kinkade expected to get Hardy out.

Suddenly the north coast of Siberia filled the screen. "I like that," Kinkade said. "I like that. Ivan won't think that it's possible for us to do. He'll be taken by surprise."

Conners did a double take, then he said, "I don't think we can do it, especially at this time of year."

"If they can get to this place," Kinkade said, using a pointer of light to indicate the spot on the map, "it's only sixty miles from Alaska. Surely there are some days when it would be possible to get a plane in and out, or a helicopter."

"But you might have to wait for weeks —"

"I want those five people out," Kinkade said. "And I intend to get them out."

"You're the boss," Conners said, throwing up his hands.

"I want to set up the rescue operation from this end," Kinkade said. "That means you'll be on sight when it goes into action. I'll notify Hardy what I want him to do."

"He'll screw up," Conners said matter of factly.

"Maybe, but then again maybe not," Kinkade said. "Remember, I'm not interested in your personal likes and dislikes. I want that team out. Give yourself a month to get everything ready. That means sometime in late January. All arrangements will be considered top secret."

Conners nodded.

"Do you want anyone assigned to you?" Kinkade asked.

"God. Because He's the only one who'll be able to bring it off."

Kinkade didn't answer.

Tracy's article on Boxer and the *Shark* came out. Boxer was surprised how much information the Company permitted Tracy to use. Boxer suddenly had requests for TV interviews and other writers wanted to do pieces on him. He turned all of them down and remained in New York for several weeks to help his mother sort out his father's estate.

On the day that he and his mother went to the offices of John Willis and Son to hear his father's will read, he was surprised to discover his father had accumulated a substantial fortune.

"The various holdings," Mr. Willis said, peering at him and his mother over the rim of half glasses, "comes to something in the order of two and one half million dollars."

Boxer did a double take.

"Your father invested in several high-tech companies that have become leaders in the industry, and he has real estate holdings in Brooklyn and Staten Island that have increased in value fourfold."

"Did you know anything about this?" Boxer asked, looking at his mother.

She shook her head. "We always lived comfortably. I never wanted for anything."

"Your father left most of his estate to you, Jack," Mr. Willis said, "with the stipulation that while your mother lives, you are not to touch any of the principal and that three-quarters of all the income derived from the investments be given to your mother."

"She can have all of it," Boxer answered. "I don't need any money."

"What you do with your share is not my affair," Mr. Willis said. "Your father's will states clearly what he wanted done with it."

Boxer nodded. By the time the session was over, he had retained Willis to be his and his mother's lawyer and Willis had agreed to find someone to manage the estate.

In the cab, on the way back to Brooklyn, his mother said, "You don't have to work anymore, if you don't want to. There's more than enough money —"

"Mom," he said, placing his hand on her arm, "I couldn't stay home. The sea is my life."

She nodded and turned her face toward the window. He leaned over and kissed her on the cheek. "You know I have to do what I'm doing. If I didn't, I wouldn't be me."

"I know," she answered softly. "I also know how dangerous it is. I don't want my son to be a dead hero."

"I'm not a hero, Mom. I just do my job."

"It takes a hero to do that job," she said.

Boxer didn't answer. He took hold of his mother's hand, leaned back and wondered if his father knew what he did. Though his father would not have said much about it, he would have been proud to read about him in the article. Very proud, indeed. Boxer smiled.

The next morning Boxer was at the hospital a few minutes before six. He waited in the lobby, near the elevators, and when he saw Louise, he called to her.

She came to him.

He took hold of her and kissed her on the lips.

"You look very much better," she said when he let go of her.

"Do you think you might be able to fix breakfast for me?" he asked, linking his arm with hers.

"Are you sure, Jack?" she asked. "The other time was — well, one of those things that happen. It might have been beautiful but —"

"It was beautiful," Boxer said. "But there was something that was left unfinished."

They moved through the automatic doors into the street. Neither one spoke until just before they reached the store where Louise shopped. Then she said, "I'd be lying if I said I didn't think about you, or how it might have been. But I didn't think you'd ever come back."

"I'm here," Boxer said.

She smiled up at him. "Lox, cream cheese and bagels," she said.

Boxer went into the store with her and paid for the food; then he picked up the bag and carried it.

"I read about you in the newspaper," Louise said as they turned down the street where she lived. "I had no idea you were so important."

"I'm only important to the men aboard the *Shark*," he said.

"And to the people you rescued," she answered.

"Well, maybe," he answered as they entered the building.

While Louise set the table, Boxer went into the living room and turned on the TV. The seven o'clock news was on. Boxer stood and watched.

"For the same price," Louise said, "you can sit down and watch it."

"I was just going to —" He stopped.

The newscaster said, "The nude body of Tracy Kimble was found early this morning near her home in Washington. The police report she had been raped and stabbed several times. There are no clues."

"Oh, my God!" Boxer exclaimed.

Louise rushed into the living room. "What's wrong?"

"The woman who wrote the article about me was raped and stabbed to death," he said, dropping down into a chair.

Louise went to him and pressed his head against her. "I'm sorry," she said.

"She was a wild, willful woman and very beautiful," Boxer said.

"Were you lovers?" Louise asked.

"No. We slept together now and then. But we weren't lovers. Not the way you meant it."

Louise knelt down in front of him. "It's not going to be any good for us now," she said. "Maybe the fates are trying to tell us something."

"You're right," Boxer said, "it won't be any good for us now. But it will be good when it happens, that I promise you. Will you be able to get a few days off around New Year's?"

"Yes, if I want them," she answered.

"You take them. Come to Washington. You'll come to a New Year's Eve party with me."

"Jack..."

"I have to go to Washington," he said. "I want the man who killed her."

"Let the police handle it," she said.

"No. But I know someone who will handle it," Boxer answered. "I'll call you in few days. You'll come down with me. I want to spend Christmas with my mother."

"Are you going —"

"I'm going to go this morning," Boxer said. "I'll take a shuttle flight down."

"Won't you even have breakfast with me?" Louise asked. "I have everything ready."

"I'll have breakfast with you," Boxer said. He leaned forward and gently kissed the top of her head.

By two that same afternoon, Boxer was standing in the morgue, looking down at Tracy. Her naked body was stretched out on a metal slab. The room was very cold and the fluorescent lighting coming from fixtures in the ceiling was very bright. Her face, neck and thighs were bruised. The stab wounds were exactly the same kind that he had seen on Dee: two were below the left breast and one directly into the heart. He nodded to the attendant and stepped away from the slab. "Has anyone claimed the body?" he asked.

"The deceased's brother," the man said. "He's flying in from Santa Fe and will be here sometime this evening."

Boxer had forgotten that Tracy, like Redfern's wife, Sue-Ann, came from New Mexico. He wrote out his name and the telephone number of the hotel he was staying at on a piece of paper and gave it to the attendant. "Tell Miss Kimble's brother to call me. Tell him I'm the captain of the submarine *Shark*."

The man's eyes went wide. "You're the man she wrote about in the article."

"That's right," Boxer answered.

"That woman must have loved you a lot," the man said.

Boxer raised his eyebrows.

"I could tell by the way she wrote about you," the man commented. "She thought you were the greatest."

The two of them had left the morgue and were now standing in the doorway of the office.

"She was a really beautiful woman," the attendant said. "I hope they get the son-of-a-bitch that put her here."

Boxer heaved a deep sigh and said, "I'm going to make sure they get him."

"If I loved a woman and someone killed her, I'd sure as hell hunt down the bastard that did it."

Boxer didn't say anything else. He left the building and began to walk. A cold and cutting wind was blowing. But he had to walk. It had never occurred to him that Tracy might have been in love with him. He had always believed she had wanted him for the same reason that he wanted her: She was a damn good lay.

Boxer spotted a cab, hailed it and told the driver to take him to his hotel. As soon as he was in the room, he phoned Sanchez at his home in the Chevy Chase district of Maryland.

"Mister Sanchez is busy at the moment," a secretary said.

"Tell Mister Sanchez that Captain Boxer is on the phone," Boxer said.

Within moments Sanchez was on the line. "Captain, I was sure you'd call as soon as you found out about Tracy."

"I want to see you now," Boxer said.

"Will you come to my home?"

"Yes."

"Should I send a car for you?"

"That won't be necessary," Boxer said. "I'll call my driver."

"Let's make it for five. You can have cocktails and then we'll have dinner here or go out, whichever you'd prefer."

Boxer was about to tell him that he wasn't interested in cocktails or dinner. But he stopped himself. He had learned that if Sanchez was anything, he was certainly a civilized human being, at least when it came to the social amenities. Otherwise he was far more cunning than any animal could be and far more ruthless. "I'll be there at five," Boxer said and put the phone down.

Petty Officer Paul Zweky was Boxer's driver. He had driven for him several times before and the two men greeted one another warmly.

"I was sorry to hear that your father passed away," Zweky said, sliding behind the wheel.

Boxer accepted the remark with an appropriate, "Thank you."

"That was some piece about you and your crew in the newspaper," Zweky said. "I mean, Captain, I sure as hell didn't know you were into all that kind of shit."

Zweky's description of his assignment as shit brought a smile to Boxer's lips. "It didn't seem like shit when I was doing it," Boxer said.

"You know what I mean, Skipper," Zweky said. "I mean that right out of ... of movies and TV."

Boxer laughed. He'd have to tell Cowly and the rest of the crew that they were living in some film made for TV.

"You know the woman that wrote that article was murdered," Zweky said.

"I know," Boxer said softly. His mood changed instantly.

"There was a picture of her in the late paper," Zweky said. "She was a good-looking woman."

"She was a very beautiful woman," Boxer agreed.

Zweky took a quick glance at him over his shoulder. But Boxer pretended not to notice. He knew what the man was thinking and it was true. He had shacked up with her more times than he could remember. And then he thought about what the man had said in the morgue. He still couldn't believe that Tracy loved him. But even more absurd than her loving him, he was beginning to wonder if he loved her. The answer really didn't matter now. She was dead. If he owed her anything, it was to find out who killed her and either bring him to the authorities or kill the bastard himself.

"We should be close to Mister Sanchez's house soon," Zweky said.

Boxer was jolted out of his thoughts. He hadn't remembered giving Zweky any specific directions other than to tell him they were going to Sanchez's house, which was located in the Chevy Chase area.

"I've driven the admiral there several times," Zweky said. "It's not an easy place to find, especially in the dark. There's a housemaid there that I've taken out a few times."

Boxer let the matter pass without commenting on it.

After a few minutes, Zweky turned off the main road and onto a narrow secondary. "It's at the end of this road. Exactly four miles from the turn-off. My lady friend told me that Sanchez owns all of the property on either side of us. There's even a lake in here somewhere."

Boxer found himself wondering if Zweky was just a driver, or was he also a member of the Company? Not that it mattered much.

Zweky stopped in front of a huge Tudor-type house, complete with wooden beams and overhanging eaves.

The door opened and a butler came out.

"Go see your lady friend," Boxer said as he left the car. "I'm going to be here for a while."

"When you're ready to leave," Zweky said, "have the butler call down to the kitchen for me."

"Just don't wind up where I can't get you," Boxer said.

Zweky grinned but didn't answer.

Boxer walked up the four steps that led to the door. "Señor Sanchez is expecting you," the man said.

Boxer nodded.

As soon as they were inside a maid took Boxer's coat and hat and hung them in a closet.

"Follow me, Captain Boxer," the butler said.

Boxer was amazed at the size of the foyer: It was easily as large as a small house. And there was a semi-circular staircase leading to the three upper floors.

Sanchez was waiting in the library: a lovely book-lined room with dark wood paneling and a fire going in the fireplace.

"It's really very good to see you," said Sanchez, crossing the room to greet Boxer. "I'm only sorry the circumstances have to be so sad."

Boxer shook his hand. Despite his initial dislike, perhaps even hatred for the man, he had to admit Sanchez had the combination of class and culture that was seldom found in a man, or a woman for that matter.

"What would you like to drink? Vodka on the rocks is your favorite, if memory serves me correctly."

"That will be fine," Boxer answered.

Sanchez went to the sideboard, opened it and fixed a drink for Boxer and one for himself. "Let us drink to Tracy's memory," he said. "She certainly was a unique woman." They touched glasses and drank.

"I want Tracy's killer," Boxer said. "I know you can get him for me."

"What I like about you," Sanchez said, "is your directness. You don't waste time."

"You know why I came here," Boxer said, "so why should I dance around the reason?"

"Have you seen the body?"

Boxer nodded. "Have you?"

"Yes. I don't believe it was rape and murder the way the police think it was. Tracy wasn't into casual pickups. She knew the man who killed her."

Boxer agreed. "She probably had sex in the car, was stabbed, stripped and thrown out of the car."

"That's about the way I see it," Sanchez said after he finished his drink.

"I don't believe it was a casual pickup either," Boxer said. "She was killed the same way Dee Long was."

"Dee Long?" Sanchez questioned.

Boxer handed him his empty glass. "I'd appreciate another one and I'll tell you all about Dee Long."

Sanchez refilled his and Boxer's glasses. "Please," he said, "sit down. You'll find it relaxing to sit in front of the fire."

Boxer chose a wing-backed chair. "Dee was aboard the *Tecumseh*. She was in my bed. I was called to the bridge. I found her dead. She had been stabbed exactly the same way Tracy was. But she was not raped. My guess is that someone came into my cabin, didn't expect to find her and —"

"Have you any ideas who might have killed Dee?" Sanchez asked.

"Hayes," Boxer said without any hesitation. "Byron Hayes."

"Ah, so that was the time you rescued him and wouldn't let him send a radio message. I know all about it. I can tell you he doesn't like you at all."

"The feeling is mutual," Boxer said gruffly.

"You seriously think he killed Dee and Tracy?"

"I think he's a mole," Boxer said. "That's really what I think."

"That's a very serious charge," Sanchez said.

"I think he killed Tracy."

"Why?"

Boxer shrugged. "Jealousy. I don't know why. But I think he did it."

"All right," Sanchez said. "I'll have him checked out. If he did it, he's as good as dead. But I really don't think he'd do it. He wasn't jealous of any man, at least when it came to their relations with women. I know he slept with Tracy and so did I, as you know. But Byron prefers men to women. He only sleeps with women because it's good for his image."

"I had no idea."

"You weren't supposed to," Sanchez said. "And there is something else you should know. For what it's worth now, Tracy loved you. She told me she did. When she was aboard the *Mary-Ann* and you were on the bridge, she said, 'God, I love that man more than I have ever loved anyone in my life.' And I said to her, 'Then tell him after this is over.' Did she ever tell you?"

Boxer shook his head.

"Sad," Sanchez said. "Very sad."

Boxer finished his second drink.

"Do you mind if I ask you a question?" Sanchez said.

Boxer cleared his throat. "Ask."

"Did you love her?"

"No," Boxer said softly. "I didn't. At least not the way she wanted me to."

Sanchez finished his drink. "Care for another one?"

"Not now," Boxer answered. "Perhaps after dinner."

"I promise you," Sanchez said, "that whoever killed Tracy will be found."

"Kill him," Boxer said. "Don't turn him over to the authorities. If you can't have one of your men do it, tell me who it is and I'll do it."

"If he is found," Sanchez said, "I'll have it taken care of."

"Thanks," Boxer said. "I owe you one."

"No," Sanchez said. "You don't owe me anything. I loved Tracy and offered to marry her. She turned me down. She said, 'I can't marry you because if Jack wanted me, I'd leave you and go to him.'"

"I had no idea."

Sanchez held up his hand. "It's all gone now," he said quietly. "That beautiful woman is gone now."

Boxer looked at the flames in the fireplace and felt the tears stream out of his eyes. He knew that he was weeping not only for her, but also for himself.

Dinner was, as Boxer expected, an elaborate affair. Complete with several different kinds of wine and an indescribably delicious ice-cream-and-brandy dish for dessert. When it was over Sanchez suggested they return to the library. "I have something to tell you," he said, "which might end the evening on a lighter note than it began." He offered Boxer a cigar from an ornately carved humidor and took one for himself. "It concerns the gold you recovered," he said, lighting up.

"What about it?" Boxer asked.

"Only a fourth of it was any good," Sanchez answered, gesturing Boxer to sit down in front of the fire again.

Boxer lit up. "I don't understand."

"Three-quarters of the bars were nothing more than gold plate."

"That's impossible!"

Sanchez smiled. "It seems like the inhabitants of India were tired of giving gold to the king of Portugal. They learned the art and technology of gilding bars of lead."

"Then all of those men died for —"

"Considerably less than Kinkade and the others thought would be there," Sanchez answered.

"Christ, I wonder if Borodine knows," Boxer said, getting to his feet. "A third of Tom's men were killed and the Russians lost more than that."

Sanchez shrugged. "There was no way for anyone to know that the Indians had found a way to fool their masters."

Boxer got to his feet. He wanted to be angry, but somehow the anger wouldn't rise.

"Naturally my share was considerably less," Sanchez said. "But the entire experience was certainly worth something."

"To you," Boxer answered. "But not to me. You weren't down with me three hundred feet below the surface. You weren't in the *Shark* when she was caught in a river of cold water, Julio," he said, using Sanchez's given name for the first time. "I know we both work for the same people. But sometimes I really wonder if they know what they're doing. I mean really know?"

"Sometimes they do," Sanchez answered. "That time they didn't."

Boxer blew a cloud of smoke toward the flames. "Kinkade must have some terrible nightmares," he said.

"I doubt if he dreams at all," Sanchez said, "at least not any dreams that he'd remember."

"Lucky man," Boxer answered. "Lucky man. All I have to do is close my eyes and I can see the sharks tear at the dead and the wounded. Yes, Kinkade is a lucky man if he doesn't remember his nightmares and luckier still if he doesn't have them, because I sure as hell do." He looked at Sanchez.

Sanchez didn't answer.

Boxer knew that Sanchez didn't have nightmares either and if he did, like Kinkade, he didn't remember them.

CHAPTER 13

The following morning Boxer received a phone call from Stark, whose first question was, "How is your mother holding up?"

"Well," Boxer answered.

"If she ever needs anything, you let me know," Stark said.

"I will," Boxer answered.

Stark paused for a moment before he said, "I want you to go out to the yard and take a look — see what has been happening to the *Shark*. She should be ready for her sea trials after New Year's."

"Will do," Boxer answered.

"I'll send your driver around to the hotel to pick you up, say, about eleven hundred?"

Boxer looked at his watch. It was oh nine hundred. He had gotten back from his meeting with Sanchez well after oh one hundred and had slept later than he usually did. "Eleven will be fine, Admiral," he said.

As soon as he hung up, he put through a call to his mother.

"I was so worried about you," she said. "I didn't know why you had to leave so quickly."

"Something to do with my boat," he lied. He was sure that now that she knew more about what he did than she previously had, she would spend more time worrying about him.

"I had a terrible dream," she told him. "I dreamt you killed someone. The way it happened a few months ago in front of the house."

"Nothing like that," he answered. Then to change the subject he said, "Stark sends his regards."

"Thank him when you see him for his kindness," she said.

"I'll be home for Christmas," he told her. "But I have a New Year's Eve party to go to down here."

They spoke a few more minutes and then said goodbye; then Boxer phoned Louise. "Just checking in," he told her.

"I'm glad," she answered. "Glad to know you're thinking about me."

"And about our unfinished business," he said.

She laughed and said, "I wouldn't let it remain unfinished if you were here."

"Listen," he said, "once I finally do climb into bed with you —"

He was interrupted by a knock on the door. It was too early for Zweky to show up. Besides, Zweky always called him from the lobby. "There's someone at the door," he said. "Hold on."

"No. You go answer it and I'll go back to sleep."

"I'm sorry if I woke you," he told her.

"I'm not. Goodbye," Louise responded.

"I'll call you again soon," he said and hung up. Then he went to the door and opened it.

"May I come in?" Kathy asked.

Boxer stepped out of her way.

She walked past him, leaving a trail of jasmine scent in her wake.

Boxer closed the door after her. "I have to shave and shower," he said. "My driver is picking me up at eleven hundred."

She faced him. "That gives us some time to talk."

"There's nothing to talk about."

"I'd say there was a considerable amount for us to talk about," Kathy said. She went to the window, looked out and commented, "Despite the sun, it's cold outside."

"I'm going to shave and shower," Boxer said.

"Go ahead. I've seen you do both before," she said.

"I don't want you here," Boxer told her. "I want you out of my life."

She nodded. "I'd gladly get out of your life."

"Then for Christ's sake do it!" he exclaimed.

"Not so easy, Jack," she answered. "It would be if I wasn't in love with you."

Boxer gave a snort of disdain.

"I resigned from the Company," she said.

"Is that supposed to mean something to me?" he asked.

"No," she answered softly.

"It doesn't matter to me what you do," he said. "I couldn't trust you. That's where it's at. I couldn't trust you."

She came directly up to him. "I know you love me," she said, putting her arms around him. "I know you want me."

"Sure," he said, pulling her arms off his neck. "But I don't love you, or more precisely, I don't want to love you. I won't let myself love you now, or any time in the future."

She moved away from him.

"Will you please go," he said.

"Once I walk out of the room, I won't come back again."

"You shouldn't have come this time," Boxer answered.

"I thought you'd understand."

"Understand!" he exclaimed, raising his voice. "I understand when I've been used."

"Yes, in the beginning. But not later on. Not now."

"I'm impressed," Boxer said. "I really am. I told you: I want you out of my life. It's over between us. Done."

"Just like that?"

Boxer snapped his fingers. "Just like that. If there's anything I know how to do," he said, "it's cut my losses."

She faced the window again. "We could have had a good life together," she said, her voice almost a sob.

"And every Wednesday, or was it Friday, you'd report to the head of your section," he said sarcastically.

"I never realized you were so hard, so unforgiving," she said, still not looking at him.

"Okay. I'll accept that. I'm hard and unforgiving."

Slowly Kathy turned around. "I won't let you do this to me," she said in a whisper.

Boxer found himself looking at a snub nose .38.

"It'll be over for the two of us," she said in a raspy voice.

She was too far away for him to grab hold of the gun.

"Your friend Tracy got hers, didn't she?" Kathy said with obvious satisfaction. "You know, I'm glad she was killed that way. Glad. She didn't deserve anything better. I wish I could have been there to watch it."

Boxer clamped his jaw together. His first reaction was anger; then suddenly he realized that Kathy was out of it. Deranged. And that if he wanted to survive, he'd have to somehow get the revolver away from her.

"I did a little checking on Tracy after she paid you that visit," Kathy said. "Did more than her share of fucking. And not only with you."

Boxer remained silent.

"Slept her way up the ladder of success."

"Kathy, listen to me," Boxer said. "Before you do something that's stupid, give me the gun."

"I know how to use it," she answered. "I was trained." She eased off the safety. "This isn't the way I wanted it."

"Do it," Boxer said. "Do it and get it over with!"

A look of confusion filled her face.

Boxer saw it. "If you want me to plead for my life, forget it. I've faced death too many times to be afraid of you."

"Not the same," she managed to say.

"You're right. It's not the same. All the other times it was doing what I was trained to do. Now it will be at the hands of a rejected woman."

"A rejected woman?" she cried.

"That's exactly what you are. I don't want you. But once you squeeze that trigger, your life is over. The Company will see to that. You know they will. I'm more valuable to them than you are. They'll put you away for years. Maybe for the rest of your life. Is that what you want?" As he spoke, Boxer moved closer to her.

"No," she answered. "They won't do that. I won't let them do that."

"How would you stop them?"

"I'll kill myself," she answered with a sob. "Yes, I'll kill myself."

"That will take a lot more nerve than to kill me," he said. He was almost close enough to make a lunge for the gun.

"I'll do it!" she exclaimed.

"It won't be what you want," he said.

Again she looked confused.

"We're not lovers ending our lives in a death pact," he told her. "You'll be nothing more than a murderer and then a suicide. If you think you'll be making some kind of statement, you can forget it."

She shook her head.

"What's that supposed to mean?" he asked.

"Hard and unforgiving," she said. "You're hard and unforgiving."

Boxer lunged at her. He tried to knock the gun toward the ceiling.

Kathy screamed.

The explosion filled the room.

Boxer felt a sledge-hammer blow in his chest. He spun to the left and dropped to the floor.

Kathy turned the gun on herself.

"Don't do it," he shouted. "Don't do it." He struggled to his feet and flung himself at her.

She fell against the bed.

An instant later the door was smashed in. Two men rushed into the room.

"She's alive," Boxer heard one of them say. Then a different voice said, "The guy's been shot."

Then Boxer began to plummet into a black void.

Boxer moved in and out of a raging black sea. When he was plunged into its depths, he used all his strength to come to the surface again, where he was at least conscious of voices and movement. He knew he was being rushed through a series of halls; then outside and, from the sounds around him, that he was being medi-vaced to the hospital. That he might die was something that he knew was very possible. If it wasn't, he would have been taken by ambulance to the hospital. He was absolutely amazed how clear his thinking was, as long as he could stay on the surface of the sea. He saw all his relationships with women for what they were: nothing but sexual bonds. Two people using each other for —

"Blood," someone said, "I'm running out of blood."

"We'll be landing in two minutes," another person shouted.

Detached, Boxer knew it was blood he needed that they were talking about. He was being moved again. He could almost see the white walls fly by. Then he was in a room with a huge overhead light.

"Breathe deeply. Yes, breathe deeply," someone said.

Boxer took several deep breaths and he was in a small sailboat with his father. The sails were set and they were running before the wind.

"So you decided to go into submarines," his father said.

"Yes," Boxer answered.

"I couldn't do that," his father said. "I've always been a surface man. I wouldn't be comfortable under the water. Up here you have the wind and sky, the sun and the stars; even the moods of the sea are beautiful. But underneath it's all darkness and quiet."

Boxer didn't answer. He knew his father understood that he didn't feel that way about being under the sea.

"Your mother tells me you're getting serious about a woman," his father said.

"Gwen," Boxer answered. "She's an actress, or wants to be one."

"Oh. It's hard for a professional officer to find a woman who'll fit into the life."

"Oh, she will," Boxer answered.

The wind suddenly shifted and the sea was running. The rain came down in cold, slashing sheets.

"I want a divorce," Gwen said.

They had just finished making love. They were still naked.

"I'm not joking," she said. "I want a divorce."

He sat up. "Just like that?" he asked.

"No, I've been thinking about it for months," she answered.

"Can't we discuss it?"

"There's nothing to discuss," she said.

"There's John. We do have a son."

"I'll take him," she said.

"Just a few minutes ago I got the idea that you loved me," he said.

"I love the way you make love; I always have. But I need more than that. I need someone who'll be with me, who will try to understand me."

"And I'm not with you and I don't try to understand you?"

"You're on your boat most of the time and even when you're not, you are in your head. You're always with it. I'm something you use to get your rocks off, whenever you happen to be in port. I never ask if there are other women, when you're away."

"I never ask if there are other men," he said.

"I'm human," she answered. "You're away for months at a time."

"Then there's someone else?"

"No, there isn't someone else," she said. "I just want a divorce. I want to go back to acting. I don't want to be married to you anymore."

"No fuss, no feathers," Boxer said. "I'll give you your divorce." He left the bed.

"Where are you going?" she asked.

"To get drunk," he answered...

Boxer opened his eyes. Everything was distorted, especially the figure and the face standing alongside the bed.

"How are you doing?"

"That you, Admiral?" Boxer asked.

"Yes. You had a narrow one."

Boxer smiled. "I knew that when the waters were black."

"The doc says you'll be fine in a couple of days."

"Did you call my mother?"

"Yes. I told her you had to go to Paris for a few days but would be home for Christmas."

Boxer nodded. "Good. Good. No need to worry her. What about Kathy?"

"She's in a hospital," Stark answered softly. "She'll be there for a long time."

"Sad," Boxer said. "Very sad."

"Is there anything I can do for you?"

Boxer was about to shake his head, but stopped himself. "I want you to call a friend of mine," he said. "Her name is Louise Ennis. Her number is in my wallet. Tell her to come down here. Don't tell her I'm in the hospital."

"I'll have her flown down," Stark said.

"Thanks," Boxer answered. "Thanks a lot."

Stark nodded. "Anything else?" he asked.

"Nothing, Admiral. Nothing else. I want to sleep now," Boxer said. "I'm very tired."

"I've worked out a preliminary plan," Conners said. "I want to run it past you, before I start calling the Air Force and Navy."

Kinkade gestured to the chair next to the desk.

"I'd rather stand," Conners said. "I'll need the map of the Soviet Union on the wall."

Kinkade opened the control drawer and flicked a switch. The large screen came down from the ceiling and the map appeared on it.

Conners moved toward the map and, with an electronic pencil, drew a circle around a small area in eastern Siberia. "From this point to our base is sixty miles. It's a remote area with two fishing villages, one on either side of the cove. Most of the year ice fills the cove. Our best shot is to fly in at treetop level, land on the ice and take them out. I'd have one of our small carriers standing offshore to recover the helicopters, rather than have them fly all the way back to the base. To

176

divert the Russians, I'd have a couple of our planes violate their airspace. That will keep their radars busy. We should be in and out of there in ten minutes, at the very most."

"How high would the helicopters fly?" Kinkade asked.

"In and out no more than sixty feet off the ground. They come in straight and leave the same way."

"What about the Russian radar?"

"That's why I need two planes to violate their airspace," Conners said. "One will fly north of the pickup point and the other south. The helicopters should be able to squeeze through the opening."

Kinkade leaned back in his chair. "You're counting on the two planes to get out of the area before the Russian fighters are scrambled."

"I've got to count on something," Conners answered.

"Why do you need more than one helicopter?" Kinkade asked.

"For insurance," Conners said. "If something happens to one, the other can do the job."

"Where will the carrier be when all of this is going on?"

"Offshore, two hundred miles to the southeast."

Kinkade pursed his lips. "The Russians are going to know something is going down as soon as they spot our planes. Someone in their command will figure it out."

Conners shrugged. "What I propose is the quickest way of bringing them out."

"Probably is," Kinkade said, pinching his lower lip between his fingers. "But there's no margin for error. We might wind up losing our people and the men who were sent to bring them out."

"If you want Hardy and the others out, that's the chance you'll have to take."

"What will be your minimum weather condition?"

"Anything less than a blizzard," Conners said. "But the weather this time of year in that area is extremely bad."

"Then this entire operation will depend on the vagaries of the weather."

Conners nodded.

"That means Hardy and the others must be ready to go at an instant's notice?"

"That's right," Conners said. "That's if they can get to the place. Our sources in Moscow say that it's just a matter of time before the KGB picks all of them up."

Ignoring Conners' last comment, Kinkade said, "Set everything up with the Air Force and Navy. I want you out there when this operation goes down."

"It doesn't require a man on sight," Conners said. "I can run it from here, via a TV hook-up."

"No. I want you there," Kinkade said. "I want you aboard one of those helicopters when they come in. Is that understood?"

"Perfectly," Conners answered. "You're making me my brother's keeper."

"Yes, I guess I am," Kinkade answered. "On sight you won't have the detachment that you appear to have now. Your life will be on the line, too."

Conners didn't answer.

CHAPTER 14

Borodine entered General Yedotev's office precisely at ten in the morning.

Yedotev stood up and extended his hand across the desk. "It's a pleasure to meet you, Comrade Captain. Your exploits are not, as you know, unknown to me. Please sit down."

Borodine nodded and sat down in the chair in front of the desk.

"I suppose you're wondering why I have asked you here," Yedotev asked.

"Yes," Borodine answered honestly.

"For two reasons, Comrade Captain. The first concerns your former wife and the second is to meet the man who Comrade Admiral Gorshkov thinks is the finest submarine commander we have."

Borodine flushed.

"We intercepted a letter from Galena to you," Yedotev said as he opened the middle drawer and withdrew the letter.

Borodine began to sweat.

"She got out," Yedotev said. "She's in Paris." He handed the letter to Borodine. "You may read it."

Borodine nodded, removed the letter from the envelope and began to read. "My dear Igor, I am sorry that I left you. But it was the only way. I could not remain in Vladivostok any longer. I could not remain in Russia any longer. I could no longer accept the policy of the government. I could no longer bear to see you risk your life for a system that has so very little to offer the people who are forced to live under it." Borodine stopped and looked up at Yedotev, who was studying him.

"She was corrupted when she was in the United States," Yedotev said. "But, please, continue to read."

Borodine lowered his eyes. "As for our relationship," Galena wrote, "it could not stand the long separations. I needed love and affection. Sooner or later you would have heard that I was having an affair with another officer at the base. This wasn't the first time I was unfaithful to you and I was prepared to face your anger when you found out.

"I doubt if we will ever see one another again. Don't judge me too harshly. Galena."

Borodine turned the envelope over and looked at the stamp and postmark. It was a French stamp and it had been mailed from Paris.

"The real problem here," Yedotev said, "is that we don't know how much she knows about your special assignment."

"Nothing," Borodine answered. "I made it a point never to tell her anything concerning my work."

"Then you distrusted her."

"No, Comrade General, I didn't distrust her," Borodine said. "I did not want her to worry about me. I did not want her to make guesses about where I was or what I was doing. She knew I commanded a large submarine. She did not know anything else."

"Am I to understand," Yedotev questioned, "that you never spoke about members of your crew, or something that happened while you were at sea?"

"I couldn't avoid mentioning the men. She saw them on base. She knew their wives."

"Would you know how she managed to get out?" Yedotev asked.

Borodine shook his head. "I have no idea. She was more resourceful than I ever gave her credit for being."

"Resourceful which way?"

"The affairs she had under my nose," Borodine said, trying to conceal his anger.

"Anything else?"

"She must have been planning to leave for months."

"Probably."

"Would you mind, Comrade General, if I smoke?" Borodine asked.

"Please do."

Borodine lit up and blew smoke down toward the floor.

"If I could only be sure that you never told her anything about the *Sea Savage*," Yedotev said, "I would rest easier."

"All you have is my word," Borodine said.

"The various political officers assigned to boats in your command were less than pleased with your politics," Yedotev said. "Practically all of them said that you were apathetic when it came to keeping your crew to the party line."

"My job, Comrade General, if I may speak bluntly —"

"Be as blunt as you want to be."

"My job was to carry out a mission and bring my boat and crew back to port safely."

"Which you did admirably. But you also have a political duty, which for the moment, I will say with equal bluntness, you failed to carry out."

Borodine didn't answer.

"I have sent several agents to Paris to find Galena and return her to Russia, where she will be tried for crimes against the state. At that time, Captain, you will be required to testify against her."

"And if I choose not to testify against her, what will happen to me?"

"Even Gorshkov couldn't protect you," Yedotev said.

Borodine said nothing.

"You may go now," Yedotev said. "But remember what I said: You will testify when your wife is brought back and tried."

Borodine stood up. He was angry. He leaned slightly forward over the desk. "Comrade General," he said in a low, tight voice, "you might as well arrest me now. Because I will not testify against my former wife. The state will have enough evidence to send her to a labor camp or have her shot. But you will get nothing from me. Absolutely nothing!"

Yedotev's jaw went slack. No one ever spoke to him that way. He couldn't make up his mind whether the man standing in front of him was a fool or braver than any man he had ever met.

Borodine threw Galena's letter on the desk. "She is no longer my wife," he said. "She is your problem, Comrade General." Then, without waiting to be asked to leave, Borodine did an about-face and left the office.

Borodine held Irena's gloved hand in his own. Snow was beginning to fall. Large wet flakes drifted down from a black sky.

"I asked you to come for a walk," Borodine said, "because I'm not sure your apartment isn't bugged and I'm very sure that mine is."

"Are you in trouble?" Irena asked, suddenly stopping.

Borodine gently pulled her after him.

"Answer me! Are you in trouble?"

"There's a strong possibility that I am," Borodine said. He explained what happened during his meeting with General Yedotev. "I just became so angry," he said. "I couldn't control myself. The words came out before I could stop them."

"And Yedotev said nothing?" she asked.

"Nothing. At least nothing I could hear. After I said what I said, I did an about-face and left the office."

"He was probably too surprised to do anything," she said. "But he is not one to forget."

"Probably not," Borodine answered. "But the truth is that I never told Galena a thing about the *Sea Savage*, or any of its missions."

"Why?" Irena asked. "Didn't you think she wanted to know?"

Borodine wasn't prepared to answer that question. It had never occurred to him to tell Galena.

"Don't you think she had a right to share that part of your life?"

"Had I told her, can you imagine what Yedotev's reaction would have been?" Borodine said.

"But don't you see, Igor, you gave Galena nothing more than your body. You kept the rest of you away from her. She had nothing but sex with you."

"By her own admission, she also had that with several officers on the base," he said sourly.

"Probably out of desperation," Irena said. "Igor, she was a lonely woman, with very little to really tie her to you."

Borodine thought about that for several minutes before he said, "You make it sound as if her defection is my fault."

"Yes," she said. "I think it is. But only because you neglected to share the major portion of your life with her."

"I couldn't tell her — I didn't even tell you about my last mission. It's not that I didn't want to, but what would be the sense? Then every time I left, you'd worry yourself sick over me.

"I do that now," Irena said, "even without being told anything."

Borodine stopped, swung her into his arms and kissed her passionately on the lips. "You worry about me and I think about you," he said, brushing several snowflakes off her face.

"I love you," she said.

He nodded. "And I love you."

They began to walk again.

"Are you angry with Galena?" Irena asked.

"No," Borodine answered. "I'm more surprised than anything else. I never really knew her."

"And she probably never knew you," Irena said.

"You're probably right," Borodine answered. "Had I known her better, I would have recognized some sign of her dissatisfaction. But I saw nothing."

"Igor, even if we never get married, I want to be part of your life," Irena said.

"You're very much part of it. You should know that by now."

"I do," she answered. "I do. But there's so much about you that you never reveal, that you keep tightly guarded."

"What I do is very dangerous," he said. "And when I come home, I don't want to talk about it."

"The admiral thinks very highly of you," she said. "I have heard him praise you several different times to the various members of his staff."

"I hold the same opinion of him," Borodine said.

"I'd like to go back to the apartment now, Igor, and make love," Irena said.

"Yes," Borodine said, "that would be very good."

Irena stopped. "Would you promise me something?" she asked.

"Anything within reason," Borodine answered.

"Share that part of your life with me that separates us," she said. "I want to know more about you than what you do in bed."

"I'll try, Irena. I really will try," Borodine answered. "But I can't promise you I will. That part of me is very, very different from the part of me that you know."

"How different?"

"Just different. Take my word for it." Suddenly, he found himself thinking about Captain Boxer. Borodine was certain that Boxer said nothing about his missions to anyone either.

"You look as if you're trying not to smile," she said.

Borodine suddenly began to laugh.

"What's so funny?" she asked.

"I was thinking about my American counterpart. Don't be so surprised that I have one," Borodine said. "He does for the Americans what I do for our government. Last mission we met. I went aboard his boat, the *Shark*. I am almost certain he tells no one anything about what he does."

"What you're saying," Irena responded, "is that the two of you are very much alike."

"Very much," Borodine answered.

"You like this man, this Captain Boxer?"

Borodine nodded.

"Does it bother you that for the sake of your country, you must be his enemy?"

Borodine shrugged. "We are professionals. We know that sooner or later one of us will destroy the other. I don't like the idea, but that is the way it is. I'm sure Captain Boxer feels the same way."

Irena linked her arm with his. "You see, you just shared something with me you probably never mentioned to anyone else."

"That's true."

"Was it so hard to do?" she asked.

"No. But only because the moment was right," Borodine answered. "I doubt if I will ever mention Captain Boxer's name again."

"But why not, if you have the need?" she asked.

"That's just it, Irena, I don't have the need. I really don't have the need to tell anyone what I do. I know that might sound strange. But it's true. And my guess is that most of the *Sea Savage*'s crew feels the same way."

They had reached the building where Irena lived and started up the steps.

Irena leaned close to him and said, "Well, at least I'll never have to worry about you telling some other man about how I am in bed."

Borodine laughed. "Never. Absolutely never!"

Yedotev was speaking on the red phone to Chernenkov. "The other two Americans have been identified as Paul Hardy and Dean Foster. They are traveling with two women and one man. We're certain the man is Boris Donskoi."

"Very good," Chernenkov said. "Very good indeed. Why don't you bring them in and we can have the kind of public trial that will —"

"I have no intentions of bringing them in," Yedotev said, "at least not yet. They are traveling eastward. My guess is that they have a rendezvous with an American ship or plane. I want the men aboard the ship or plane, too. And if I am patient enough, I will get everything I want."

"Sometimes it's better to settle for a half a loaf of bread than wait for a whole one."

"We are not talking about bread," Yedotev said. "We are talking about the destruction of a major American espionage effort."

"It's in your hands," Chernenkov said. "But this time, General, when you take them alive, keep them alive so that they can be of some use to the state."

"I'll do my best," Yedotev said.

"For your sake," Chernenkov said, "I hope your best is sufficient for our cause."

The line went dead.

Yedotev went to the bar, where he poured himself a vodka. His intuition coupled to his years of experience told him he was right about Hardy and the others. They were going to try to get out of the country through the east and to do that they'd have to rendezvous with a ship or plane. That's when he'd close in on them; that's when he'd get them. "Then," he said aloud, "then I'm going to find a way to bring Chernenkov down. Bring him here for interrogation." That thought excited him. He poured another vodka, drank it as quickly as the first, then went back to his desk and decided that it was time for Tanya to understand the real reason why he had her transferred to his office. He switched on the intercom and told her to come into his office.

CHAPTER 15

Boxer put the phone down. He had just finished telling his mother that he wouldn't be home for Christmas. He had lied and had said that he was being sent on an assignment. He didn't want her to see him with the bandage on his left shoulder. That would cause her more worry and grief than his missing Christmas. He pursed his lips. The shoulder with its new tantalum ball joint was stronger than it had been. But it was still sore and swollen and would be that way for at least another two to three weeks, according to the doctors.

Boxer was just about to walk away from the phone when it rang. He picked it up. "Boxer here," he said.

"Sanchez here," Julio answered. "Surprised you, didn't I?"

"Yes," Boxer admitted.

"I'm down in the lobby. Would you mind if I came up, or would you like to meet me in the bar?"

"The bar would be fine," Boxer said. "I'll be down in five minutes."

"Take your time," Sanchez said and hung up.

Boxer slipped off the bathrobe he was wearing and put on a pair of jeans and a turtleneck shirt. A few minutes later he entered the bar, which was just beginning to get busy with the after-work cocktail crowd.

Sanchez was seated in a small booth with a round yellow candle on the table.

"You look good for man who recently was shot," Sanchez said. He stood up and offered his hand.

Boxer shook it and asked, "Is there anything you don't know?"

"Lots," Sanchez answered with a smile.

They sat down. Sanchez summoned one of the bargirls. "A very dry martini," he said. "Tell the barkeep to use Tanqueray gin. And my friend here wants a —"

"Vodka on the rocks," Boxer said.

"And bring two plates of those hot hors d'oeuvres that the newspapers rave about," Sanchez told the bargirl. A big smile showed on his white teeth. As soon as they were alone, he leaned across the table and said, "That play we spoke about last time has come up with a very different character in the lead role."

"Oh!"

"Hayes was definitely out of the running," Sanchez said.

"Positive about that?"

Sanchez nodded.

"Then who had the part?" Boxer asked.

"A heretofore unknown. A doctor with a double role."

"Klee?"

Sanchez nodded.

"But he's on the *Tecumseh*," Boxer exclaimed.

"He's been with the Company for years," Sanchez said, removing a cigarette from a gold case. "He has an excellent reputation."

The bargirl returned with their drinks and two dishes of hors d'oeuvres.

"Charge it to room fourteen ten," Boxer said.

"Nonsense!" Sanchez exclaimed. "This is my treat."

Boxer shrugged.

"We'll probably have more than one," he said, looking up at the bargirl.

She gave him a professional smile. "I'll be here when you want me."

Sanchez nodded. "I just might want you," he answered.

"For drinks, I mean," she said coyly.

"Oh, absolutely," Sanchez responded. After a pause, he added, "For drinks."

"I'll be here," she told him again and rolled her hips as she walked away from the table.

"You never stop hunting, do you?" Boxer asked.

"Don't tell me you do," Sanchez said.

Boxer lifted his drink. "To hunting," he toasted.

Sanchez grinned. He touched his glass to Boxer's and drank. Then he said, "Klee knew exactly where to stab."

"But why?"

"Jealousy," Sanchez said.

"But I thought you said he had a double role?"

"He does. But nothing is more sinister than a sexual psychopath. He wanted Dee and when she refused him, he decided to kill her. It was easy to mess up your papers and make it look as if someone was looking for something."

Boxer finished his drink. "He practically told me what you just did."

"I wouldn't doubt it," Sanchez said.

"But why Tracy? He didn't even know her."

"You're wrong, Jack. He did know her. He read her article about you."

"Holy Christ! Are you telling me what I think you're telling me?"

Sanchez nodded. "Remember, he had seen her with you aboard the *Tecumseh*."

"I need another drink," Boxer said, looking around for the bargirl.

"She's coming," Sanchez said.

"Do it again," Boxer told her.

"All around," Sanchez added.

Alone again, Boxer said, "How the hell did you put all of this together?"

"It doesn't matter how," Sanchez added. "You have the picture. Do you want to —"

"What would stop him from killing any woman he might see me with?"

"Nothing, I suppose."

Boxer rubbed a hand over his beard. "You're absolutely sure."

"Yes."

"Would the police be able to act on your information?"

"No. But only because of the way it was obtained. It would be called entrapment."

Boxer leaned forward and placed his elbows on the table. "Take the bastard out," he said in a low, tight voice.

"Are you sure that's what you want?"

"I'm sure," Boxer answered, looking straight into Sanchez's black eyes. "If you can't do it, then I will."

"No problem," Sanchez said. "No problem at all."

Boxer leaned back. He suddenly felt very tired.

The bargirl returned with their second round of drinks.

"When do you finish here?" Sanchez asked.

"Four," she answered.

"I'll be outside in a black limo," Sanchez said.

She smiled and walked away.

"I'm going to have one hell of a night."

"Here's to you having a hell of a night," Boxer said, raising his glass.

"Strange," Sanchez said, after he drank, "that after the way we met, here we are someplace between friendship and —"

"Conspiracy," Boxer said. "Somewhere between friendship and conspiracy."

"You can still change your mind."

Boxer shook his head. "Have him taken out," Boxer said. "He already killed two women. He's not going to have the chance to kill a third."

"Vengeance is mine, saith the Lord," Sanchez said.

"No," Boxer said, "this time it's mine."

Sanchez raised his glass and nodded.

In time to meet the one o'clock flight from New York, Zweky drove Boxer to Washington International Airport.

"You sure you don't want me to meet your lady friend?" Zweky asked as he pulled up in front of the Eastern Airlines shuttle building.

"Stay in the car," Boxer said.

"What about her baggage?"

"What about it?"

"Admiral Stark doesn't want you to —"

"Look, stop treating me as if I were something delicate. I'm not. I'm perfectly fine."

"Skipper," Zweky said, "if anything happened to you the admiral would have my ass on the fire."

"Nothing is going to happen to me," Boxer answered and he moved forward in his seat to open the door.

"I'll get it, Skipper," Zweky said.

A few minutes later, Boxer joined the group of people waiting at gate two for incoming flight thirteen zero five. Though he had spoken to Louise every day in the past two weeks, this would be the first time he would see her since the morning he'd learned about Tracy's murder. He had invited her down to spend New Year's Eve and a few days more with him before he was scheduled to take the *Shark* out for sea trials.

Through the big glass window, Boxer watched the plane taxi up to the mobile ramp. Many of the people who were waiting moved toward the gate door, but he remained where he was.

A stream of passengers came through the door, then he saw her.

She was wearing a dark gray pants suit, and a light gray belted coat was draped across her shoulders. She was looking to the left and then to the right. Obviously trying to find him.

Boxer went straight to her. "Am I the guy you're looking for?" he asked.

"Where were you? I didn't see you," she said.

"Here," he answered and, taking her into his arms, he kissed her on the lips.

"People are looking at us," she managed to say.

"Let them look," he answered and kissed her again.

"Jack, please. This isn't New York."

He let go of her and picked up her bag. "This all you brought?" he asked.

"I have another one that has to be picked up in the baggage claim area," she said.

"We might as well go down there," he said, taking hold of her hand. "But it'll probably be fifteen or twenty minutes before the baggage is put on the carousel. How was the flight down?"

"Smooth as silk," she answered as they started toward the baggage claim area.

"The day after New Year's," Boxer said, "we'll drive down to Hilton Head and spend three days there."

"That would be wonderful," she said.

The flight number was listed above the carousel, but it was empty.

"How are you feeling?" she asked.

"Good. Very good," he answered.

"No pain?"

He shook his head. "A bit stiff when I get up in the morning. But that quickly goes away."

"When Admiral Stark called me," she said, "I was so frightened I couldn't talk. He kept asking me if I was there. He even asked if I could hear him."

"He told me," Boxer said. "By the way, you'll meet him New Year's Eve."

"Oh!"

"He's only an admiral," Boxer said. "There's the baggage. Give me your ticket stub and wait here."

Five minutes later, Boxer pulled a large brown soft pack from the carousel and brought it back to where Louise was standing. "You must have packed a set of weights in here, or several lead bowling balls."

"Just clothes," she answered.

"Nothing that heavy could be just clothes," Boxer said, picking up the soft pack with his right hand and the other valise with his left. "You'll just have to hang onto me somehow," he said.

"Oh, don't worry, I will." And she took hold of his belt with her right hand. "You sure you can carry both bags?" she asked.

"It's good exercise," Boxer answered as they started to walk.

The moment Boxer walked out of the terminal, Zweky shouted, "Skipper, I'll get them."

"My driver," Boxer exclaimed, as he put the bags down. "He now thinks he's my mother, too."

Zweky stopped short. His jaw dropped.

"Louise," Boxer said. "This is Paul Zweky. Zweky, this is Louise Ennis."

Zweky nodded respectfully and picked up the bags.

As soon as Boxer and Louise were in the car, she leaned close to him and whispered, "I don't think he approves."

"Don't be silly," Boxer answered, but he knew she was right. "Listen," he said, "I know a great seafood restaurant right on the river. How would you like to have dinner there tonight?"

"I'd like it very much," she answered.

Boxer took hold of her hand and squeezed it. "I'm glad you could make it down here."

"I couldn't pass up the opportunity to finish what we started," she said.

"Not finish," Boxer said. "Begin."

She laughed. "Alright," she answered. "Begin."

Her laugh and her voice had a soft lilt that Boxer liked.

"You're not going to believe this," she said, "but this is the first time I've been south of the Mason–Dixon line since I was ten years old."

"Are you telling me that you've never been to Washington before?"

"Never," she answered.

"Then we have some serious sightseeing to do," Boxer said.

"Chief, did you hear that? This lady has never been down here before."

"I heard," Zweky answered.

Boxer caught something in Zweky's tone that was close to rudeness.

"I really would like to visit the National Gallery," she said.

"You can see anything you want," Boxer said. "Can't she, Chief?"

"Yes," Zweky answered.

"You just name it," Boxer said, "and we'll go."

She leaned closer to Boxer. "I never believed this would really happen," she said. "When you invited me down, I thought you were just being kind."

"You're joking!"

Louise shook her head. "No, I mean it. Kind of like you were paying me back for breakfast and —"

Boxer put his finger against her lips.

With her eyes riveted on his, Louise opened her mouth and gently swirled her tongue over his fingertip. A burst of heat came into Boxer's groin.

"Skipper," Zweky said, "we're coming up on the hotel."

Boxer looked at his watch. "It's almost two," he said. "By the time you unpack, it will be two-thirty. Suppose you pick us up at three, Zweky, and we'll drive over to the Lincoln and Jefferson memorials." Looking at Louise, he asked, "Would you like that?"

"I'd like to see them at night," she answered. Then in a whisper, she said, "There are other things I'd like to do first."

Boxer grinned. "Okay, Zweky, delay picking us up at three. Make it five."

"Sure," Zweky answered as he pulled over to the curb and stopped.

The hotel doorman opened the door and helped Louise out of the car.

"Send the luggage up to room fourteen ten," Boxer said to the doorman. "Louise, wait for me in the lobby. I have to take care of something. I won't be long."

She nodded, turned and walked into the lobby.

"Get into the car," Boxer told Zweky.

"What?"

"In the car," Boxer said.

Zweky went around to the driver's seat and Boxer sat down next to him. "Okay, Zweky, I'll lay it straight out. Miss Ennis is my guest. I don't care what you think about it. She's my guest and I want her treated with as much respect as you give me. If you can't handle it, I'll have someone else assigned. Now you tell me which way it's going to be?"

"I'll handle it," Zweky said.

"Make sure you do," Boxer told him, "or you'll find out just how tough I can be."

"Aye, aye, Skipper," Zweky answered.

Boxer left the car and walked into the hotel lobby.

"What was all that about?" Louise asked as he came up to her.

"Zweky has to take the car to the government motor pool and have it checked out," Boxer lied. "He was supposed to have it done this morning." Relieved that Louise accepted his explanation without comment, he guided her into a waiting elevator.

"What are you drinking?" Boxer called out to Louise as soon as he heard the shower stop.

"Whatever you are," she answered.

Boxer removed the vodka from the small refrigerator and poured three fingers into two different glasses. He added two cubes of ice to each glass and for a few moments swirled each drink around. Then he set them down on an end table and looked toward the bathroom.

Louise was standing there. She wore a white satin belted housecoat.

"I want to draw you," she said.

"Now?" he teased.

"Some time while I'm here," she answered, moving toward him.

Boxer lifted the glasses and handed one to her. "You make the toast," he said.

She hesitated.

"Go on," he urged.

Louise glanced over her shoulder at the bed. "To — I was going to say love, but it's not that, at least not yet. Might as well call it what it is. Right?"

"Right."

"To good sex," she toasted.

"There's nothing wrong with that toast," Boxer said, touching her glass with his. "To good sex!"

They entwined their arms and drank.

Boxer put his glass down on the dresser; then he took hers and placed it next to his. "You smell good," he said, drawing her to him.

She put her arms around his neck. "Hold me," she said in a low voice. "Hold me, Jack."

He pressed her to him and kissed her passionately on the lips. She gently bit his lower lip, opened her mouth and pushed her tongue against his.

Boxer moved his hands around her back and down over the cheeks of her ass. He could feel the heat of her body through the satin.

"Jack," she whispered. "Oh, Jack!"

He opened the top of her gown and exposed her breasts. He kissed the erect nipple of one and then the other. Her skin was smooth.

She tousled his hair.

He eased her away from him, undid the belt and slipped the housecoat off. Her body was far more beautiful than he had thought. He had always seen her in a white uniform. Naked she was totally different.

"Do you like what you see?" she asked.

"Very much," he said.

He started to unbutton his shirt.

"Let me do that," she said, moving closer to him.

Once she was done, Boxer scooped her into his arms. He kissed her neck and her lips before he put her down on the bed.

She moved aside to make room for him. "You turn over on your stomach," she said.

"Why? What are you going to do?"

"Turn over on your stomach and close your eyes," Louise purred.

Boxer rolled onto his stomach and closed his eyes.

"Relax," she said softly. "Relax."

He could feel her position herself between his legs. Then he felt her hands on the back of his neck.

Using the tips of her fingers and only the gentlest of pressure, Louise massaged his neck and shoulders. "How does that feel?" she asked.

"Nice," he answered. "Very nice."

"It would feel even better if I had some cream or baby oil," she said. Her fingers glided down his back and around his flanks.

She kissed his shoulders and the broad of his back.

Boxer uttered a deep sigh of pleasure. "You're going to spoil me forever," he said.

"Maybe that's my purpose," she answered.

"It's a good way to be spoiled though," Boxer said.

"One of the best ways I know," she answered.

Suddenly he had an intense desire to feel all of her against him. Taking hold of her face between his hands, he drew it down to his and kissed her passionately on the mouth, while his hands moved down her silky body.

She opened her mouth.

With delight, Boxer slid his tongue over hers.

She eased her mouth away from his. "If you let me," she said in a low voice, "I'll really drive you wild."

"That's something you don't need permission to do," Boxer told her.

Afterwards, Boxer wrapped his arms around Louise. "Do you think we finished the unfinished business?" he asked.

She raised her hand and looked at him. She said, "I'd like to think we just began it. What about you?"

"Me, too," Boxer answered. "I'd like to think that we started something between us."

"We did," Louise whispered.

CHAPTER 16

The Redferns' New Year's Eve party was in full swing. All of the *Shark*'s officers were there, and so was Admiral Stark, Mr. Kinkade and Senator Sam Ross, Tom's father-in-law.

Boxer discovered that Louise was a very good dancer. She moved effortlessly, whether it was a simple fox trot or disco. And though she danced with several of the other male guests, she always came back to him.

"Having a good time?" Boxer asked, holding her close for a slow number.

"Oh, yes!" she exclaimed. "But best of all I like the way your men look at you."

Boxer laughed and turned her around. "That's because they're all nuts."

"That's because they love you," she answered.

"No," he said, "that's because I love them."

"I believe that," she said resting her head against his chest. "You know," she said, "most of the men did a double take when they first saw me, but as soon as they realized I was with you, everything was all right."

"They're not used to seeing a black woman —"

"With a white officer."

Boxer went into a walk step. "Something like that," he said, bringing her back to him.

Louise tilted her head up. "You know," she said, "it would never work. It's okay for what we have, but not for anything else."

"Did anyone ever tell you that you talk too much?" he said, kissing the tip of her nose. "And, I'm beginning to realize, you worry too much."

She lowered her head. "It's not easy not to think about you," she told him.

Boxer had no ready answer. But in the few days he had spent with her, the thought had occurred to him that he might want something more from her than a casual relationship. Suddenly he felt someone tap him on the shoulder and heard Cowly ask, "May I cut in?"

Boxer looked over his shoulder.

"Skipper, the admiral would like to see you in the upstairs study."

Boxer nodded and let go of Louise. He said, "Take good care of her."

"Will do, Skipper," Cowly answered, taking hold of Louise and moving away with her.

Boxer crossed the dance floor and saw Sue-Ann. "Great party," he said.

She smiled broadly at him. "I'm glad you like it."

"I do," he said and started up the long, curving flight of steps that led to the upper floor. He had been in the study several times before and knew it was the second room, immediately to the right of the steps. He rapped on the door twice.

"Come in," Stark called out.

Boxer opened the door and walked into the book-lined study. Stark was there, so was Kinkade and the senator. He closed the door.

"A drink?" the senator offered. "We're having brandy."

"The same," Boxer said.

The senator handed him a snifter. "It's very good brandy," he said.

Boxer nodded and, cupping the glass in his hands, he swished the liquid around.

"I think we have to clear the deck," Stark said, "or we'll just fuck ourselves up."

"What the admiral means —" the senator started to say.

"I know exactly what the admiral means," Boxer said. "Let Kinkade run his operation and I'll command the *Shark*."

"That's a mite blunt," the senator said.

"I don't tell him how to run the Company. I don't want him telling me how to run the *Shark*. Besides, I thought all this crap was settled the last time we met."

"Oh, it is," Stark said. "I and the senator thought the two of you should shake hands and —"

"I'm ready to shake Kinkade's hand any time," Boxer said and he moved toward him. "Even now." He extended his right hand.

Kinkade lifted his.

The two of them shook hands.

"Smile," Boxer said to Kinkade. "After all, for better or worse, we're in the same organization. Right?"

"I will give you all the professional support, I can," Kinkade said, finally speaking. "But never count on me for friendship."

"Never did," Boxer answered. "And never will." Then he raised his snifter and said, "To the crew of the *Shark*."

The three of them drank.

"Now if you'll excuse me," Boxer said, "there's a beautiful lady waiting for me."

"There is one other thing," Kinkade said.

"Yes?"

"Doctor Peter Klee was killed yesterday."

"Oh."

"Hit and run," Stark said.

Boxer nodded.

"Nothing to say about it?" Kinkade asked.

"I hardly knew the man and what I knew, I disliked."

Kinkade nodded. "No expression of sorrow or sympathy?"

"None, Kinkade. I save that for the men I lost going for a treasure that was mostly lead."

Kinkade flushed.

"Sanchez told me," Boxer said. "Could you imagine what the men downstairs might do if I told them? Think about it, Kinkade. Now, if you gentlemen don't mind, I'll leave."

"What's this about the gold?" Stark asked.

"Kinkade hasn't told you?" Boxer asked.

"No."

"I'll let him tell you," Boxer said. "I do have a lady waiting for me." He put the snifter down on the desk and walked to the door. Just before he opened it, he turned and said, "I'll spare you the trouble of an investigation, Kinkade. I gave the order to have Klee taken out. He killed Dee Long and he killed Tracy Kimble. See you gentlemen downstairs."

Boxer opened the door, walked out into the hallway and closed the door behind him. For a few moments, he stood very still; then he took several deep breaths. When he was sure he was completely steady, he started down the steps.

At midnight the horns started to blast, the lights flickered and, on the lawn, for those who would brave the cold, the Redferns set off a beautiful fireworks display complete with Roman candles.

Boxer put his jacket around Louise and watched the fireworks display from the steps. She stood in front of him and he held her around the waist.

She leaned her head back against his shoulder. "If I could make two wishes," she said, "do you know what I would wish for?"

"No idea," he answered.

"That tonight would go on forever," she said. "It's like a storybook come true."

Boxer hugged her. "For you it's a storybook, for women like Sue-Ann, it's the way they live."

She put her hand over his. "And that you take me back to the hotel and make love to me. Does that shock you?"

"No. But I'll tell you something that will," Boxer said.

"Oh!"

"I want to leave now," he said.

She smiled up at him. "I'm ready."

Boxer turned her around to him. "Then let's do it."

"Just like that?"

He nodded. "Come inside and I'll get your coat from one of the servants."

An hour later they walked into the lobby of the hotel. Boxer stopped at the desk and asked if there were any messages for him.

"None," the desk clerk said and wished him a happy New Year.

"The same to you," Boxer said. Walking back to Louise, he said, "Why don't we stop at the bar for a drink."

"I wouldn't mind that," she said.

He took hold of her hand and walked into the bar. It was crowded, but there was space for them at the bar.

"I don't mind standing," Louise said. "Besides, we're not going to be here long."

Boxer nodded and led her to the bar. There was a bowl of peanuts and pretzels directly in front of him. "Have some," he said, helping himself to the peanuts.

Louise picked up a pretzel.

"What are you drinking?" the barkeep asked.

"Vodka on the rocks," Boxer answered.

"I'll have the same," Louise said.

The barkeep quickly delivered their drinks.

Boxer raised his and was about to toast Louise, when she suddenly gasped. "What's wrong?" he asked.

"Let's get out of here," she answered.

"But —"

"Please!"

Boxer dropped a five-dollar bill on the bar, nodded and started to leave.

"Honey, when you're finished with him," the man next to Louise said, "I'll be waiting down here for you."

Boxer stopped. "Was he bothering —"

"Please, Jack, let's go," Louise said.

"I was just offering her some additional business," the man said, facing Boxer. "She's a working girl. Now aren't you, honey?"

Boxer's brow furrowed. The man was slightly taller than himself. Had a ruddy complexion and wore a Stetson and boots.

"This woman is with me," Boxer said.

The man laughed. "Don't get yourself ruffled about that. I know that, mister. But that's for now. Later I'd like her to be with me."

Boxer realized that several other people were now looking at him and the man at the bar.

"I don't think you understand what I am saying," Boxer said. "This woman is with me."

"You keep saying that." The man laughed. "I know that. But like I say, later —"

"She's my wife," Boxer growled. "Do you understand that?"

Louise touched his sleeve. "Let's go. Please."

"Mister," Boxer said, "I want to hear an apology."

"What?"

"You heard me, mister," Boxer said. "I want to hear an apology."

"For what?"

"I'll ask you once more."

The man was off the stool. He swung at Boxer with his right hand. Louise screamed.

The blow knocked Boxer to the floor. The man stood over him. "Wife shit! You aren't going to be able to fuck her for a month of Sundays." He started to kick Boxer.

"Stop him," Louise screamed. "Stop him."

"Naw," another man said, "let them settle it."

Boxer rolled away and sprang to his feet.

The man threw his right fist again. Boxer moved close, grabbed the man's arm, lifted him off the floor and hurled him against the wall. Boxer didn't wait until the man was on his feet. He grabbed hold of his head and smashed it against the wall. "He'll have a bad headache when he wakes up," he said.

"Hey," one of the men complained, "you're not giving him a sporting chance."

"No," Boxer answered, "I'm not. If I did, I'd break every fucking bone in his body. Barkeep," Boxer called, dropping a ten-dollar bill on the man, "here's a few dollars to take care of this sack of garbage." Then he straightened his own clothing, took Louise by the hand and said, "Let's go."

"Yes," she whispered, "let's go."

Facing one another on their sides, they had made love and now they rested in each other's arms.

Boxer slid his hand down Louise's naked body. She ran her finger over the scar on his right shoulder.

Neither one had said a word since they left the bar. They went up to the room, undressed and silently made love.

"I'm sorry about what happened," she whispered.

"It wasn't your fault. Just the fault of a stupid man," Boxer answered.

"I was frightened," she said. "I thought he had hurt you."

"He kicked like a mule," Boxer said. "I guess I'll have a few black and blue marks."

"You didn't have to tell him I was your wife," she said, touching his face. "That really made him angry."

"I guess it did," Boxer answered. "But it was the only thing that I could think of. I mean, I suddenly thought that if you were my wife, I'd have fought the son-of-a-bitch. I wanted him to know that you meant something to me and that was the one thing that came to my mind."

She buried her face in the groove of his neck. "I love you," she whispered. "I know it's nuts. That we're together because each of us wanted the other. That's okay. But I love you."

"I'm not worth it Louise," he said. "Not worth it for any woman who wants something more than just a good time now and then."

She drew slightly away from him and propped herself up on one elbow. She said, "I didn't come to you a virgin. You don't know what I've done, or where I've been, or whether I'm worth anything more than a good time. I didn't ask what you're worth, Jack. I just know what I feel when I'm with you. I know I love you. I didn't even ask you to love me back. I —"

Boxer pulled her down to him and kissed her. "I love you," he said.

She smiled. "That's nice to hear," she told him.

"But I'm still not worth it," Boxer said.

"Let me be the judge of that," Louise said.

CHAPTER 17

Boxer stood on the outside bridge of the *Shark* and watched the few remaining members of the crew come aboard. Cowly stood next to him and nearby were several other members of the bridge detail.

A raw wind was blowing from the northeast and there was a chop in the bay. Boxer looked at his watch and checked it against the instrument panel clock. Both read 0555. The *Shark* was scheduled to cast off at 0600. The deck detail were already standing by at the bow and stern lines. Unlike other boats, the *Shark* never lay alongside a mother-ship, or another boat. She was too big.

"With or without Mister Bart Simmons," Boxer said, referring to the new lieutenant assigned to the *Shark*, "we'll sail."

"Stand by at the lines," Cowly said over a bullhorn.

Suddenly a silver-hued Jaguar pulled up.

"That's him now," Cowly said.

Boxer grunted as he watched Simmons, a tall, young black man, get out of the car followed by a woman at least a head shorter. The two of them embraced, kissed and then Bart started to run for the boat.

Simmons was assigned to fly the *Shark*'s newly installed helicopter, a machine that Boxer didn't particularly want aboard, since it required a redesign of the forward part of the hull and lessened the space assigned to Tom's men. But it was a completely new kind of helicopter and both Stark and Kinkade wanted it tested. "Let's move her out," he told Cowly.

"Cast off all lines," Cowly ordered.

The chief of the forward lines waved.

"Forward lines off," Cowly told Boxer. A moment later the signal came from the chief of the stern detail. "Stern lines off."

Boxer keyed the EO. "Give me one two zero zero rpms reverse," Boxer said.

"One two zero zero rpms reverse," the EO answered.

Responding immediately, the *Shark* began to ease out of her berth.

Simmons pounded toward her and leaped onto the deck, just as the bow cleared the end of the wharf. Like a cat, he landed upright, saluted the flag and grinned up at the bridge.

"Have Mister Simmons report to me as soon as we're out in the bay," he told Cowly.

"Aye, aye, Skipper," Cowly answered.

"Helmsman," Boxer said, "come to course six four degrees."

"Coming to six four degrees," Mahony answered.

Boxer switched on the MC system. "All electron section officers, run standard operations tests on your equipment. DCO, test all operating systems."

One by one the reports came in that all systems were functioning.

Boxer keyed the RO. "Do not report any surface target closer than two thousand yards."

"Roger that, Skipper."

Boxer keyed the EO again. "Give me ten knots forward speed."

"Aye, aye, Skipper. Ten knots forward speed."

The *Shark* swung around.

"Helmsman, come to course seven five degrees," Boxer said.

"Coming to course seven five degrees," Mahony answered.

The *Shark* headed south, toward the entrance of Chesapeake Bay.

Boxer filled his pipe. As soon as he had it lit, he leaned against the side of the bridge. As much as he enjoyed being on land, as much as he enjoyed being with Louise, this was really his life. He looked around. The sky was blue and spotted with some flat cirrocumulus clouds in the northeast. Several large container ships were following him out and a supertanker was coming in. It reminded him of the *Tecumseh* and he said to Cowly, "The *Tecumseh* has been ordered north with us. We are going to get in and out of her in the Arctic under the best and worst conditions."

"Why?" Cowly asked. "The Russians know about us and they must surely know about her."

Boxer shrugged. "Stark wants to see if it can be done."

Cowly made a face.

"That's the way I feel about it," Boxer said. "But the admiral has been pretty good to us, so I didn't kick about it. The ice might give us some trouble. But I don't think we should have any trouble doing it."

"I hope not," Cowly answered.

The radar officer keyed Boxer.

"Yes?"

"Target bearing two eight zero degrees. Range four thousand five hundred yards. Speed four zero knots. Closing fast."

"Helmsman stand by to take evasive action," Boxer said coolly.

"Target bearing two eight zero degrees. Range three thousand eight hundred yards. Closing fast."

Boxer was about to key the EO and increase the *Shark*'s speed, when the COMMO keyed him. "Skipper, just received word from the CONN to heave to and prepare to take on passengers."

Boxer moved away from the side of the bridge and trained the bridge binoculars on the approaching craft. It was a forty-foot hovercraft. He keyed the RO. "Next time you give me a target," he said sharply, "I want it ID'd immediately."

"Aye, aye, Skipper," the RO answered.

Boxer turned to Cowly. "Who's RO now?"

"Mister Wagner," Cowly answered.

"Have the section officer keep an eye on him," Boxer said. "I don't want any slip-ups."

Cowly nodded.

Boxer keyed the EO. "Heave to."

"Roger that, Skipper," the engineering officer answered.

"Cowly, have the deck detail prepare for boarding," Boxer said.

Within minutes the *Shark* hove to. The hovercraft was only five hundred yards away.

Boxer, though curious about the visitors, didn't voice this curiosity aloud. He watched the hovercraft come slowly to rest in the water about fifty feet off the starboard side and then ease its way alongside. Two suitcases were passed from the deck of the hovercraft to the deck of the *Shark*.

"Looks like we're going to have visitors for a while," Cowly said.

Boxer scowled, but remained silent.

Two people leaped from the hovercraft to the deck of the *Shark*.

Suddenly the skipper of the hovercraft came over the MC. "Good sailing," he said.

Boxer switched on the *Shark*'s MC. "Thanks," he said.

The two crafts drifted away from each other.

"Get those people below," Boxer said over the MC. Then he keyed the EO. "Give me one zero knots," he said.

"One zero knots," the EO answered.

Boxer turned to Cowly. "I'm going below to see what we have aboard. Let me know when we leave the bay."

"Do you want to run fully surfaced all the way out?" Cowly asked.

Boxer nodded. "Too much traffic to go out any other way," he said. "You have the CONN." Anxious to see who had come aboard, he went into the hatchway and hurried down the steps.

As soon as he reached the bridge, Boxer saw Sanchez. The other person was turned away from him.

"Captain Boxer," Sanchez exclaimed, extending his hand, "it's really a pleasure to see you!"

Even as Boxer shook Sanchez's hand, the other person turned around. It was a woman.

"Captain," Sanchez said, "may I present Meagan Thomas."

"A pleasure," Meagan said, offering her hand.

Boxer nodded.

"Ms. Thomas is with the *World News*," Sanchez offered.

"I've been assigned to do a story on your crew and your boat," she said in a soft, sensuous voice.

"By whom?" Boxer asked, letting go of her hand.

She smiled at him and opened her shoulder bag. She handed him an envelope. "It's all there."

"I'm sure it is," Boxer said, taking the envelope from her. He looked at Sanchez. "I suppose you have a similar envelope."

Sanchez dug inside his jacket pocket. "Signed by Mister Kinkade," he said, handing the envelope to him.

"We'll be with you for the duration of the *Shark*'s sea trials," Meagan said. "I am to have free access to every part of the *Shark*."

"That's in the letter," Boxer said sarcastically.

She smiled at him.

Boxer had two choices: He could put up a fight, which would probably get him nowhere and only irritate Kinkade even more, or he could accept the visitors as gracefully as possible. He decided to accept them. Besides, he owed Sanchez and this was as good a way as any to pay the debt. "Under no circumstances," he said, "are either of you to interfere with the operation of the boat. You may ask questions, but if those questions involve secret equipment, or any other classified material, you will not be given any answers. Ms. Thomas, before you leave the *Shark*, you will submit to me whatever you have written or recorded."

"But that's censorship!" she complained.

"Yes," Boxer answered. "But we depend on the equipment aboard the *Shark* to keep us alive and we wouldn't want the wrong people to know anything about it."

She hesitated for a few moments before answering, "Yes."

Boxer summoned Ensign Koss. "Escort Mister Sanchez and Ms. Thomas to the two cabins aft of my own."

"Aye, aye, Skipper," Koss said.

Boxer nodded. "Mister Koss, see that they have proper clothing. Coveralls will do fine. And provide them with eating cards."

"Aye, aye, Skipper."

Suddenly Boxer realized that Simmons was on the bridge, too. He fixed his eyes on him for a few moments; then he shifted them back to Sanchez and Meagan. "Mister Koss will take care of you," he said.

"Thank you, Captain," Meagan said.

Sanchez thanked him too, then he and Meagan followed Koss off the bridge.

"Well, Lieutenant Simmons," Boxer said, "I'm certainly pleased that you finally got here. We were going to sail without you."

"That certainly would have been a bad scene, Captain," Simmons answered. "You probably would have had to stop somewhere between here and wherever we're going and I would have had to jump. Then a few of your men would have had to come get me. I don't mind the jumping," he said, with a broad smile, "I mind the getting wet."

Boxer rubbed his beard. "You figure this whole exercise is for your benefit, don't you?"

"No, sir," Simmons answered. "It's for the benefit of that bird I fly. That bird, Captain, can be released from one hundred feet down, while you're doing forty knots. It breaks surface just like a missile. Gets up about one hundred feet; then if everything is working right, it becomes a helicopter with enough stuff on board to knock out a destroyer and enough fuel to keep me up there for an hour. Then I come down and you pick me up. But first I destroy the bird."

"Ah, so that's how it works!" Boxer exclaimed, with mock astonishment. He had been briefed on the operation of the helicopter three days before it had been put aboard.

Simmons raised his eyebrows questioningly. Then he started to laugh. "Captain, you knew about it all the time and you let me run off at the mouth."

"Mister Simmons," Boxer said, "the officers of the *Shark* were due on board at twenty-four hundred hours."

"Damn it!" Simmons exclaimed. "I told Lee that and she said that didn't apply to me. I was just a helicopter jockey, not one of the ship's crew."

"That's what Lee told you?" Boxer asked.

"Absolutely, Captain," Simmons answered. "Besides, I was having such a good time with her, I figured that —"

"Mister Simmons," Boxer said in a flat voice. "You are an officer aboard the *Shark*. You will from this instant forward act like an officer. That means obeying every rule and regulation that the other officers follow. Do you understand?"

"Sure, Captain," Simmons answered.

"I mean, do you really understand?" Boxer growled. "Because if you don't and you fuck up, just once, I'll make sure you never fly again. Do I make myself clear?"

"Yes, Captain," Simmons answered with a snap.

"See the boat's EXO for your duty assignments," Boxer said.

"Captain, helicopter jockeys don't pull regular ship's duty," Simmons said.

"This is not a regular ship," Boxer answered curtly. "This is a boat and you'll pull whatever duties are assigned to you. Is that understood?"

Simmons came to attention and saluted. "Yes, sir."

"You can cut that shit out," Boxer said. "We don't salute aboard the *Shark* and I'm referred to as Skipper. Now stow your gear away and get into your work uniform."

"Aye, aye, Skipper," Simmons said.

Boxer nodded and turned away, focusing his attention on the COMCOMP. All operating conditions were normal.

"Stark," Kinkade said, "Conners just spoke to me. He has a no-go situation up. The Russians have increased their patrols."

"You sure as hell can't use anything on the surface then," Stark answered.

"That was my feeling, too," Kinkade said, helping himself to a cigar and lighting it, before continuing, "I'm going to order the *Shark* in."

Stark was silent.

"Did you hear what I said?" Kinkade asked.

"I did and I'm against it," Stark said. "She'll have to surface and —"

"No other alternative," Kinkade replied. "I want those people out. I can't have two of our agents fall into the hands of the KGB. I can't risk that."

"But you're risking the *Shark* and its entire crew to get two men out."

"Two men and three very important scientists," Kinkade said.

"Have you spoken to the President about this?"

"Yes, and he agrees with me," Kinkade said. "This is the kind of mission that we had in mind when we came up with the idea for the *Shark*."

"What about air cover for the time that they're on the surface?" Stark asked.

"Can't do," Kinkade said. "They'll have to be in and out within a matter of minutes. We can't risk an incident with the Russians."

"If all of this is already set up, why did you bother to call me?" Stark asked.

"The President wanted me to keep you informed."

"I'm informed," Stark said angrily. He slammed the phone down.

As soon as the *Shark* was out in the open ocean, Boxer set a course into the AUTONAV and NAVCLOCK that would bring the *Shark* through the Denmark Strait and into the Greenland Sea. He maintained an operating depth of 250 feet.

Within four days the *Shark* was off the northeast coast of Greenland.

Neither Sanchez nor Ms. Thomas caused any difficulty. He sometimes saw them at mess and once they asked permission to visit the bridge, which he granted.

Boxer, though aware that Meagan was a good-looking woman with long brown hair, wasn't interested in her. Somehow the chemistry just wasn't there. And to his surprise, he found himself actually yearning for Louise. He had not had that particular feeling for a woman since the first days of his marriage to Gwen.

During the four days out, dozens of tests were run on every one of the old and new systems, including a water jet system that could be used to increase their speed to fifty to fifty-five knots in an emergency. It functioned well, but created a severe vibration in the stern section of the boat.

At 0830 of the fifth day, COMMO keyed Boxer. "Skipper, we have a priority-three message coming through for you."

"Roger that," Boxer said. "Transfer to the COMCOMP."

"Transfer completed," the COMMO said. "Out."

Boxer put the message through the decoder and put it up on the screen.

DATE: JAN. 6TH, 1997
FROM: KINKADE
TO: CAPT. J. BOXER, SHARK
PROCEED IMMEDIATELY TO LAT. 70° N., LONG. 170° 23'15" E... YOU WILL RENDEZVOUZ WITH A GROUP UNDER THE COMMAND OF PAUL HARDY ... RETURN THEM IMMEDIATELY TO U.S. BASE.
    SIGNED
    KINKADE.

Boxer looked at the message with disbelief. "Cowly, read this," he said, gesturing toward the screen.

"Holy shit, that's mainland Russia!" Cowly exclaimed.

Boxer switched on the map selector, dialed in the coordinates and pressed the display button. Instantly a Mercator's projection of the area came into view. Then he pressed a sequence of buttons. A three-dimensional view of the area filled the screen.

"A cove with low hills on all sides," Cowly said.

Boxer touched two more buttons. "Forty feet at its deepest part. But this time of year it's probably covered with five-foot-thick ice."

Cowly agreed.

"We'll burn our way through with the laser," he said, "or just break through with our own force. The ice isn't the problem. The problem is that we don't know what the Russians know. If they have any idea that we'll be there, you can bet they're going to try and stop us from leaving."

"That's for sure," Cowly answered.

Boxer keyed the COMMO. "Send the following message to Kinkade: Will proceed as ordered. ETA seventy-two hours. Need exact rendezvous time. Most tests on boat not completed. Deep dive test not completed. Helicopter not flown. Laser not tested. Still have two civilians on board. Estimated chances for successful completion less than thirty percent... Sign my name."

"Roger that, Skipper," the COMMO answered.

Boxer set up the computer for an accurate TA. The answer he got was seventy hours. "That's maintaining our present speed of forty knots," he said to Cowly.

"Any reason to go faster?" Cowly asked.

"Not unless Kinkade comes up with one," Boxer answered. "But once we get those people aboard we're going to have to really move. That means using the new water jet system. It should give us a flank speed of five five knots."

"That's fast!"

"We're going to need every bit of that fast," Boxer said. "Every fucking bit, especially if the Russians pick us up."

"Are you going to tell the crew?" Cowly asked.

"I'm going to do that right now," Boxer said, switching on the MC. "Now hear this. Now hear this. This is the captain speaking. The *Shark* has been ordered into Russian territorial waters to evacuate a team of American agents. Our arrival time is set for seven one hours from now. Major Redfern, please report to the bridge immediately. Lieutenant Simmons, report to the bridge immediately. All other personnel, remain at your stations. In exactly six zero hours from now, we will go to general quarters and remain at general quarters until further notice. That is all."

All of the officers from the nearby CIC section turned to look at him.

"You didn't exactly give them good news, or make them feel comfortable," Cowly said.

"I don't feel particularly comfortable myself," Boxer answered.

Redfern came up to the bridge, followed a few seconds later by Simmons. "I'm here, Skipper, on time."

Boxer ignored him and said, "Tom, pick a team of men to leave the boat and go out on the ice to cover it. There just might be some mortar crews and/or field pieces behind those hills," he said, pointing to the three-dimensional display on the screen.

"We could set up a few of our own," Redfern answered.

"Do it," Boxer said.

"I'll go out with De Vargas and two squads."

"Fine," Boxer said. "I'll have my FCO ready with surface-to-surface missiles and our 20mm guns on deck."

Redfern nodded.

Boxer turned to Simmons. "I want your bird in the air," he said. "I need all the cover I can get."

"Negative on that, Skipper," Simmons said.

Boxer's jaw went slack, then he scowled. "Mister, did you just say, 'negative'?"

"That's just what I said, Skipper," Simmons answered. "I'm a test pilot. I don't know anything about flying cover or —"

"Then you'll learn," Boxer answered. "The moment you're up there, you'll learn. Your job, mister, is to supply cover for my boat. You have two choices: to do it, or to stand court-martial when we return to the states. This boat and everyone on it will be exposed to enemy fire for as long as we're on the surface. That means we can be sunk. You're going to be part of the team that makes sure that won't happen."

"You don't like the colour of my skin, do you, Skipper? Well, Skipper, Captain, or whatever else you prefer to call yourself, I'll take the court-martial. My orders were to test fly that bird, not to fight in it."

Boxer could feel the anger rise in him. But he fought it down. "I don't like wise guys," he answered. "I don't like any man who refuses to fight when fighting is the only way to save my boat and my crew. "

"Like I said," Simmons answered, "you just don't like me."

"You're wrong, Lieutenant Simmons," Boxer said, looking straight at him, " Now, go to your quarters. You're under arrest."

Simmons executed an about-face and left the bridge.

Boxer looked over to Cowly. "Believe that?"

Cowly shrugged and said, "I heard it, so I guess I have to believe it." Then he added, "Mister Sanchez and Ms. Thomas request permission to speak with you."

"Send them up," Boxer said, wiping Kinkade's message from one screen and the maps from the other.

Sanchez and Meagan came directly up to him and Sanchez said, "I don't imagine there's any way we can be put off?"

"Not unless you're willing to freeze to death," Boxer said. "We're moving below the Arctic ice pack now. On that pack I would guess the temperature is well below forty degrees below zero, with a wind-chill factor that probably makes it feel like seventy below. That's if a blizzard isn't raging. Once we come up, I have no idea what the weather will be, or for that matter anything else. My orders are to evacuate a group from Siberia. That's Russian territory. We'll be inside Russian territorial waters. If they don't know we're coming, they'll surely spot us somewhere along the way."

"Are you telling us that you don't think the *Shark* will survive?" Meagan asked.

"I'm trying to tell you that we'll be very lucky if we survive," Boxer answered.

Sanchez looked at Ms. Thomas. "Just think of the story this will make," he said.

"It won't make a story," Boxer told them. "This mission is a highly classified one. Nothing will be written about it."

"You're joking!" Meagan exclaimed.

Boxer shook his head. "I am not joking, Ms. Thomas. I don't joke about such things. In not too many more hours, this boat and its crew go on battle status. Until then you have exactly the same privileges as before. But once we go to general quarters, I must ask you and Mister Sanchez to remain either in your quarters or in the mess area. Now if you'll excuse me, I have a great many things that must be attended to."

Meagan was about to protest, but Sanchez touched her arm and looked straight at Boxer, saying, "It is better to do what he tells you to. He has a bad temper."

"A very bad temper," Boxer added.

"Well, so have I," Meagan said. "I just don't —"

"Meagan," Sanchez said, "he doesn't give a fuck what you do or don't want to do. He wants you to do what he wants you to do. Now come with me." And taking her by the hand, he led her off the bridge.

"Mister Sanchez seems to know you," Cowly commented with half a smile.

"We've gotten to know one another," Boxer said. He stood up and stretched. "Take the CONN, Mister Cowly. I want to talk to the men."

Cowly moved to the COMCOMP and sat down.

"It's going to be a very long seventy or eighty hours," Boxer said.

"Maybe we'll be lucky," Cowly answered.

Boxer shrugged and left the bridge. He needed to talk to his men as much as they needed to hear him. They were a part of him, an extension of him. Their fears were his and he was afraid.

CHAPTER 18

Colonel Stepanovich was seated at his desk. Directly in front of him sat General Yedotev, who had arrived a few minutes before.

"I didn't come here to run an inspection," Yedotev said. "I came here to continue an operation which I have been personally running for some time now."

Stepanovich shifted uneasily in his chair.

"You have in your area two Americans and three Russians who are trying to escape from Russia."

"Here in Vladivostok?" Stepanovich asked.

Yedotev scowled. "A large map of your area of command, please."

Stepanovich picked up a phone, stabbed two buttons and barked out the order for a map. "It will be here in a matter of moments," he said.

"We have tracked these people," Yedotev explained, "all across Russia and now we know they're here."

Stepanovich nodded, though he hadn't any idea of what his commander was saying.

A sudden knock at the door brought his eyes to it. "Come," he said.

"Your map, Comrade Colonel," a young woman said, moving into the room.

Stepanovich nodded and thanked her.

"Didn't know you had such attractive women in this part of the country," Yedotev said.

"Her name is Luba. I can arrange a meeting for you, if you would —"

"Why does that name mean something to me?" Yedotev asked.

"She was the agent assigned to Captain Borodine," Stepanovich answered.

Yedotev nodded. "Perhaps a meeting to congratulate her would be in order. But later. Now we have important business to take care of. Unroll the map please." He stood up and walked around to the back of the desk. "The people we want are here," he said, placing his blunt forefinger on a small cove in the Arctic. "They are in a cabin, waiting to be taken out. They were going to go out from this point," he said, moving his forefinger to a place nearer to Vladivostok. "But we beefed up our air and sea patrols so that nothing could get through, and the weather has been our ally." He moved his finger back to its original position. "We know they are here."

"May I ask who they are?"

Yedotev shook his head. "All of them are enemies of the state. Now, we know that nothing can fly them out, or sail them out, at least on the surface. Therefore, we are sure that they will be taken out by submarine. And because we know that the American equivalent of our *Sea Savage* has put to sea and we have monitored a series of transmissions from the polar regions in a code that is new to us, we have concluded that the *Shark* is on its way here to take out the people we have been tracking. But that makes the *Shark* more important than the people. We can sink the *Shark* and capture the people at the same time."

Stepanovich felt very uncomfortable with Yedotev bending over him. For one thing the man's breath was foul and secondly his cologne was overpowering. Several times he tried to stand but each time, Yedotev blocked his way. Suddenly

Yedotev started to pace. And Stepanovich immediately took the opportunity to stand.

"Comrade Chernenkov wants a public trial and we're going to give him what he wants, eh, Comrade?"

"But if the weather —"

Yedotev held up his hand. "What the Americans can put under the sea so can we. At this moment the *Sea Savage* is preparing to get underway and head for that very cove where we expect the American submarine to arrive."

"But I was not informed —"

"On my orders, Comrade. I had Captain Borodine taken from the arms of his mistress and flown here, without ever being told where or why he was being taken. The same for the entire crew. Their orders are sealed and will not be opened until they clear the harbor. I did not want to risk a leak to a double agent, or possibly an American spy."

Stepanovich was overwhelmed by his commander's ability to organize things and act.

"And you, Comrade, will share in the glory once this operation is brought to a successful conclusion," Yedotev said.

"But what role can I play?" Stepanovich asked. "You seem to have things so well organized."

"I do," Yedotev answered. "I pride myself on that ability. I even have field pieces placed around the cove, should the *Shark* surface and come close to shore. But for you to earn your share of the glory, you must accommodate me."

"Certainly."

"I want you to set up a headquarters for me somewhere along the shore of that cove and completely out of sight of where the Americans are."

"What?"

"It shouldn't be too difficult. All I need is an Arctic tent, a good radio and an expert operator."

"Comrade General, it is not difficult, it is impossible."

Yedotev scowled. "I did not hear you," he said.

"Comrade General, with all due respect, we don't even have an idea what the weather is. Our nearest weather station is three hundred kilometers away."

"I expect to be flown there in exactly two hours," Yedotev said.

"Yes, Comrade General," Stepanovich answered.

"And while you are out of your office attending to the necessary details for my flight, I will take the opportunity to personally thank that woman Luba for her good work. I do not wish to be disturbed until everything is ready; then you may call me on the phone. Do not come directly to the office. Is all of this clear, Colonel?"

"Absolutely clear, Comrade General."

Yedotev nodded. Suddenly he was frightened. His career, and therefore his life, depended on the success of this mission.

Despite the roaring fire in the hearth, the cabin was cold enough for their breaths to steam. The two women huddled together in front of the hearth. Donskoi was against the wall.

Hardy and Foster were standing near the far wall. Both had heard the sounds during the last few hours and knew that something was happening on the other side of the hills.

"My guess," Foster said, "is that they brought troops in and are waiting before they close in."

"If that was the case," Hardy said, "they'd have been here by now. No, something else is going down."

"But what?"

Hardy shrugged. "If I was a betting man, I'd bet that what we heard was the sound of artillery being moved into place."

"But why?"

"To blast whatever lands to fly us out," Hardy said.

"You sure it's going to be a plane?"

"What the hell can get in and out quickly? The cove is frozen; it will probably land there."

Foster shook his head. "So they let us go this far —"

"Haven't you thought that everything was just too easy? Even when our plans were changed and we wound up here. It shouldn't have happened that way. We should have been captured."

"What are you two talking about?" Natalia asked.

"The weather," Hardy answered.

She laughed. "Always a topic for conversation," she answered. "Come by the fire and warm up a bit. It must be forty degrees colder where you're standing."

Hardy and Foster moved toward the fire.

"I could use some food," Donskoi said.

"There's some canned soup. You can prepare it yourself," Nicole answered.

"You want soup," Hardy said, "you go make it. Otherwise stay where you are and keep quiet."

"A regular KGB man!" Donskoi said. "No, worse. Much worse."

Hardy and the others ignored him. He offered Natalia a cigarette.

"It's your last," she said.

"Take it."

"No."

"I'll share it with you," he offered.

"That I'll accept."

Hardy broke the cigarette into two equal pieces and handed one to her. Then he struck a match and held it for her. "When this is over," he said, lighting his own half, "I'd like to share much more than a cigarette with you." He spoke matter-of-factly.

Natalia took a deep drag on the cigarette and slowly let the smoke escape from her nostrils. "Yes," she said. "I have been thinking the same thing now for several days."

Hardy nodded and blew smoke toward the fire.

Foster and Nicole smiled at them.

"I guess we're engaged," Hardy said, taking hold of Natalia's hand.

"Yes, I think we are," she answered.

Hardy removed the glove from her hand, kissed the back of it and put the glove back on. "That makes it very official," he said.

"And so does this," Natalia said, kissing his forehead.

The four of them laughed.

CHAPTER 19

Borodine held the *Sea Savage* just out of sight of the Russian coast. His orders were to proceed with all possible speed to Latitude 71° E., Longitude 170° 23' 15". There he was to intercept and destroy any American vessel found in that vicinity. He was not to leave the area until ordered.

When Borodine had showed Viktor the orders, the EXO had shrugged and said, "We probably have some sort of new base up there, or some exercise is taking place that the command is nervous about."

At the time the explanation seemed to be a perfectly logical one, but Borodine had three days to think about it and now, as he sat in front of the COMCOMP, he came up with another idea. "Viktor?" he called.

Viktor left the CIC and went to the COMCOMP.

"I know why we were sent here," Borodine said. "I've been thinking about it since I read the sealed orders. What you suggested was logical."

"So?"

"What I'm going to suggest isn't logical at all. But I think it's somewhat close to the truth."

"Go ahead."

"To stop someone, or maybe more than just one person, from leaving Russia," Borodine said.

"Send us all the way up there for that?"

Borodine nodded.

"That's crazy!"

"Maybe crazy, but look at it. I mean, really look at it. Our orders are to destroy any American vessel, right?"

"Yes."

"What would an American vessel be doing up there this time of year?"

"Spying?"

"Yes. If there was something to spy on. And if there was, how much spying could be done in the weather that is going on above us?"

"Not much," Viktor admitted.

"But if someone wanted to get out, where would the last possible exit place be? I'll tell you: where we are going, that's where."

"Then you think we'll find an American ship up there?"

"I think we'll find the *Shark*," Borodine said. "Anything on the surface would be too risky to send. No, if my thinking is correct, then the only vessel for the job is the *Shark*."

"What's our ETA?"

Borodine ran his fingers over several keys. Ten hours came up on a small screen.

"We'll go to battle stations in five hours," Borodine said.

Viktor nodded.

"In the meantime," Borodine said, "I'm going to take her down to one thousand feet and run a few tests on our imaging system. This time we'll be able to see the *Shark*, as well as hear it."

"My guess is that they could see us as well as hear us," Viktor said.

Borodine nodded. "With any luck we'll see them first and get our torpedoes off first. But even if that doesn't happen, it gives us a better chance to survive."

"That's true," Viktor said.

Borodine switched on the MC system. "Stand by. Stand by. We are going from our present depth of two zero zero feet to a new cruising depth of one zero zero zero feet. The dive will be automatically accomplished. DO stand by to monitor manual system."

"Standing by," the DO answered, "Comrade Captain."

"Commencing dive," Borodine said, dialing the new depth to the DDC.

A slight sound of rushing air filled the *Sea Savage* as more water flooded into the ballast tanks. The red diving light came on. The EDPI showed a five-degree angle for the forward and stern diving planes.

Borodine watched the bubble indicator: The bubble moved slightly forward. The *Sea Savage* was down at the bow. The DDRO was moving rapidly: fifty feet deeper, then a hundred. "DO report," Borodine said.

"Three zero zero feet and still going down," the DO said.

Borodine nodded and switched on the UWIS just as a huge whale was crossing the bow of the *Sea Savage*, some two hundred yards away. "Look at that!" he exclaimed.

Viktor peered over his shoulder and gave a long, low whistle. "Now that's really beautiful!"

"Igor," Viktor said, addressing him familiarly, "the men are grumbling about the way they were brought back to the boat."

Borodine nodded. "I didn't and don't like it. But I guess it was done for security."

"That's the word I've given out."

"In addition to myself, you and Petrovich know where we're going," Borodine said. "But the crew is smart enough to know we're in northern waters."

"They know," Viktor said.

"Passing through nine five zero feet," the DO announced.

Borodine gave his attention to the instruments in front of him. The LI began to ease back to its level position. The DPI was beginning to move toward its null position. The red diving light went out and a yellow one came on. It began to flash, went out and a green light came on. Borodine switched on the MC. "Dive completed. DO stand down. Dive completed."

"Roger that, Comrade Captain," the DO answered.

Borodine put his hand over the mike. "I'll tell the crew where we're going and why," he said. "It will help them to understand why they were taken from their homes by the KGB."

"Good idea," Viktor answered.

Borodine cleared his throat. "Now hear this. Now hear this. This is your captain speaking. We are going into the Arctic to sink an American ship that is in our territorial waters. There is nothing more I can say, except to wish all of you good luck."

Boxer was resting in his cabin. His eyes were closed, and the lights were dimmed. He felt himself beginning to doze when Lieutenant Howe keyed him from the bridge.

"Skipper," Howe said, "you wanted to be notified when we approached the line of Russian sound detectors. According to our charts we're twenty thousand yards away."

"Roger that," Boxer said, sitting up and moving to the MINICOMCOMP. "I'll take it from here."

"Aye, aye, Skipper."

Boxer keyed the boat's electronic officer. "Time to test our electronic sound simulation equipment."

"Aye, aye, Skipper," the EO answered. "What are we going to simulate and when?"

Boxer rubbed his beard. The new equipment could simulate any previously recorded sound, whether it was produced by a ship or sea creature. The idea behind it was to confuse the enemy's sound pickup devices. "What's the estimated range of the Russian pick up?"

"Twelve to fifteen thousand yards, depending upon the water temperature," the electronics officer answered.

"If we play something that they know isn't there, they'll know we're trying to get through, or just testing them."

"According to our SO and visual ID there are a great many whales around. We could play the sounds they make."

"Alright, do it," Boxer said. "But tell the SO to be on the lookout for any targets. We don't want to be surprised."

"Aye, aye, Skipper."

Boxer switched off the MINICOMCOMP and returned to his bunk. He had been on the bridge for ten consecutive hours and now his neck and shoulder muscles ached. Knowing that the tension would mount swiftly within the next few hours, he closed his eyes and took several deep breaths. He was almost dozing when two light raps brought him to complete wakefulness. He sat up. "Come," he said.

Meagan opened the door and hesitated.

"Come in," Boxer said, standing up.

"I didn't mean to disturb you," she said. "I could come back another time."

"It's alright," Boxer said. "Come in."

She nodded, walked into the cabin and shut the door behind her.

Boxer gestured to the chair in front of the MINICOMCOMP. "Please," he said, "sit down." He took a pipe from the rack on the shelf above his bunk and filled it. "What can I do for you?" he asked.

"I'd rather stand if you don't mind," Meagan said.

Boxer realized she was wearing a coverall and that her hair was pulled back and held with a piece of blue ribbon. He lit the pipe and blew smoke from the bowl.

"I've never been in a situation like this," Meagan said.

"Neither have I. Neither has any man on this boat," Boxer told her.

She looked down at the deck. Her breathing was very rapid. "You don't understand," she said in a whisper. "I'm frightened." She looked straight at him. "So frightened I want to scream. I wasn't prepared for this. I feel as if I'm being smothered to death."

"I understand what you're saying," Boxer answered. "I even know what you're going through. It takes time to get used to living in a boat."

She shook her head. "I could never, never get used to it. And knowing that we might be attacked and —"

"Ms. — "

"Please call me Meagan," she said.

"I can't tell you not to think about it," Boxer said. "But remember, every man on this boat wants to live. We're all professionals."

She nodded. "That's what I tell myself."

"Believe it," Boxer said.

Suddenly tears began to stream out of her eyes. "Help me," she sobbed. "Help me!" She rushed to him and threw her arms around his neck.

Boxer put the pipe down and embraced her. "I'll ask the doc if he has something to settle you down."

"No. No. That will be worse. If something happens, I won't be able to escape. No, no. I don't want anything."

Boxer wanted to promise her that nothing would happen to her. But he couldn't do that for her, or anyone else aboard the *Shark*. The mission was dangerous, very dangerous.

"Just promise me," Meagan said, "that if anything happens, I mean, if we are sunk, that you won't let me die from drowning or from suffocation. Promise me that?"

"I promise," Boxer said.

She eased out of his embrace. "You're not just saying that to make me feel better?"

"I promise to shoot you myself," he said, "if we go down."

She nodded. Boxer picked up his pipe.

"There's one more thing," Meagan said.

"Yes. What is it?" Boxer asked, relighting his pipe.

"It can't happen here and maybe it will never happen," she said. "But I want to sleep with you."

Boxer swallowed a mouthful of smoke and started to cough.

Meagan walked to the door. "I'm sure other women have told you the same thing," she said. "I just wanted you to know that I find you very attractive."

"Thank you for the compliment," Boxer managed to say.

She nodded, opened the door and walked out of the cabin.

Boxer was on the bridge. The *Shark* had reached its destination.

"Skipper," Cowly said from the COMCOMP, "the UWIS show ice in every direction. The SO comes up with the same definition."

"Prepare to activate the LGN," Boxer said. "We'll have to burn our way through."

"LGN activated," Cowly said, throwing two switches.

The lights dimmed, then resumed their former brightness.

Boxer keyed the EO. "How's the power situation?"

"Using more than usual," the EO answered. "But no problem."

"Reduce speed to zero knots. Just enough RPMS to hold her steady."

"Roger that," the engineering officer answered.

"Fire laser," Boxer said.

"Laser firing," Cowly answered, activating two more switches.

"What's it look like?" Boxer asked.

"Come see for yourself, Skipper," Cowly said.

Boxer moved to the COMCOMP and looked at the UWIS screen. The ice one hundred feet above the *Shark* was breaking up. "Stand by to surface. Surface on manual. Stand by. Diving planes up zero five degrees."

"Diving planes up zero five degrees," the DO said.

"Blow forward ballast."

"Forward ballast blown," the DO answered.

"Blow aft ballast," Boxer ordered.

Suddenly the lights went out. The red fire light began to flash. An instant later the emergency klaxon sounded.

"Switch to emergency power," Boxer ordered.

"Emergency power on," Cowly said, throwing the switch. The light came back on.

"Kill that klaxon," Boxer ordered.

The horn went dead.

The EO keyed Boxer. "Fire, Skipper, in the cable. Smoke coming out fast."

"Blow main ballast," Boxer said.

"Main ballast blown," the DO answered.

Sanchez and Meagan came running toward the bridge.

"Keep those people away from here," Boxer said.

Two officers intercepted Sanchez and Meagan.

"Skipper," the EO said. "The smoke is bad down here."

"We'll be on the surface soon," he said, watching the depth gauge. "Going through five zero feet now."

The DCO keyed Boxer. "Main cable to the laser is burned out."

"Can you get to it?"

"Yes. But the laser will not be able to fire again."

"Roger that," Boxer said.

A green light began to flash. "Surface," Boxer said. "Surface. Open number four and five hatches. Activate foam. I want clean air into the engine room as quickly as possible."

"Roger that," Cowly answered.

Within minutes freezing air rushed into the *Shark*.

Boxer went out on deck. It was night. To the south lay the headland of the cove. He keyed Redfern. "Tom, come up on deck."

"Roger that," Tom answered.

Boxer scanned the shore with his infrared glasses. The cabin was visible.

Redfern scrambled through the hatchway.

Boxer handed him the glasses. "There's the cabin," he said. "The people we want are inside."

"From here to there is about two miles, maybe less," Redfern said.

"But we're not going to be here," Boxer said. "I can't risk sitting here. Even with our sail down, we're easy to spot. You move your men over to the right. According to the latest satellite photographs, the Russians have something behind the hills. Probably a few pieces of artillery. Have part of your team take those out on the eastern side of the cove. If you can, use them against the pieces on the other side of the cove. Just drop a pattern. That should create enough confusion for the other part of the team to get the people out of the cabin. You bring them across the ice. Five miles from where we are now."

"Are you sure that there's ice out there?" Redfern asked.

"If there isn't, you're going to be in big trouble," Boxer said.

The EO keyed Boxer. "Skipper, the fire is out and the smoke is cleared. Request permission to close hatch number four. It's too fucking cold with it open."

"Close it," Boxer said.

"Aye, aye, Skipper," the EO answered.

"Have your men ready to move out in twenty minutes," Boxer said.

"Sure thing, Skipper," Redfern answered.

Boxer scrambled down the open hatchway. "Mister Cowly, Major Redfern and his team will be going ashore in one eight minutes. Prepare to dive as soon as they leave the boat."

"Aye, aye, Skipper," Cowly answered.

"Skipper," Cowly said, "MET shows a storm front coming in."

Boxer nodded. He had been watching the barometer drop within the last few minutes. "Tom and his men have got to get out before we can move."

"They're going to be in trouble if the ice begins to shift," Cowly said.

"Nothing I can do about it. I can't wait around to see what goes down."

Redfern came up to the bridge. He was dressed in a storm parka and face mask. "Ready to go," he said.

"Tom, you've got some weather coming up," Boxer said.

Redfern glanced at the barometer. It was down to 29.05.

"You should be in the midst of a blizzard within minutes after you leave us," Boxer said.

"Makes it easier to take out those guns," Redfern said.

"Target," the SO reported, "bearing two eight zero degrees. Range sixteen thousand yards. Depth three zero zero feet. Speed thirty-two knots. ID the *Q-21.*"

"Move!" Boxer said.

Redfern rushed toward the hatchway, undogged it and flung it open. His men hurried up and out of the *Shark.*

"Cleared," Redfern reported over the radio.

"Good luck," Boxer said and hit the klaxon twice. "Dive," he said over the MC. "Dive. Dive on automatic control." He dialed in two zero zero feet into the electronic dive-control system.

Boxer watched the depth gauge. The *Shark* was going down fast. Her bow was tilted down fifteen degrees. All her tanks were flooded.

"Making three zero zero feet," Boxer said over the MC. He switched on the UWIS. The *Q-21* was still out of range. "Stand by forward torpedo room."

"Forward torpedo room standing by," the TO said.

"Taking helm off automatic. Mahony, take the helm," Boxer said.

"Course six four degrees," Mahony answered.

"Come to new course two eight zero," Boxer said.

"Coming to two eight zero," Mahony answered.

"Forward torpedo room arm and load four torpedoes," Boxer ordered. "Set for electronic control from COMCOMP." This was something he didn't really want to do, but if he didn't blow the *Q-21* out of the water, he'd run the risk of having the *Shark* blown out of the water by it. "Stand by to fire simultaneously."

Boxer adjusted the COMCOMP to control the four torpedoes' guidance system. The information would be passed to the guidance systems from the data processed by the UWIS system. Suddenly the *Q-21* came onto the screen. It appeared as a long, dark shadow without much definition.

The TO in the forward torpedo room keyed Boxer. "Skipper, we're getting intermittent signals from the target."

Boxer pushed the electronic resolution button. The image on the screen became larger by a factor of ten. "Fire," Boxer ordered.

"Torpedoes fired," the TO reported.

The bow of the *Shark* lifted slightly, then quickly readjusted itself.

Boxer watched the torpedoes head toward the *Q-21*. Suddenly the screen went blank. "What the fuck is happening!" he shouted. "TO, what have you got?"

"Nothing. Return signals not coming in," the TO answered.

Boxer keyed the DCO. "What the fuck is happening with our electronic fire control?"

"Everything is in order, Skipper," the DCO answered.

"The UWIS went out. No, it's back on. Hold it ... the torpedoes lost the target; they're past it. Stand by. Stand by to dive again. The Russians have to know we took a shot at them." He reached over to the AUTODISYS and dialed one thousand.

The SO keyed Boxer. "Target bearing two eight zero degrees. Range ten thousand yards. Depth four zero zero feet. Speed forty knots and closing fast."

Suddenly the all-too-familiar ping of the *Q-21*'s sonar sounded through the boat.

Boxer looked at Cowly. "I hope the Russians weren't waiting for Tom," he said.

"Target," the SO shouted. "Target two eight zero degrees. Torpedo. Torpedo closing fast."

"Come to course three six zero," Boxer said.

"Course three six zero," Mahony answered.

Boxer keyed the EO. "Give every bit of speed you can."

"Flank speed," the EO answered.

"Torpedo still holding course two eight zero degrees," the SO said.

Boxer keyed the fire control center. "Activate electronic screen."

"Electronic screen activated."

Boxer looked at the DDRO. "Passing through nine zero zero feet," he said.

Suddenly the SO said, "Two targets coming from two eight zero degrees. Range ten thousand yards. Speed five five knots. Christ, they're minisubs."

Boxer picked them up on the UWIS. "Minisubs," he called out to Cowly.

"Closing fast, Skipper," the SO said.

"Going to five zero zero feet," Boxer said, making the necessary adjustments to the dive control system.

"We're not going up fast enough," the SO said.

"Forward and aft torpedo rooms. Arm all torpedoes for independent homing."

The two fire-control officers repeated the command.

"We've got to take those two out," Boxer said. "We don't have time to launch our own. If we get to the surface, we might have a chance to fight."

"That means breaking through the ice," Cowly said.

"We don't have any other chance."

"Torpedoes in forward torpedo room armed and set," the TO reported.

A split second later, the TO in the aft torpedo room reported. "All torpedoes armed and ready, Skipper."

Boxer took a fix on the two minisubs with the UWIS and fed the information into the computers aboard the torpedoes.

Both torpedo officers reported the torpedoes' guidance systems were operating.

"Forward torpedo room fire," Boxer ordered.

"Torpedoes fired," the TO reported.

"Aft torpedo room fire," Boxer said.

"Torpedoes fired," the TO reported.

Boxer gave his attention to the UWIS. One minisub disintegrated. The sound of the explosion rolled over the *Shark*. "One is moving in on us," Boxer said.

"Torpedo. Torpedo. Torpedo," the SO shouted.

The explosion rocked the *Shark*. The lights went out. Boxer hit the emergency switch. The lights came on again but very dim.

"Skipper," the DCO said, "we took one between the engine room and the stern. Water coming in."

Boxer hit three switches. "Sections eleven, twelve and thirteen sealed off," he said over the MC. "Blowing all ballast. Diving planes set at two five degrees."

The *Shark*'s bow began to tilt up.

"Skipper we're settling by the stern," the DCO said.

Boxer keyed the EO. "I need that jet power now to make it to the surface."

"Stand by," the EO answered.

"We're putting out max power," he said. "Two driveshafts appear to be damaged."

"Give me that power!" Boxer said.

"Power coming on," the EO answered.

Boxer's eyes were glued to the DDRO. The numbers started to move up. "Cowly, check for survivors in sections eleven, twelve and thirteen," he said in a monotone.

"None," Cowly answered.

Boxer glanced him. "How many dead?"

"Twenty-three, including four crew members and nineteen from the strike force."

Boxer clamped his jaw. Focusing through blurred vision on the DDRO, he wondered why Borodine hadn't come in for the kill.

Redfern and Alvaro De Vargas lead the strike team of twenty-four men quickly across the ice. By the time they reached the shore it was snowing heavily, and the wind was blowing at thirty knots.

"We're not going to try to knock out the guns," Redfern said. "In this weather they're useless."

"I sure as hell won't be able to find those guns," De Vargas answered. "We're lucky if we find the cabin."

"I brought along an infrared sensor," Redfern said, holding up a small telescope-like device. "The cabin is over there. About two hundred yards. Pass the word to spread out and encircle it. I don't want any surprises."

De Vargas pulled up alongside Redfern again. "I ain't never goin' to complain about the jungle again," he said.

"Sure you are," Redfern answered.

They worked their way over a small rise and through the falling snow. They could see the cabin.

"Spread out," Redfern said. "Don't fire unless I give the order."

"I'd make it to be about two hundred yards away," De Vargas said. "There's smoke coming from the chimney. I hope they have something hot to drink."

"You won't have time to piss," Redfern answered, "let alone drink."

They moved forward at a crouch.

"So far so good," De Vargas said.

Redfern nodded. The cold had already penetrated his thermal clothing. Where his breath touched the face mask, ice had formed.

"Tom," De Vargas asked, "why haven't the Russians taken these guys? They gotta know they're here, don't they?"

"We're betting they don't," Redfern answered.

"It's a piss poor bet, if you ask me," De Vargas answered.

"Fuck all, I lost the damn house!" Redfern exclaimed. He scanned the area in front of him with the infrared detector. "Okay, it's off to the right about fifteen yards."

De Vargas used a hand-held radio to pull the men to the right. "There it is!" he exclaimed.

Redfern halted the men and keyed on the radio. "We go in on a regular assault basis. De Vargas and I will take the door. The rest of you cover the outside. If there's any trouble, open up with everything you have; then make for the rendezvous point. All of you know where it is. Good luck." He switched off the radio and put it back in its pocket on his pack. "OK, Lieutenant, let's go." He began to run for the house.

De Vargas kept up with him. "We're making a hell of a lot of noise in the snow," De Vargas said.

Redfern didn't answer. The door was in front of him. He threw his weight against it. It burst open.

Two shots exploded in front of him. He was lifted off the floor and fell back.

De Vargas opened up.

The men around the cabin began firing.

"Enough. Enough!" a man shouted from inside the cabin.

De Vargas stopped firing and radioed his men to cease firing. "Get up here immediately. The major caught a couple," he said. Then he walked into the smoke-filled cabin. Besides the CIA man and the civilians there were two Russian officers and three enlisted men.

"I'm Paul Hardy," one of the men said.

"Dean Foster," the other man said.

De Vargas didn't ask about the civilians. "Who shot the major?" he asked, looking at the Russians.

No one answered.

He looked at the Americans. "Who shot him?" he asked.

"Take them scientists back with you," Hardy said. "And I'll —"

"You got it all wrong, Mister Hardy. I'm going to do it. Here. Now tell me, who shot the major?" He turned to one of the men bending over Redfern. "As soon as I get the civilians out, kill all of the Russians."

"I shot him," one of the officers said.

"Who are you?"

"General —"

De Vargas pointed his rifle at him, lowered it and squeezed off two rounds.

General Yedotev's knees shattered. Screaming in pain, he dropped to the floor. The women were too horrified to scream.

"The major is dead," one of the men from the team said.

"You sure?"

"I'm sure."

"Get his equipment and tags. Leave nothing the Russians can ID," De Vargas said, "and set him on the table here. Take the rest of these people out and start moving toward the rendezvous point. Take this fucking general with you."

"Sure thing, Lieutenant," the man answered.

Alone De Vargas looked down at Redfern's body. "Not much to say ol' buddy. Not much at all. You were the best damn officer I ever knew. Maybe the Russians will give you a decent burial. Maybe not. Now it don't matter what happens to you." He stepped back, saluted and hurried out into the blinding snow. "Let's get the fuck out of here," he shouted over the sound of the wind.

"You'll never make it," Stepanovich said in Russian.

"What did he say?" De Vargas asked.

"We'll never make it," Hardy said.

"Tell the fucker if we don't, he won't," De Vargas answered.

"Hey, Lieutenant," one of the men said, "got movement on the ridge to our right."

De Vargas scanned the hilltop with the infrared scope. "A dozen Russians comin' toward the cabin," he said. "We'll stop here an' wait 'til they're inside. Butch, Joe and Zimpy set up your stove pipe and get ready to lay down a pattern."

"You're not going to fight them?" Hardy questioned.

"No. My stove pipe team is goin' to kill them," De Vargas said.

"But there are probably several dozen more where they came from!"

"Yeah, probably. Too bad we can't get to them," De Vargas answered. "OK, Butch, you got less than a minute to do it. Figure you got one zero zero yards."

"Got it, Lieutenant," Butch answered.

A dull thwap sounded; then a moment later there was an explosion and a fountain of snow leaped up in front of the cabin. Another thwap went off, followed by a second explosion that joined with the first.

"Cease firing," De Vargas said. "You got 'em. Let's go." He moved forward to lead the group onto the ice.

Borodine was at the COMCOMP. "Boxer still has torpedoes," he said.

Viktor leaned over to look at the UWIS screen. "He's moving toward the surface."

"We'll be there waiting for him," Borodine said. "Maybe we can save some lives. Maybe he'll see the hopelessness of his situation and surrender."

"Would you, if you were where he is?" Viktor asked.

Borodine shrugged. "It's hard to answer that," he said. "But probably I wouldn't. Probably I'd fight."

"That's what Captain Boxer is going to do," Viktor said.

Borodine nodded and hit the klaxon once. "Stand by to surface. Stand by to surface," he said over the MC system.

"Minisub returning," Viktor said.

"Have it surface with us," Borodine answered. "She'll be retrieved as soon as we reach the surface."

Viktor relayed Borodine's orders.

"Minisub acknowledges your orders," Viktor said.

"Going to auto-control," Borodine said, setting several switches in new positions. "Diving planes at zero five degrees," he said. "Main ballast blown."

The *Sea Savage*'s bow rose up. Borodine watched the bubble indicator: It was off center now.

The SO keyed Borodine. "Target bearing eight four degrees. Range six thousand yards. Speed one zero knots. Depth two five zero feet."

Borodine checked the UWIS. The *Shark* was clearly visible. She was leaking oil, or some other viscous fluid. A long streak, like dirty bunting trailed after her. She was a dying boat with no hope of being saved.

Except for the whirring sound of the blower system and the constant pinging of the *Q-21*'s sonar against its hull, the *Shark* was silent. The men stood at their stations with their eyes focused on the instruments in front of them.

"One five zero feet. And still going up," Boxer announced in a monotone. He checked the DDCO net. Three sections had been blown out. There was no doubt in his mind that if they had been deeper, maybe even a hundred feet or fifty feet, they would have gone to the bottom. He keyed the EO. "How are we holding up?"

"Another two minutes on the jet system," the EO answered.

"Make it five and we all might be alive," Boxer answered.

"It won't be any damn use to us again."

"If we go down again," Boxer said, "nothing will be any damn use to us again. We'll be dead."

"Pushing for five," the EO answered.

"We could lighten up a bit by getting rid of our torpedoes," Cowly started to suggest.

Boxer shook his head. "Borodine has to come in for the kill. I want to be ready for him. Maybe we can get a few licks in before we take the final one."

"Then you don't see us getting out of this?" Cowly asked.

"Not likely," Boxer answered. "But we sure as hell are going to try!"

Cowly pointed to the DDRO.

"Passing through one zero zero feet" Boxer announced. He checked the time-to-surface clock, or TTSC. Because of the damage it would be off a bit, but not by much. It read .02 minutes.

"Five zero feet," Boxer said over the MC. That wasn't much depth, but with the kind of damage they had, it had to be the surface or nothing. "Twenty-five feet. All hands stand by. We'll come up through pack ice and it might be rough. Stand by. The bow will break out first, then fall back. One zero feet. Raise sail. Raise sail."

"Sail going up," Cowly responded.

Boxer breathed easier. If the sail had jammed they would have lost their surface and air radar.

A green light on the SCRAM panel began to flash, another on the COMCOMP. A bell began to ring.

The *Shark*'s bow slammed its way through the ice floes.

"Christ," Cowly exclaimed, "that sounds like we're being torn apart."

"Surface," Boxer announced. "Surface. Deck details to hatches two, three, four and five. Bridge detail stand by. Go!"

The men began to cheer.

"Stow it," Boxer said. "We're still in deep shit." He grabbed his parka. "I'll take the CONN from the bridge, Cowly. Join me up there."

Smiling broadly, Cowly answered, "Aye, aye, Skipper."

Boxer rushed up the steps. The hatch had already been opened. Even before he pulled himself up on the bridge the snow came rushing in.

"Skipper, there's a fuckin' blizzard going on," one of the men said.

Boxer didn't answer. He looked toward the aft section. All that remained of the hull was twisted steel. "Get some men into those sections and pull out the bodies."

"Aye, aye, Skipper," a chief answered.

The EO keyed him. "The jet system is burned out."

"Roger that," Boxer answered.

Almost immediately the COMMO keyed him. "Skipper, I have Captain Borodine on an open frequency."

"Patch him in."

"Captain," Borodine said. "I know your condition. I have seen you and I ask you to think about saving your own life and the lives of your crew. Your situation is hopeless."

"Captain, I will take my chances," Boxer answered. "But I appreciate your offer."

"Skipper," the COMMO said, "the transmission went dead."

"Roger that," Boxer said. "Try to raise Redfern. I want to get those people aboard as soon as possible."

"Aye, aye, Skipper," COMMO answered.

The *Q-21* smashed through several large floes of pack ice.

The green light on the COMCOMP began to flash. "Bridge detail topside," Viktor ordered.

"I'll take the CONN," Borodine said. "Let Popov stay below. You come topside with me."

"Comrade Captain," Captain 3rd Class Uri Karenski said, "I would consider it an honor to accompany you to the bridge."

Borodine looked at the man. He had completely forgotten about him. He was tall, thin and colorless. He was the *Sea Savage*'s new political officer. He had been standing nearby since the *Shark* had been picked up by the UWIS and he hadn't intruded once, either in the conversation between him and Viktor, or —

"This my first trip to the Arctic and I would like to see it," he said with a smile.

Borodine nodded. "Permission granted," he said, and grabbing his outer wear from a nearby hanger, he hurried up to the bridge.

"Not more than fifty meters visibility, Comrade Captain," one of the junior officers said.

COMMO keyed him. "Comrade Captain, message coming through from CO on land."

"Read it."

"Americans attacked and killed several soldiers. Kidnapped General Yedotev and district commander Colonel Stepanovich. Their casualties, one dead. Signed Major Babonos."

"Roger that," Borodine answered. "No reply." He turned to Viktor and relayed the contents of the message, then he said, "They're out here. Somewhere they're going to make contact with the *Shark*."

The radar officer keyed Borodine. "Target bearing three eight degrees. Range four thousand yards. Speed ten knots. ID the *Shark*."

Borodine slapped Viktor on the back. "We're almost within kissing distance. Helmsman, come to course four four degrees," Borodine ordered.

"Aye, aye, Comrade Captain, coming to new course four four degrees."

"I want to get close enough," Borodine exclaimed, "not to miss a surface shot."

Karenski nodded.

"COMMO, try to make radio contact with the *Shark*," Borodine ordered.

"Aye, aye, Comrade Captain," the communications officer answered.

"Skipper, De Vargas is on," the COMMO said.

"Have you picked us up yet?" Boxer asked.

"Six one degrees from us. One thousand yards. Skipper, there's about six zero zero feet of open water between us."

Boxer keyed the RO. "Team six one degrees from us. Give me a sweep."

"Got them," the RO said.

"Lock on them. Interface with NAVCOM," Boxer ordered. "Mahony, stand by. Helms switching over to RC."

"Roger that."

"Helm on RC," the radar officer reported. "ETA one one minutes."

"Tell Tom to stand by to come aboard," Boxer said.

"Skipper," De Vargas said, "the major bought it."

"Say again," Boxer said.

"The major is dead," De Vargas said.

Despite the static, Boxer heard the message. He swallowed hard. "Tom is dead," he said to Cowly.

Suddenly the sky exploded into shimmering sheets of green and blue light.

"What the fuck is that?" Cowly asked.

Before Boxer could tell him it was the aurora borealis, the RO keyed him again. "Target bearing three one six degrees. Range two —"

"What the hell happened?"

"Screen went blank," the RO said.

"That's got to be the *Q-21*," Cowly said.

"No doubt about it. She's coming in for the kill. Coming close because she can't see us in this storm." He keyed the FCO. "Get your SSMS ready to fire."

"Roger that."

"Skipper, the screen came back," the RO said. "Range one thousand yards and closing fast."

"Feed bearing and range data to FO computer," Boxer said.

"Interface with FOCOMP completed," the radar officer said.

"FCO set SSMS for air burst. Two five feet above target," Boxer said.

"Roger that."

Another explosion of color lit up the sky.

"Skipper," the RO said, "closing fast with the edge of the ice."

"Roger that," Boxer answered. He switched on the MC. "Deck detail, stand by to board team. Stand by to board team."

The bulkhead door on the port side of the sail was flung open and six men rushed out on the forward part of the deck.

"COMMO, find out if De Vargas has made visual contact with us," Boxer said.

"Skipper," the FCO said, "all birds armed and ready to fire."

"Fire two," Boxer said.

A red light flashed on the bridge COMCOMP; then two roaring sounds and the birds were away. Their long tails vanished immediately in the driving snow.

"Skipper," De Vargas said, "you're in sight. Shooting two red flares."

Boxer glanced at the missile countdown clock. The green turned to red.

Two thunderous explosions rolled out of the falling snow. An instant later two red lights hung in the air.

"Stop all engines," Boxer told the EO.

"All engines stopped," the EO responded.

"Helm going to manual," Boxer said, throwing a switch. "Mahony, ease her toward the ice. Six six degrees should do it." Boxer turned on the *Shark*'s high intensity searchlight and swept the ice until he had De Vargas and the other members of the team in the brilliant yellow cones. "Stand by, De Vargas, to come aboard," Boxer said on the MC.

The two women were handed to the members of the deck detail, then the wounded general. Everyone else scrambled up the side and onto the deck of the *Shark*.

Boxer keyed the EO. "Give me whatever you can," he said.

"Twelve knots maybe," the EO answered.

"Do it," Boxer answered.

Suddenly the sky erupted in sheets of brilliant colors.

"Skipper," the RO said, "the surface system is out."

"Mahony, come to course four eight degrees," Boxer said.

"There she is," Cowly exclaimed, pointing to the *Q-21* off the portside.

"Mahony, come to course two seven degrees," Boxer said.

"Coming to course two seven degrees," Mahony answered.

"My guess is that Borodine's radar is having trouble too. He must be as surprised to see us as we are to see him. We're going to try and ram him. He'll guess that as soon as he realizes we're turning toward him." Boxer switched on the MC. "All hands rig for crash. All hands rig for crash."

The RO keyed Boxer. "New target five five degrees. Range twenty-five thousand yards. Speed eight hundred knots. Altitude forty-five thousand feet."

"Could be one of theirs," Cowly said. "Borodine might have called for it."

Boxer keyed the COMMO. "Any radio traffic between the *Q-21* and —"

"Negative, Skipper."

"Use the Gamma frequency and code FireHatch," Boxer said. "Make contact with that plane and patch me in."

"Roger that," the COMMO said.

"Mahony," Boxer said, "come to course five five degrees."

Mahony repeated the course.

"Cowly, have some of Tom's men bring Simmons up here," Boxer said.

The *Shark* began to swing onto her new course.

Boxer keyed the aft torpedo room. "Arm and load four fish," he told the TO.

"Roger that," the TO answered.

"Skipper," the COMMO said, "I have the pilot on the scrambler."

Boxer picked up the mike. "This is Captain Jack Boxer, skipper of the submarine *Shark*. We are under attack. I repeat, we are under attack. Need your assistance now!"

"Where the hell are you?"

"Will give you radio and radar signal to follow down," Boxer said.

"Need verification," the pilot said. "Have lost my radio compass due to atmospheric disturbances. Need verification."

"No time now."

"Have your signal on scope."

"Will help?"

"Roger that," the pilot answered.

Borodine was on the bridge, peering through the blinding snow. The *Sea Savage*'s surface radar was out and the best he could do was guess that the *Shark* was somewhere in front. In order to be able to kill her, he needed to see her, either with his eyes or with radar.

"There," Borodine suddenly shouted. "There she is. Helmsman —" He realized the *Shark* was coming straight at the *Sea Savage*. He keyed the EO. "Flank speed. Flank speed."

"Flank speed," the EO repeated.

"Helmsman, come to course one three four degrees," Borodine said.

"Comrade Captain," the RO said, keying Borodine, "target bearing five five degrees. Range fifteen thousand yards. Speed eight hundred knots. Altitude forty-five thousand feet."

"Roger that," Borodine answered. "It must be one of ours." He keyed COMMO. "Send signal to aircraft using the Star frequency and the code. Then patch me into the pilot."

"Roger that," the COMMO answered.

"Skipper," RO said, keying Boxer, "target turning."

"Roger that," Boxer answered.

"Simmons is here," Cowly said.

Boxer didn't bother to look at him. "I want you to fly your helicopter now. I want you to go up and confuse the shit out of the Russian radar." He faced him. "That's an order, mister, and we're in a combat situation."

Simmons nodded.

"Get going," Boxer said.

"Skipper," COMMO said, "pilot says we're on his radar."

"Am I still patched in to him?" Boxer asked.

"Roger that."

Boxer picked up the mike. "My helicopter is going up. He'll be below you. Your target bearing and speed is now being transmitted to your radar."

"On screen," the pilot answered.

"She's all yours," Boxer answered.

"Coming down for kill," the pilot answered.

"Roger that," Boxer said.

"Comrade Captain," the COMMO said, "I can't raise the pilot. Several transmissions between the American submarine —"

Borodine saw something explode out of the *Shark*.

"Target," the RO said, "five five degrees. Altitude twenty-five thousand feet. Speed nine hundred knots and closing fast. Target five five degrees. Altitude one five zero feet and stationary. Target —"

Borodine hit the klaxon three times. "Crash dive. Crash dive," he shouted over the MC. "Crash dive. Coming under air attack!" He dropped through the hatch and rushed to the bridge. The *Shark* would live to fight another day. "Making one thousand feet," he said, putting all systems on automatic control.

Two explosions hammered down on the *Sea Savage*, rolling her off to the portside. Then two more went off above her. But she was already too deep to feel their effect.

The huge U.S. fighter bomber flew low over the *Shark* and dipped its wings in salute.

Boxer ordered Mahony to come to course two eight degrees. "We're safe for now," he said to Cowly. "But it's a long way home and we have to sail a damaged boat through a hostile sea."

"I'm not complaining," said Cowly.

"I didn't think you would." Boxer grinned.

A NOTE TO THE READER

Dear Reader,

If you have enjoyed the novel enough to leave a review on **Amazon** and **Goodreads**, then we would be truly grateful.

Sapere Books

Sapere Books is an exciting new publisher of brilliant fiction and popular history.

To find out more about our latest releases and our monthly bargain books visit our website:
saperebooks.com

Printed in Great Britain
by Amazon